Yours, Always

I sat at the table and opened the letter, pulling out the paper gingerly, so it wouldn't fall apart. It took me forever to manage to get the sheet open without tearing it.

The writing inside was more faded than it had been on the outside, just a sepia tracery on the yellow page. I had to turn the light on over the kitchen table to be able to read what it said.

Dear Jacinth, it said. *I had hoped things would never come to this pass.* Pass was underlined five times. *But I'm afraid my husband knows. Or at least, he has enough reason to suspect. Sometimes he looks at me in such a way that I'm not sure I can stand it (far less survive it). I will meet you next week, at seven thirty, at the fruit stand. I will bring the baby. I am afraid the time has come to take you up on your offer and leave as soon as possible. Yours, always, Almeria.*

I looked at it, and I confess I felt shocked. Victorian people—and I was almost sure that the letter was at least a hundred years old—weren't supposed to have complications like a husband, while being someone else's "always."

Berkley Prime Crime titles by Elise Hyatt

DIPPED, STRIPPED, AND DEAD
FRENCH POLISHED MURDER

French
Polished

Murder

ELISE HYATT

BERKLEY PRIME CRIME, NEW YORK

THE BERKLEY PUBLISHING GROUP
Published by the Penguin Group
Penguin Group (USA) Inc.
375 Hudson Street, New York, New York 10014, USA

Penguin Group (Canada), 90 Eglinton Avenue East, Suite 700, Toronto, Ontario M4P 2Y3, Canada
(a division of Pearson Penguin Canada Inc.)
Penguin Books Ltd., 80 Strand, London WC2R 0RL, England
Penguin Group Ireland, 25 St. Stephen's Green, Dublin 2, Ireland (a division of Penguin Books Ltd.)
Penguin Group (Australia), 250 Camberwell Road, Camberwell, Victoria 3124, Australia
(a division of Pearson Australia Group Pty. Ltd.)
Penguin Books India Pvt. Ltd., 11 Community Centre, Panchsheel Park, New Delhi—110 017, India
Penguin Group (NZ), 67 Apollo Drive, Rosedale, North Shore 0632, New Zealand
(a division of Pearson New Zealand Ltd.)
Penguin Books (South Africa) (Pty.) Ltd., 24 Sturdee Avenue, Rosebank, Johannesburg 2196,
South Africa

Penguin Books Ltd., Registered Offices: 80 Strand, London WC2R 0RL, England

This is a work of fiction. Names, characters, places, and incidents either are the product of the author's imagination or are used fictitiously, and any resemblance to actual persons, living or dead, business establishments, events, or locales is entirely coincidental. The publisher does not have any control over and does not assume any responsibility for author or third-party websites or their content.

PUBLISHER'S NOTE: Neither the publisher nor the author is engaged in rendering professional advice or services to the individual reader. The ideas, projects, and suggestions contained in this book are not intended as a substitute for consulting with a professional. Neither the author nor the publisher shall be liable or responsible for any loss or damage allegedly arising from any information or suggestion in this book.

FRENCH POLISHED MURDER

A Berkley Prime Crime Book / published by arrangement with the author

PRINTING HISTORY
Berkley Prime Crime mass-market edition / May 2010

Copyright © 2010 by Sarah Hoyt.
Cover illustration by Jennifer Gennari.
Cover design by Rita Frangie.
Interior text design by Kristin del Rosario.

ISBN: 978-0-425-23346-7

BERKLEY® PRIME CRIME
Berkley Prime Crime Books are published by The Berkley Publishing Group,
a division of Penguin Group (USA) Inc.,
375 Hudson Street, New York, New York 10014.
BERKLEY® PRIME CRIME and the PRIME CRIME logo are trademarks of Penguin Group (USA) Inc.

PRINTED IN THE UNITED STATES OF AMERICA

10 9 8 7 6 5 4 3 2 1

Acknowledgments

Thank you to Doctor Tedd Roberts for assistance with pharmacology research.

Thank you to my editor, Ginjer Buchanan, for work beyond the call of duty on this one.

And as always, thank you to my family and my critique group for putting up with the insanity.

CHAPTER 1

The Fast and the Electrically Furious

We were thirty years old—and, in his case, thirty plus a little more than six months—when I came to the sad conclusion that I would have to murder my friend Benedict Colm.

This was as sad as it was necessary, but there was no escaping the fact as my son, Enoch—whom I call E in an attempt to save him therapy bills as he gets older—came speeding into the living room, atop Ben's Christmas gift to him.

The gift was a toy electric motorcycle with a top speed of ten miles per hour, an acceleration that might seem impossible for a small boy to achieve in a home that was less than seventy feet in either direction, but that E managed, quite often.

I heard the horn blare a moment before E came riding in and, with the practice born of two weeks of terror, dove behind the sofa, while Ben, who stood square in the middle of the living room, his arms crossed on his chest, became an impromptu traffic circle.

E sped around him once, twice, then headed the other way, at increased velocity.

"What do you mean you'll have to kill me?" Ben asked obtusely, looking at me. "And what are you doing behind the sofa?"

I crept out and up to stand on the sofa itself, having learned that a large piece of furniture was the best defense against the toddler version of the fast and the furious. "Isn't it obvious?" I said as, from the kitchen, there came a now-familiar series of sounds indicating that E was either rearranging the kitchen chairs to use as slalom cones or simply hitting them and dragging them along with sweet disregard for what it might do to chair legs and seats.

I dropped to sit on the sofa, shaking slightly, with what I figured was a form of post-traumatic stress disorder only not particularly post, since the stress had started just over two weeks ago when E had first unwrapped the fully charged electric motorcycle.

"If you were likely to have children," I told Ben darkly, "I'd already have started payments on the realistic drum set with electronic amplification."

"You are making no sense at all," Ben said, in that even tone that made me want to strangle him with my bare hands—even though I was aware that would be one of the stupidest ways to kill him, as I would be immediately discovered. "What can the possibility of my having children have to do with this? Besides, surely you remember I used to have a garage band. In the unlikely event I ever have a child, I'd be happy if you gave him or her a drum set."

I think that was when I picked up the nearest object—

a collection of mystery short stories, leather bound, weighing in at about three pounds, a Christmas gift from my parents—and flung it at his head. I missed, of course, just as E came back through the door from the dining room, in time to ride over the book and break its spine.

"Well, you shouldn't have thrown it at me," Ben said, looking baffled when I howled in outrage. He picked up the book and tried to smooth the broken spine.

Ben stood six-three in his stocking feet, with reddish-blond hair and the sort of face that is pleasant to look at rather than handsome. Because this was the weekend and also still part of his Christmas vacation, he was in what he considered his relaxed attire: dark green pants, with a broadcloth shirt, a cashmere pullover just a shade darker than his pants, and the sort of tie he considered playful and holiday-like—in this case green, with a barely discernable red dot. I would bet that were I to lift his sweater I would find his tie had been precisely arranged to fall just over the top half of his belt.

I thought, not for the first time, that it was a very good thing that Ben was gay because any woman worth her salt, forced into a romantic relationship with someone so unflappable, exact, and unemotional-seeming would have done the sensible thing and put a steak knife through his heart.

"Not your steak knives," he said, when I communicated this sentiment. "They'd never get past the rib cage. You never sharpen them." He set the abused book on my coffee table, which is thirdhand and made mostly—I think—of spit and cardboard. The legs bowed under the weight of the book, which wasn't exactly a surprise, since they bowed under the weight of a coffee cup.

Ben and I had been best friends since middle school,

when I was Lancelot, Galahad, and *La Belle Dame sans Merci* rolled into one—or actually, considering that my parents were the owners of the largest used/new mystery bookstore west of Kansas, Miss Marple, Poirot, Perry Mason, and Nero Wolfe—forever running off in defense of those younger than I or those in peril of some sort. Or again, perhaps not, since the only small, young, or shy teenagers that those four were likely to rise in defense of would be those who had been unjustly accused of murder, while I ran to the defense of any smaller person who was being bullied or otherwise abused or ganged up on by people bigger than them.

At five foot five—which was to be my adult height—and weighing less than a hundred pounds, soaking wet and with lead in my pockets, I'd been constitutionally incapable of sleeping at night if I thought that someone, somewhere, was getting away with committing blatant injustice against his fellow man or woman, or snively, pimply middle school kid.

Ben had first come to *my* rescue when I'd taken on three bullies—each of whom were twice my weight—at once and had insisted on helping me despite my outraged howls that I had them surrounded.

We'd been best friends ever since and cooperated in an unusual way—I charged in and got way over my head, and he jumped after me to rescue me and incidentally finish off whatever dragon I'd been fighting. But now, I thought, staring at him, my eyes misting with tears, I would simply have to kill him.

"Why on earth are you crying?" Ben asked, as E came back in and whirled around him three more times, before speeding back out to the dining room, causing a hollow sound in his wake that I was afraid was the knocking down and breaking of the potted plant my boyfriend's mother had given me for Christmas.

"Because I really am going to hate having to kill you. And then, you know, at your size and in the middle of winter, with the ground frozen solid, there is no way that I can dig a hole large enough to bury you in. And that means that either you'll be found right away, and I'll have to figure out a system of misdirection so they think someone else is the culprit, or I'll have to figure out a way to dissolve your body, so I can flush it down the drain or something." I thought a moment. "Given how dirty that bathtub was when I moved in, do you think there would be any noticeable difference if I used it as a container to dissolve you in muriatic acid?"

He sighed heavily. "Don't you think that buying enough muriatic acid for that purpose would call attention in and of itself? Besides, from what I've read, it doesn't dissolve the body completely. You'd end up with clogged drains, and they'd find pieces of me in the plumbing." He had to shout the last part because E had come back for a whirl around the living room and, this time, was blaring the horn continuously, which created a sort of siren effect. "Besides, your neighbors upstairs would probably complain about the smell."

"Why not?" I said, as the siren receded toward the kitchen, followed by a series of thuds that meant that E was trying to open the door to the bathroom by dint of knocking on it with the front wheel. "They have already complained about the noise. Which means I'll get evicted before the month is out and I have no idea if the security deposit will cover impact marks on the bathroom door." I brightened up, as the noise indicated that E had hopped directly from the motorcycle onto the toilet, which was, at least, an improvement over the last time, when he'd brightly informed me that the bike was plastic and washable. "Where did you say your ex lives now? I wonder if I might simply make it seem like he did you in. I mean, the police already know he set fire to the inside of your condo when you broke up."

"Only that part of the police force that is currently dating you," Ben said tartly, and then in the tone of one defeated, "Fine, fine, fine, fine. Do you want me to take the boy out for a spin on the sidewalk, to tire him out, so he can stop terrorizing you?"

"Would you?" I asked, as the horn/siren started up again. "That is ever so sweet of you."

Ben rolled his eyes as he reached to the toppled coat tree and grabbed E's little, black leather jacket, which was the other part of Ben's Christmas gift. "Why is this coat tree brok—oh, never mind," he said, as E rode the electric motorcycle straight into his leg and stopped with a thud. In Ben's defense, he didn't even flinch. Calves of steel. Clearly his daily workout was doing something.

He got the jacket on E in a single movement, reminiscent of a matador's wrangling a bull in full-charge, and then took advantage of E's momentarily puzzled state to say, "Come on, E, we're going for a ride outside."

"Outside!" E said. He had just recently started talking in front of people who were not his mother—that is to say, most of the world—but he seemed to think the function of his vocal cords was to enable him to become part play-back machine and part question generator.

Ben handled this with more aplomb than I managed. He said, "That's right, outside." And with a bright and horrible smile, he reached over and flung the front door open, which allowed E to dart out of it on his electric motorcycle at top speed.

I heard the sound of the motorcycle going down the front cement steps, and then E's battle cry. Ben darted out the front door. "Wait!" I heard him scream, shortly followed by, "Not on the street. Not on the street."

I closed the front door and relished the relative quiet of a toddler-free apartment. I wasn't in the least worried that Ben would let E play in traffic. I had long ago laid down the rules for their outings together without my supervision and that was that, if Ben broke E he would give birth to the replacement, and I would make sure that this happened, no matter what the physical impossibilities.

Able to hear myself think for the first time in more than a week, I thought I would go out back to my work shed and make room for the piano I was going to refinish for my boyfriend's birthday.

Which is why I was alone when I found the letter.

CHAPTER 2

Of Rats and Pianos

I was picking up the plant in its miraculously unbroken pot and setting it back atop the windowsill when the phone rang. Since the plant wasn't long for this world from the moment it had entered my house, I sort of patted at the dirt, shoved the pot into a corner of the sill, and rushed off to track down the phone.

It's not that I put the phone in weird places. It's more like it gets tired of waiting for someone to call and starts roaming around the house, finding ever more inventive places to hide. This time I got it on the third ring because it was only behind the toaster. "You should have known I'd catch you!" I said. "You were only two feet from the base."

"Dyce?" the voice on the other side said.

Fortunately I'd lived with my nickname long enough that I knew this wasn't a plea from Gamblers Anonymous. "Were you talking to the phone again?"

The voice was Cas—Castor—Wolfe's. He was my first boyfriend after two years of being divorced, and we'd been dating six months. Which didn't give him the right to know that much about me.

"Never mind," he said in the sort of tone that implied that other, normal women didn't chase their phones all over the house. Which, frankly, either meant their phones were far better behaved than mine, or that they were phone-whipped. But Cas didn't give me a chance to reply. Instead he said, "The guys will be there to deliver the piano any minute now. I told them to come through the backyard gate."

"Right," I said.

"Are you sure you can refinish it?" he asked. "It's in pretty bad shape."

"No problem," I said, which translated roughly to "I sure as heck hope so."

But by the time I made it out the back and into the yard, to unlock the door to the shed that was one of the reasons I lived where I did, I wasn't sure at all.

The truck was already there, maneuvering over the ten feet of dead grass and remains of snow in the backyard. It was a beat-up truck, painted an indifferent brown that mingled well with the patches of dirt. On the side of it, it said *Starving Students Moving* in the kind of writing that suggested a drunken midnight and a can of spray paint. Only, it was more like several cans of spray paint, since the *S* was in pink, but in the middle of the *V* it changed to black, then turned yellow on the *D*, and finished in glorious orange after the *O*. In fact, whoever had used the orange was so enthusiastic that it dotted off to the front of the truck and only quit in front of the wheel well, though I suspected the ground had been spray-painted as well.

The guys who jumped out each door of the truck as soon as it stopped didn't look like they were starving. They also didn't look like college students, unless the category was expanded to include those students who had gone on a trip into space in the eighties, had failed to come down to Earth, and hadn't yet realized that twenty years had gone by.

The bellies protruding out of their too-short T-shirts and above their too-tight pants definitely had taken twenty years and a lot of beer to develop.

"Yo," the nearest one said. "Is this where we drop the piano?"

In these circumstances, I'm always possessed by the ghost of my grandmother, the last woman in my family who put any stock in the term *ladylike.* I straightened myself up, which meant I reached these guys' chests, but never mind. Morally, I was standing on a mountain. "If you please," I said. "It should go in the workshop."

I think I was a little surprised they didn't look at me like I was a total nut. Instead, they climbed onto the back of the truck and started untying the piano, which was covered in a confusion of ropes that looked like a cat's cradle.

While they were doing that, I went into the workshop, leaving the door open. Mind you, it was a workshop. It was also where I earned the living that kept E and me in roof, food, and clothes.

Having tried three majors on for size, I'd left college to get married. That course of study had proven as much a success and now All-ex—couldn't be any more ex unless I killed him, something I considered two times a week and three times on Sunday—Mahr and I were divorced. I'd turned to the furniture-refinishing talents I'd picked up while trying to furnish the house on a shoestring, to keep up my side of E's upkeep and my own. So, the food often defaulted to pancakes, my clothes sometimes came from flea markets, and the apartment was in the sort of neighborhood that made Ben worry about my safety. But I was managing. I was on my own.

And it all happened in this little shed, with its chemical-and tool-filled shelves; its worktable made of four sturdy kitchen cabinets topped by a big, heavy board; and its pegs on the wall, that held my protective suit—resistant to most chemicals—my goggles, and my ear protectors.

When the guys came in carrying the piano, I was trying to drag the worktable to one side, which was easier said than done. First, because I had some pieces awaiting refinishing by the wall. Second, because cabinets and plywood top and all, the worktable outweighed me by quite a bit, even without the cans of stain and varnish I had stashed under it.

I'd managed to push it maybe five inches—okay, two—when one of the Starving Students said, "Whoa, there. Let us do that."

They pushed the table as far as it would go without moving the tea cart and the leather-topped desk by the wall. The blonder of the two—though it might just have been white hair shining from within his mullet that gave that impression—said, "What do you keep under there, little lady?"

He could have chosen a less appropriate thing to call me, since little I am, but *lady* is open for debate. Before I realized it, my mouth said the first thing that crossed my mind, "The body of the last guy who asked that question."

I don't know if they thought I was crazy or if they believed me. This sort of stuff tends to sound much more plausible when you're in a girl's workshop, surrounded by cutting and power tools.

Whether they thought I spoke the truth or that I was the rudest woman on Earth, they went ahead and brought the piano in and left it where the worktable had been. When I turned around to give them the twenty bucks I had in my pocket for that purpose, they were already hurrying to their truck, slamming both doors behind them.

"Your husband already paid us," the less blond one said, out the window, as they tore out of the backyard, in a shower of half-melted ice and clods of earth and dead grass.

Since All-ex wouldn't be caught dead near such a rag-tag outfit and, in fact, would probably pay ten times as much to have white-glove movers do whatever needed to be done, I assumed they meant Cas.

Which was just as well, I thought, as I came back to the workshop and took a look at the piano, because All-ex would also not be caught dead near a piece of furniture in this condition. And for once, perhaps he would be right.

To begin with, the piano was painted—in patchy, irregular bits—the sort of pink that suggested someone had melted a lot of cartoon horses or perhaps a lot of little girls. And it was covered in dirt. Opening the keyboard cover revealed ivories as yellowed as an old man's teeth.

But the inside of the keyboard cover was not painted, and it had the name stenciled on what I was almost sure was rosewood. It said *Steinway* in golden letters. And that had been the problem.

You see, Cas Wolfe is a manly man of the sort that—Ben tells me—one imagines sitting at home growing his chest hair. He works one of those dangerous professions that every little boy dreams of doing and every little girl dreams of marrying—in his case, investigator in the Serious Crimes Unit of the Goldport Police. He drives a four-wheel-drive

vehicle, and he calls it a *vehicle*, too. He climbs tall mountains. He runs for miles every morning. He likes going to the
range with his dad and his brother on the weekend, and the
least manly thing he will admit to is fencing at the Goldport
University Club on Saturday mornings. And that doesn't
really count, because while some guys might sneer at fencing, every girl knows that the Three Musketeers were no
sissies. Besides there's just something inherently right about
a big muscular guy with a big, gleaming sword.

But Cas has a dark secret. He plays the piano, having
learned from his grandmother, who gave private lessons.
Now that he had his own place, a few blocks from mine,
in downtown Goldport, he'd been dreaming of owning of
a piano of his own. His grandmother's Steinway had gone
to—he said—his least favorite aunt. And though Cas did
pretty well, a really good piano was hard to afford on a
police officer's salary.

I'd heard him sigh and moan long enough. I'd gone
with him from store to store, playing pianos, trying them
out. There was no piano-selling store, between downtown
Goldport and Pueblo, ranging from piano-manufacturer
outlets to thrift stores, that he and I hadn't visited. But the
pianos we found fell into two categories: the ones that
were too far gone to be recovered and the ones that were
too expensive.

So, when we'd found this piano at a flea market, Cas
had immediately looked at the back, at the soundboard,
which he said was intact, then opened the keyboard cover
and fingered the keys.

It had started innocuously enough. "The soundboard is
not cracked," Cas had said. He had that excited little-boy
gleam to his eye, a look guaranteed to melt the hearts of
mothers and girlfriends.

I'd looked at the piano, which looked dismal but not too bad, in the half dark of the old movie theater's lobby. "Wouldn't it be too hard to tune, though?" I said.

"Nah. I used to help my uncle tune grandma's piano. . . ."

He'd walked around, making *um* sounds, and poking at things, then said, "Mind you, it will need all new felts, and the ivories need cleaning and, of course, it needs to be cleaned inside, too, and tuned." Then he'd looked closer at the open keyboard cover and sighed. "And it's a Steinway, too. Looks like one of the early ones." He'd sighed. "Only, I don't think it can ever be made presentable. That pink paint looks like melted plastic or something. Even if I could make it play properly, I'd be embarrassed to have it in the living room."

This was when I lost my mind. I'd looked at the wrecked piano and said the first thing that came to me, which happened to be, "I can refinish it, if you can tune it."

I realized how far out on a limb I'd climbed when Cas gave me a sobering look. "Are you sure?"

"Of course I'm sure," I said, all the while wondering what exactly I'd taken in my morning coffee.

Now I decided whatever it was had to be potent, because there was no way I knew what to do with this mess.

Aren't pianos supposed to be French polished? he said. *They are,* I'd said. *You know how to do that?* he asked. *Of course,* I said.

I groaned. I knew how to apply French polish just like I knew how to fly. First method, buy a ticket in an airliner. Second method, grow wings.

This is another fine mess you've gotten us into, I thought vaguely, as I took a deep breath and contemplated the dismal, plasticky expanse of dusty, filthy piano.

In these circumstances, my grandmother has a way of coming to my rescue. Oh, not literally, since the dear lady had been dead for years, and even someone of her disposition couldn't defeat that kind of handicap. But the kinds of things she'd told me and taught me came to mind when nothing else would do. And what came to mind right now was that there wasn't anything so hopeless that a good cleaning wouldn't take it a fair way toward being solved.

I'd had a sink installed in the workshop, though there was no pipe in there, of course. Instead, I had a large plastic barrel with a faucet on it, leaning on a shelf at the back of the sink. There were some chemicals for which the best antidote was rinsing in plenty of water. I now grabbed a rag and wet it in the water, then took it back to the piano, and started washing a corner of it. Which, well . . . made the plasticky expanse look a brighter pink.

Right.

I went back to the shelf and grabbed one of the patent paint removers. Normally I used a bit of denatured alcohol and paint thinner mixed together, but I had a feeling the bright, bright pink cover was polyurethane and I didn't believe in hitting my head against walls.

So instead, I wet the tip of an old paintbrush and applied the furniture-finish remover to a corner of the piano.

Which is when I heard a squeak. It sounded like . . . a wheel out of joint. In fact, my first impulse was to think of the wheel of E's bike, which almost made me dive behind the piano. But then the squeak didn't sound again. So I thought it was a trick of my ears.

I grabbed the five-point painter's tool and tried to pry at the plastic paint that was bubbling up beautifully. Beneath it, there was gleaming silver. Right. I applied paint remover—again.

I opened the keyboard cover and got a rag moistened with water, and started wiping the keys, then went back and prized at the little bit of the silver paint off to reveal white. I put a bit more paint remover on, and went back to wipe the keys some more. They took a lot of wiping, as the rag kept coming away dark brown.

As I wiped, I couldn't help pressing the keys of course, and every time I did, there was a squeak as an echo.

I stepped back and frowned at the piano. The squeak continued—at first faint, then with increased urgency. *Squeak, squeak, squeak.*

It was undeniable that the sound was coming from inside the piano. But I was fairly sure pianos didn't squeak. Not absolutely sure, mind you. After all, Cas had said he needed to change the felts and what not, maybe there were also rubber parts inside the piano that needed changing. Or perhaps oiling . . .

I stared at it for a moment, but had to admit nothing was going to get done as long as the piano continued to squeak at me.

So I looked closer at the upright panel between the bottom of the keyboard and the pedals. I thought that it would have to be removed, anyway, so Cas could do whatever it was he wanted to do with felts and what not. So, eventually, he was going to have to open the bottom. And if it was rubber or something, I'd just give it a shot of oil and not be distracted as I was cleaning.

I grabbed the electric screwdriver from the shelf. There were four screws holding the panel in. It was only a moment's work to remove them and pull off the panel and—

Somehow, I'd dropped the wood panel, and I was on the other side of the shed, my body pressed flat against the wall, while my hands tried to figure out a means to escape backward into it.

Because inside the piano was a litter of papers, newspapers, and—rats.

Don't ask me how I knew they were rats. They were mostly pink and small and crawling all over one another. But I knew they were rats. And the instinctive reaction forming in my gut wanted me to climb on a chair and pull up the skirt I didn't have on and scream, "A rat, a rat!"

It took me several deep breaths before I realized that while these were probably rats—or mice, or perhaps guinea pigs or rabbits, though those were less likely to go wandering about inside old pianos—they were, in fact, tiny, pink, furless, and clearly harmless. Also, there were at least six of them, so screaming, "A rat," would not only be futile but also seriously understating things.

Continuing to take deep breaths—because the oxygen is likely to make you a little drunk, I guess—I forced myself to get closer. Yep. Rats or mice. Probably rats, because I had the idea mice were smaller at this stage of development—though the only baby rats I'd ever seen were the ones we dissected in biology—six of them. In a nest made of papers and other bits of rubbish.

As I moved nearer I thought the little things were actually kind of cute. In fact, they reminded me of E when he was born, all big head and flailing limbs.

Considering how often I'd called All-ex a rat, perhaps there was a reason for the resemblance. But unlike E, these baby rats were in a pile, and all of them seemed to be trying to dig under the others, trying to get down into a warm or safe place. . . .

The sane thing to do, I thought, was to kill them or something, right? But how did one kill baby rats? Poison? Or smack their little heads with the screwdriver. The idea made me cringe. They hadn't done anything wrong. Okay, so probably Cas would say they deserved death for nesting inside a piano, but if rats understood pianos, then the world was too complicated for my taste.

But if I left them there, I had a feeling they'd die, anyway, from cold or hunger or something.

So . . . they needed some place warm. Most babies did. And also food. And then I'd call wildlife rescue and ask them to find a foster mother or something. Mom had done that when she'd found a baby squirrel in the attic storage area of the bookstore.

I still was not particularly fond of the idea of touching them. After all, they could have plague or salmonella or retrovirus or whatever. However, I also couldn't let them die. So I put on my dust mask—to ward off the retrovirus thing—and I put on my heavy gloves, and then I dug underneath, trying to get all of the little rats and the nest, too.

It wasn't as easy as it sounds, because as I had all six in the space between my hands, I felt another one flail underneath, so I had to reach farther.

When I was done, the mess of newspaper and paper and wiggling baby rats didn't fit in my hands. So I grabbed a clean paint tray and dumped it all in it, covered it with a rag, because I was going to have to cross the space outside where the temperature was in the thirties, and ran, holding the tray, out of the shed and into the back hallway of the house, then along it to the kitchen, where I set the tray on the table.

The rats were still wiggling around wildly, and I considered putting them in the oven on warm, but I had the vague idea that it might prove to be a bad move. So I did what anyone else would do. I figured they were too young to actually walk. They seemed to be wriggling around on their bellies. I'd put them in a shallow, oven-proof glass dish.

I couldn't quite bring myself to put the mess of bits of paper and dirty stuff in it, though, so instead I used kitchen towels. I moved the babies, one by one into the dish, atop the towels.

Then I got my warming tray, put towels on top of it to mitigate the heat somewhat; set the dish atop the towels, and covered it with another towel.

They continued to squeak, but it didn't speed up or anything, so they were probably okay.

I grabbed the paint tray and shook the mess of papers into the trash.

And there, right on top of it all, a letter fell. It was so old that the envelope looked almost mustard yellow and the addresses were sepia-toned.

But it was a letter, and I couldn't throw a letter away. I fished it out of the trash and looked at it, realizing it was indeed very old.

CHAPTER 3

Wildlife and Secrets

The letter was addressed from someone named Almeria to Jacinth Jones, on Wisteria Court. I looked at the envelope a good long time, because Wisteria Court was just around the corner from me. Well, five blocks down, another of the neighborhoods populated almost exclusively by students living ten or twelve to a dilapidated Victorian. I guessed when the letter had been written the neighborhood was quite different.

Temptation to open the letter and read it warred with hesitation to pry into the lives of others. I opened the envelope just enough to see that there was indeed a letter inside. The whole thing was so fragile, though, that I was afraid it would fall apart in my hands. I set it down on the table and told myself maybe I would take it to the library or the downtown historical society. Or I might try to track down the descendants of Jacinth Jones. Surely they'd be the appropriate people to give the letter to.

Right now I had more important things to do. There was no wildlife rescue listed in the phone book, but the library gave me a name. I dialed it. And was met with incredulity. "Rats?"

"I think so. They could be mice." I thought about it a moment. "Large mice, with strangely shaped heads."

There was a long silence from the other side. "Rats aren't wildlife you know?" the person said. He sounded uncertainly male, like boys do when they stop growing but their voice hasn't caught up with their bodies yet. His kept cracking on the heights of incredulity. I thought he must be a high school student, putting in his required volunteer hours. "They are, in their own way, as domesticated as cats and dogs. That's why we don't advise taking them to the wild and setting them free."

I actually took the phone away from my ear and looked at it, to make sure it was indeed the phone and not some other sort of audio device of a prepared lecture. "I don't want to release them to the wild. They're babies!"

A throat cleared impatiently at the other end of the line, and then the voice, nasally high, asked, "How old did you say they were?"

"I have no idea," I said. "They're pink, they have no fur. Their eyes are closed. You tell me."

There was a long rustle, papers being shuffled and moved maybe. "They sound," he said at last, "like somewhere between newborn and a week old."

I looked at the dish. The babies were still squeaking under the dish towel, and still moving but the movement was less frantic. I wondered if they were warm enough?

Too warm? "Good to know," I said impatiently. "But I really need to give them to someone experienced in looking after rats."

"We don't have anyone," he said. "Most people . . . er . . . kill rats."

Which I completely understood, given my reaction on finding them. I might even have brought myself to do it, had they been adult. Though this was doubtful, since during the very brief suburban idyll of my marriage I'd found out I had trouble even buying ant poison to clean up the anthills in the yard. "Right. But I don't want to kill them. I want to raise them."

"Perhaps . . ." he said, hesitantly, "if you call pet shops? My book says that the best care for rats is a foster mother. They might know breeders who have a foster mother with a litter the right age."

"That's it?" I said.

"I'm afraid so," he said. "Rats are outside our provenance." And, as if he just couldn't help himself. "We also don't care for cockroaches."

Hah hah!Funny. I would have told him so, but he had hung up.

Cursing under my breath, I looked through the phone book again. Three pet shops. Bird Beauty, the first one, seemed vaguely horrified I wanted to do anything at all with rats. Apparently rodents were beneath them. They sold birdseed, they informed me—only birdseed. Gourmet birdseed.

I hung up wondering what kind of birds were gourmets. And did they take their seed with caviar.

Next up on the list was Fluffy Friends animal store. They treated me to a long diatribe on the evils of pet shops that actually sold pets and tried to intimate I was running a rat mill. I informed them, primly, that I didn't even own a loom, and hung up.

But, of all three of them, the worst was the third, Pets To Go. As soon as I mentioned, tentatively, that I'd found a litter of baby rats, they said, "Alive?"

"There wouldn't be much point calling you if they were dead."

"Well, we can't give you much," the guy said. "Only fifty cents apiece."

"Oh," I said, since I hadn't been thinking of money at all. "So you have a foster mother?"

"No, no, no. As food."

"You're going to give me fifty cents for the rats to eat?"

A long exasperated sigh was my answer. I had a feeling he was thinking I was the ultimate in dumb from the sneering tone in which he said, "No. Fifty cents per rat as food for pet snakes."

I hung up on him. Look, I realize that snakes have to eat, but I wasn't about to sell baby anything to be eaten alive. I still had to sleep with myself at night.

Right. This left me with—well, it left me with a bunch of baby rats that I didn't want to kill, but who were going to die if I didn't take care of them as surely as if I killed them. So . . . I had to figure out how to feed them and look after them. I had the vague idea that if I looked on the Internet, I could find a dozen sites telling me how to care for rats. The problem was that my laptop had died shortly after my marriage, and I had yet to find the money to replace it. Ben had a laptop, of course, but not at my house.

I called Cas—at work, something I rarely did. I got the

receptionist I always thought was much too cheery for what she actually said, "Goldport Serious Crimes Unit! How may I help you?"

Though it always seemed to me like she was the perky teen operator at a catalogue-ordering center, I refrained—at great cost in will power—from telling her she could mail me three murder cases and five burglaries. Something for which I felt I should get a medal. "I'd like to speak with Officer Wolfe, please. Tell him it's Dyce Dare."

There was the muffled shuffling talk that one hears when someone else has covered the telephone receiver with a hand. And then there was Cas's voice, "Hi, Dyce. Are you ready?"

For a brief, disturbed moment, I thought that he expected me to have the piano all done now. Then I remembered we were supposed to go out to dinner, which was part of the reason that Ben was at my place. Because he was supposed to babysit E. Of course, he was not supposed to arrive three hours early, alphabetize my pantry, color code my hairpins, and generally make himself a borderline OCD nuisance. Except that this was how Ben behaved when he was between relationships. "Oh. That. Not yet."

"Oh," he said. "But we have reservations for six."

I looked at the clock. It was five thirty. This meant that Ben and E had been gone for more than two hours. Weird. Normally they didn't stay out that long. Mind you, I wasn't worried that something had happened, because Ben was very competent at keeping people safe, having practiced on me for years. On the other hand . . .

"Ben took E out," I said. "And they're not back yet."

There was a little silence, and then Cas said, "On the electric bike?"

"Well, E hardly has any room to ride in the house."

There was a low chuckle. "Dyce, you're a mean, vengeful woman."

"I do what I can," I said modestly. "But right now I need you to look up how to take care of baby rats for me. Would you?"

There was another silence. "Uh—Dyce, I don't think you should lock Ben in your shed and let rats loose on him. I mean, you can, of course, but I wouldn't advise it. I am an officer of the law and I—"

"No. If I were to lock Ben up with rats, they'd be big rats. With sharp teeth. Trained to chew on ties."

"Dyce!"

"Well . . . he did give E that thing. But no, you see, I found a litter of baby rats in the piano."

"Pet shops will buy them for—"

"No."

"I see." I heard him tapping the keyboard. "Um . . . looks like you need to put them somewhere on top of a heating pad on the lowest setting, and shield them with towels, you know, so they don't get burned."

I looked at the dish. "Check."

"Oh, good. You're also supposed to give them baby formula. Using an eyedropper."

"I don't—" I started.

"I figured. I'll stop by the supermarket on the way there." I heard him close his laptop. "I'll be there in about . . . twenty minutes. Can they wait that long?"

"I hope so," I said. "See you soon, then."

Having hung up, I was left with nothing more to do. It wasn't like I could feed the babies until Cas arrived. That meant . . . I looked at the letter. Part of me—the part that had been raised by my grandmother—informed me sternly that ladies don't read other people's correspondence. But judging by the color of the paper, the color of the ink, and the pointy, old-fashioned handwriting, I suspected whoever had written this letter, and whoever was supposed to receive it had long been dust in the ground. And come on, I told Grandma's shade. If people didn't read other people's letters, there would be no histories. No biographies. No blackmail. No indictments for conspiracy. All sorts of productive enterprises would never happen.

I sat at the table and opened the letter, pulling out the paper gingerly, so it wouldn't fall apart. It took me forever to manage to get the sheet open without tearing it.

The writing inside was more faded than it had been on the outside, just a sepia tracery on the yellow page. I had to turn the light on over the kitchen table, to be able to read what it said.

Dear Jacinth, it said. *I had hoped things would never come to this pass.* Pass was underlined five times. *But I'm afraid my husband knows. Or at least, he has enough reason to suspect. Sometimes he looks at me in such a way that I'm not sure I can stand it (far less survive it). I will meet you next week, at seven thirty, at the fruit stand. I will bring the baby. I am afraid the time has come to take you up on your offer and leave as soon as possible. Yours, always, Almeria.*

I looked at it, and confess I felt shocked. Victorian people—and I was almost sure that the letter was at least a hundred years old—weren't supposed to have complications like a husband while being someone else's "always."

Still sitting at the table, staring at the letter, wondering at the long-lost love affair behind it, I heard the front door open and Ben's all-too-brisk voice saying, "That's it, E. You bring Pythagoras in."

Pythagoras? Since I heard the bike almost immediately,

I assumed they'd named it, though it seemed like a truly bizarre idea. Then there were sounds of E dismounting, and moments later, Ben's forced-cheerful voice from the dining room. "Dyce, we're home. Sorry to be late, but I—" He stopped at the door to the kitchen. "You didn't have to make dinner. I figured I'd take E for burgers or something." He crossed the kitchen as he spoke, and lifted the dish-towel. And jumped back.

"Dyce, what the hell? I'm not eating that."

"Good," I told him. "You'd have to pay me fifty cents a piece!"

"What?"

"Please cover them. Cas is getting formula and an eye-dropper to feed them."

"They're rats!"

"Yes, I found them in the piano."

"Ew!"

"They're just babies. Don't tell me I should have killed them."

"I wasn't about to tell you anything of the kind. I've known you for almost twenty years." He made a low whis-tle under his breath. "Uh . . . so . . . you're raising them."

"That's the general idea."

"And then?"

"I don't know," I said. "Put an ad in the paper. Sell them or something. For more than fifty cents, so people don't feed them to snakes."

Ben pulled a chair away from the table and sat down in it. At this moment, E came bounding in, pulling at my shirt. "Mom, mom, mom. Mom!!!! Cat."

Ben ran his hand backward through his hair, opened his mouth.

"No, honey. They're rats."

E looked confused. He shook his head. "Cat. Peegrass!"

Ben closed his mouth with a snap, then drew in a deep breath. "Uh . . . no, uh . . . he means cat."

"What?"

"Well . . . you see, we found this cat, two blocks away, choking and foaming at the mouth. So we took him to the vet. He'd been given poison. So the vet induced vomiting. So, the cat didn't have a chip or a tag or anything, and he's really sweet. Big black tom. So E and I . . . *wethoughtwe'dkeephimandbringhimhome*."

"What?!"

"Peegrass E's cat!"

"Benedict Colm, are you out of your ever-loving mind?"

He put a finger inside his collar, as if it had suddenly gotten too tight and actually stammered, "Well, well, y-you see, E really liked him, and he wanted to keep him. I couldn't say no!"

"Oh, right, hide behind the toddler." I didn't know whether to laugh or cry. Rats, cats, toddlers, oh my. "You know I never got along with cats."

"Only Fluffy. And that's because you set her on fire when you were five."

"I didn't set her on fire," I said. "I just lit the quilting frame and tried to get her to jump through it. If she'd been quick about it, and I hadn't had to use the shoelace, she'd not have caught fire."

"Shoelace?"

"Whip. I didn't have a whip. Couldn't be a lion tamer without a whip. I had to try something. And anyway, Fluffy never forgave me. She had to take Valium whenever she saw me. And she piddled in my bed whenever I stayed at Mom's."

"Which is probably why it's best for everyone that she's gone to a better place."

I abstained from pointing out I wasn't sure that Mom's fireplace mantel was a better place, since that's where Fluffy's ashes were, inside an urn shaped like a Persian cat. At least the urn didn't hiss when it saw me.

"So now you can have Pythagoras. Really, he's a very sweet cat!"

"If he's so sweet, why don't you keep him?" I asked.

"Because he's E's cat."

"Peegrass E's cat!" my son the traitor said, nodding vigorously.

"Right, agree with Ben, why don't you?"

"Aguee wid Ben!"

"So, Mister Colm, why can't you take Peegrass yourself?"

Ben squirmed. "He's black!"

"And? Is your condo color segregated?"

He looked at me like I'd taken leave of my senses. "He would clash horribly with my rugs and the sofas. It's all white or red! He'd be completely out of place."

Since this concept of color-coordinated pets had never occurred to me, I was silent for a moment. Before I could tell him to dye the cat a more appropriate color, E had run out of the room and returned carrying a plastic cage with a metal grate door.

He sat the cage on my knees, so that I had to put out a hand to balance it. It weighed at least fifteen pounds. E grinned at me. "Peegrass!"

Pythagoras the cat looked at me through the cage. He was huge and black, and looked exactly like a baby panther. A baby panther in dire need of a corner to hide himself in.

He was apple-headed, with a big, round cranium and the sort of jaw that says, "I can crush you with one bite."

However, his green eyes had an intensely blue center, and crossed ever so slightly. And the expression in his eyes said, "I'm sorry. I hope I'm not trespassing." And, "Could you please direct me to the nearest corner where I may cower and piddle quietly on myself?" He looked—if such were possible—like a much younger feline version of Woody Allen.

I sighed. I could kick him out into the cold cruel world. Sure I could. Right after I strangled the baby rats with my bare hands and danced on their little corpses.

"Peegrass good cat!" E said.

"Mmmeeeee?" Pythagoras said, in what was clearly, "I'm not intruding, am I? Pay no attention to me. I'll just sit here and cross my eyes at you." He put a paw out through the bars and touched my hand, with every claw retracted.

Right. "Ben, I'm never going to forgive you. Never, ever, ever, ever. What am I going to do with a cat and seven baby rats?"

He opened his mouth, and I could tell he was considering telling me that one sort of solved the other, but thought better of it, which meant that despite all appearances, Ben had the capacity to learn. "Uh," he said. "The . . . the rats are a temporary thing, right? I could . . . I could stay here and . . . uh . . . cat-sit. You know, to make sure they don't . . . uh . . . come in contact. Until we find homes for the rats!"

It was at this moment that the love of my life walked through the door. Cas Wolfe is slightly taller than Ben and has the sort of face that makes you think he's very, very ugly, until that is, you realize the reason his features don't work together is that each of them is perfect. And he has a smile that melts snow and makes all the little plants perk up and flirt.

He was giving me that smile as he looked from the carrier, to me. "Nice," he said. "Are you opening a pet shop as a sideline?"

"I see nothing escapes you," I said, putting the carrier down.

"Of course not," he said, setting the bag from Youngling Foods on the table, and leaning down to half pick me up off my feet and kiss the living daylights out of me. I'd been kissed before Cas Wolfe had ever kissed me, and it was entirely possible I'd be kissed after, but I was fairly sure no one else could kiss me like he did. For one, I was fairly sure he kept a time-distortion device in his pocket. As his lips closed over mine, his arms crushing me against his muscular chest, his tongue darting into my mouth, I felt as though time had stopped. Like in those old movies, when someone presses a stopwatch and everything around them stops, and only they are intensely alive. By the time he sat me down, I had no idea what he was talking about, as he added, "It's my training in the police."

And then he proceeded to take charge, the way he normally did, "Here's the formula," he told Ben, setting the formula can—ten times as large as all the rats combined—on the table, with a printout and one of those droppers one uses for giving medicine to children. "The instructions are on the paper, Ben. They say you have to feed them pretty much every couple of hours, though. Or whenever they squirm and cry."

"Me?" Ben said.

"You. Because I'm taking Dyce out to dinner."

CHAPTER 4

Policemen in the Night

"How long is Alex going to be away?" Cas asked, as we got out of his car in the driveway outside my home.

He'd taken me to dinner and dancing—both conveniently provided by the same restaurant—and we'd talked very little about my present situation. Except for his laughing over my house going to the cats and the rats and offering me a dog to complete the set.

But now, as he opened the door for me, and held my hand walking to the house, his mind clearly had returned to essential matters and there was no matter more essential than the fact that All-ex had been out of town for two weeks now. Normally we shared E's custody, more or less evenly. But All-ex was out of town, visiting the family of Mrs. All-ex for the holidays. This meant that Cas could not spend the night—a decision we'd both made when E was staying with me, so as not to confuse him.

So the best we could do was hold hands—his very warm, large hand enveloping mine—and walk to the front door. Where he stopped, wrapped his arms around me, and kissed me for keeps. As soon as he'd let me go, and I could breathe again, I said, "Why don't you come in?"

"Uh," he said. "Better not. With . . ."

"Ben is here. You're not going to seduce me in front of Ben."

Cas nodded once. He looked at me like the guy who's been lost in the desert for a week and now comes across a case of bottled water, a nice juicy steak, and chocolate cake for dessert. "Why must your ex have three weeks of vacation?" he said. "It's not fair. Next time make him take E!"

"I don't think Michelle's parents would like E," I said. And besides, unleashing E on unsuspecting strangers who had never done me any harm probably rated up there as a karmic offense.

"Come in, have some tea or coffee, or something," I said, and opened the door, mindful that Ben might be behind it looking through the keyhole. Okay, so he hadn't done that since my first date with Cas, but you never knew.

However, Ben wasn't behind the door. He wasn't in the living room or in the portion of the dining room that I could see. And then I heard it—two male voices from the kitchen. Neither of them E's.

I frowned. Ben wasn't seeing anyone at the moment. Which accounted for his having plenty of free time to hang out at my house, alphabetizing my spice rack and color-coordinating the paper napkins. And while he had a varied and extensive circle of friends, he did not usually bring them to my house. Unless, of course, someone needed something relating to work, or a friend had an emergency. Even then, I had trouble believing that Ben would be willing to let someone come here, to what he considered slum housing. He'd be more likely to package the rats, the cat, and E and go meet them wherever.

So I hurried into the kitchen. And stopped. Ben was sitting on one of the chairs, legs casually crossed, a dish towel laying across his arm, presumably to protect his sleeve, because on the sleeve rested a baby rat, whom he was feeding with the eyedropper.

Sitting on the chair across from him, a similar dish towel draped over his right arm, a baby rat resting tummy up on it, while the other hand rubbed said tummy with a cotton ball was . . . I narrowed my eyes, quite unable to decide whether it was Apollo or Bacchus. I was sure it was one of them because I'd seen pictures of ancient friezes: the aquiline nose, the dark tumbled curls, the full lips. Of course, the friezes didn't show the five-o'clock shadow and very few carved Greek divinities wore anything resembling a polo and a pair of jeans. But I figured that was a matter of detail and understood, all of sudden, why he was here. Clearly Ben had got exasperated while looking after the animals alone, and decided to invoke supernatural help.

The stranger looked very Apollo as he rubbed the rat's tummy, but when he looked up at us there was a spark of Bacchian mischief in his dark eyes. "Hi, Cas," he said. And got up carefully, so as not to disturb the baby rat. He dropped the cotton ball, grinned wide, and extended a hand to me. "And you must be Dyce."

"Uh, yes," I said, allowing my hand to be squeezed in his. Standing, he was just a little shorter than Ben, which again brought up the whole Apollo thing. Someone so Mediterranean-looking shouldn't be so tall. "Uh . . ."

"This is my idiot cousin, Nick," Cas said. "I've told you about him."

"Nick?" I said, confused. Cas had exactly three family members in Goldport. The rest of them lived spread out throughout the state. His parents, I'd met. His cousin—whom he never named—had been out of state for the last six months, and so I hadn't had the pleasure. The only thing I knew about the man, was that they'd been friends as kids and that his cousin was gay. I looked at Ben with a slight frown, but Nick was talking, "Stravos Nikopoulous," he said, with a disarming grin. "But I find people have an easier time just saying *Nick*. Besides, I got tired of being shoved into lockers as a freshman and *Nick* calls a whole lot less attention."

"Uh . . . yes . . ." I said, still looking at Ben who gave me an almost imperceptible shrug, which meant "I didn't do it, and I don't get it, either."

"I came over," Nick said, divesting himself of the dishcloth and setting the baby rat gently into a large aquarium on the kitchen counter—a dry tank with what looked like a mass of cotton wool at the bottom and little pink wiggly bodies nestled in it. "Because the vet called about, uh . . . Pythagoras being poisoned? I couldn't get an answer on the phone, so I stopped by on the off chance someone was home and I could ask a few questions. And then . . . uh." He looked at Ben. "Mr. Colm needed help with the rats."

Behind his back, Mr. Colm rolled his eyes and said, "I've put E to bed, Dyce. And Pythagoras is with him. I put Pythagoras's box in the bathroom. And these damn rats are always hungry. You finish feeding and rubbing their tummies, and the first one is hungry again."

"I told you they were just like E," I said. "Rubbing their tummies?"

"To give them a bowel movement," Nick said, and coughed. "It's an unusual occupation."

I leaned against the sink. I had a feeling there was more going on here than I was being told, and besides, Cas was leaning on the sink and had that look in his eyes that said, "I love it when a plan goes well." Was the love of my life playing matchmaker? "Uh . . . you wanted to ask about the cat? Is he yours?"

The grin again. Honestly, the man could solve the energy crisis just by smiling like that. "No, no. I'm sorry, I didn't explain myself properly. I'm Officer Stravos Nikopoulous of the Serious Crimes Unit of Goldport Police Department."

"*Officer* Nick," Cas said. "Joined the force a month ago, and we now trust him to investigate crimes against cats. If he promises to be very careful and follow the rules."

Officer Nick made the sound normally transcribed as *thp*, which I was fairly sure was not part of any regulations, but when I looked at him, he was grinning again and shaking his head at Cas.

"Serious crimes?" I asked, before any more breach of officer-like protocol occurred. At the table, Ben had picked up a cotton ball and was rubbing the squirming rat. "Uh . . . the cat—"

Nick nodded decisively and actually pulled a notebook from the back pocket of his jeans. Now, how in hell he'd managed to get that notebook into a pocket that seemed to fit tighter than a second skin, I didn't know. But he flipped through it. "There have been a series of poisonings, and . . . and other dead cats and dogs in this neighborhood, and the police have been tracking them very carefully."

Now, I knew that Goldport Police Department didn't really have much to do. The average number of murders per year was maybe four, though in the past two years there had been more like ten. However, those had been part of mass murders, and therefore all tied together into one or two incidents. And I hoped the trend wasn't about to continue. My parents might be thrilled to live in the capital of small-town crime, but I didn't share their fascination with murder, fictional or otherwise.

Given the average number of murders before that, I completely understood there might have been mission creep and that, for all I know, mailbox bashing and wheelies on the lawn might now fall to the Serious Crime Department. But Cas must have guessed my thoughts, because he jumped in. "In a way animal cruelty is borderline," he said. "Normally we'd let the beat officers deal with it. They're more likely to follow the leads because of whom they know in the neighborhood. But when the case is not easily solvable and goes on for months, and when it seems to be serial . . ."

"Yeah," Officer Nick said, and for once he didn't smile. "We find that serial animal abuse is often a . . . well . . . a warm-up act for a mass murderer."

"Oh, not another one," I said.

"Well, look at it this way," Cas said. "If we hadn't had those cases, we wouldn't have the money to hire Nick, after he finished his training."

"I hardly think that's compensation," Nick said. "Though I was glad to come back to Goldport."

Ben perked up, as he put the rat in the aquarium next to its siblings. "Where did you work before?"

"In Goldport," Officer Nick said, ruefully. And to Ben's look of confusion, he replied, "As a systems analyst. Tech. I was laid off a year ago, there didn't seem to be anything in the area, so I went through an intensive law-enforcement course in Denver. I thought I would have to work in Denver, but I'm glad to have come back." He gave Ben an indecipherable look—or at least indecipherable by me—then said, "At any rate I was . . . I came to ask Mr. Colm how he found the cat and to see if it was recovering. We've asked all the vets in this neighborhood to call us whenever something like this happened, so we can keep track of the cases."

I had the strong impression that normally keeping track of the cases was done by phone, at most. I also had the strong impression that Mr. Colm's turned back was being given a very careful once-over, even as Officer Nick folded his notebook, which I gathered had been more or less an official-looking prop—and slid it back into his pocket, before clearing his throat and saying to Ben's back, "I guess I should go, since I have the information I needed and . . . er . . . you don't need my help with the rats anymore."

"Oh, come on," Cas said. "You're off duty, aren't you? This was an off-duty call. Stay and have some coffee."

"Uh . . . I don't know if . . ." He looked at me.

This, of course, was my cue. "I'd be happy for you to stay. I met Cas's parents over the holidays, and I'm glad to finally get to meet you." I did my best imitation of his smile back at him. I got a huge smile, with hints of relief, then he looked back at Ben who was keeping his back resolutely turned and was fiddling with the rats. "But I have to go check on E. So if you would make coffee, Cas!"

I walked around through the dining room to the living room, and then through my bedroom into E's. E was asleep in the little bed I'd got him recently—made of plywood and shaped like a race car—going for a song at the flea market. He was lying on his side, his arm over Pythagoras, who was awake and who gave me a "please don't kick me out" look, as I leaned in to kiss E. He looked so pathetic that I petted his head. "Of course not, Pythagoras."

E smiled and mumbled, "Peegrass," and the cat looked even more apologetic, as though he were afraid I'd be jealous of him. I petted him. "Just don't pee floor," I whispered, as I pulled a light blanket over E, and went back to the kitchen.

Where Ben, to what should not have been my surprise, had claimed the coffee-making honors. It shouldn't have been a surprise because—possibly because of how much time he'd spent at my house in the last six months, and his exasperation with my coffee—his gift to me had been a huge, industrial-looking coffeemaker, that could make coffee, espresso, latte, and—for all I knew—dance, do dishes, and sing the blues.

Officer Nick—or, I guessed, since he was off duty, just Nick—was trying resolutely to keep up a conversation, which was being met with mumbles and occasional nods from Ben. I wondered if he'd been playing this hard to get while we were gone, too, and felt like shaking him. Okay, not that I think that Ben should fall for every guy who talked nice to him. And not that I even knew if Nick was hitting on him. But Nick was trying to establish some sort of conversation, and being if not rebuffed at least mostly ignored.

"Normally," Nick said, and cleared his throat, "I prefer Greek coffee, you know, with the grounds in."

"I'll be quite happy to pour the grounds in the cup," Ben said, and I couldn't tell if his answer was playful or ill humored.

Clearly Nick didn't either, because he gave a half chuckle and said, "No, it has to be a particular kind of coffee for that, not just . . ." He petered out and moved forward to help Ben retrieve the cups—tall ones, so I presumed we were having coffee, not espresso—from the cabinet above. A short-lived cooperative effort, since there were only four cups, and each of them got two and set them on the counter, and then Nick had to step back.

"Nick's parents own The Golden Fleece in Denver," Cas said. He sounded helpful, but he still looked very amused. "They used to have a restaurant here, but they moved there when Nick was in his last year of high school. So he stayed with my parents and me for his senior year."

I don't have any idea what either Cas or Nick expected Ben to do with this information, but what he did was start passing out coffee cups and sort of herd us toward the table, where he proceeded to set out sugar and in a blue glass creamer, which he'd also given me, cream. He looked grave as he brought coffee spoons to the table and sat down.

There were enough chairs, because Cas had given me two more for Christmas, to complement my initial two. He said that sooner or later E would start sitting at the table, not in a high chair, and Ben came over often enough.

Ben hesitated before sitting down. I got the impression he didn't like the only seat open, which was between Cas—who had claimed the seat next to me—and Nick. He had a slightly mulish look on his face that reminded me of when his mother tried to interfere with his attire in high school. I knew that Ben was stubborn enough that any pressure met its proverbial immovable object in him.

"So," I said, as silence lengthened, "you got an aquarium and a cat litter pan?"

Ben nodded. Apparently the silent treatment would also extend to me.

"Before or after Officer Nick arrived," I asked him, now determined to needle him out of his silence.

"Before," Ben said. "That's why I wasn't here when he called. When I came home with E and Pythagoras, he was parked at the curb, waiting."

"I didn't have anywhere else to be," Nick said, apologetically. "I'd left work and I thought I'd stop by on the way home." He frowned slightly. "I live alone, so I wasn't delaying anyone's dinner."

If there was just a hint of something in his look at Ben, it went completely unanswered. Ben sipped his coffee in silence.

Once more it was left to me to fill the conversation gap. "I found a very old letter today," I said. "It seems to talk about, well, if not a murder, then a situation that could have lead to it. I told Cas at dinner that I was sure there had been a murder and we should investigate."

"And I told her we had enough trouble with present murders, without imagining old ones," Cas said with a smile.

"Uh . . . yeah . . ." Nick said. "I doubt we would have the resources . . ." He sipped his coffee. He was still frowning.

"What was that all about?" I asked Ben as the door closed behind Goldport's finest.

"What?" he asked. The way he asked it—sulkily—told me he knew quite well what I was talking about. He had brought the small suitcase that he normally used when he was spending a couple of nights. He'd also brought a pair of sheets and a light blanket, with which he was transforming the sofa into a bed. I would probably have been offended at his bringing bed clothes from home, if I didn't realize he was doing it to save me money and time. He owned a washer and dryer—and most of the time sent his laundry out—while I had to tote the dirty clothes and E to the Laundromat around the corner.

How he could be at the same time so considerate and so pigheaded was beyond me. "You know very well what. Poor Nick!"

Ben gave me an intentionally blank stare. "What, because he has a penis, I'm supposed to go over like nine pins?"

"Oh, for heaven's sake," I said, picking up the mystery book from the coffee table and doing my best not to throw it. "He was trying to be friendly. Make small talk."

Ben glared. "He was trying to be way too friendly. Does your boyfriend think that just because his cousin is gay I will obviously be smitten with him?"

"You seemed to be doing fine when we came in."

Ben shrugged. "He was helping with the rats. I needed an extra pair of hands."

I bit my lip, to abstain from giving the reply that crossed my mind.

He sighed—his well-known sigh of exasperation that he deployed whenever he didn't know what else to say to me. "Look, Dyce, he's not my type, okay?"

"Oh, of course not. Your type is blond and imbecilic. To such stunning success."

"Dyce!" he said. It was the warning voice, the one that told me I was about to cross all boundaries and risk having him at the very least sulk at me for weeks.

"Fine!" I said. "Are you going to look after the rats during the night?"

"That's the idea," he said. "That's why I'm staying. I put the screen cover that came with the aquarium over them and I got them a little heat thing the pet shop recommended. Mind you, I don't think Pythagoras will try to hurt them, but it's safer to have the cover on."

There was nothing left for it, but for me to slink off to bed.

Where, after a few minutes, I heard a *mmmmmr,* followed by a *euuu* as the heavy body of a less-than-aerodynamic cat landed on the top of the bed. I turned around to watch him walk hesitantly toward me. It was the first time I watched a cat pick his way, as if unsure of himself. When he got close enough, he reached out with claws retracted and tapped my arm with his paw. It was the sort of tap that meant, "May I cuddle?" the meaning as clear as if he'd spoken. I turned his way. "Come on."

Pythagoras jumped up and started kneading at my arm, making a sound like a faulty motor. It was rather nice, and something Fluffy had never done.

I woke up to a sound like . . . digging. For a moment, in utter confusion, I thought someone was digging a grave. Don't even ask why I was dreaming of graves. I just was. Then the sound of digging and flying earth became the sound of scraped plastic. Paws. Scraping on plastic. I realized it was Pythagoras, in the bathroom, digging in the box, and apparently trying to dig through the bottom of the box to China.

For the first time it occurred to me that my son might not see a difference between the litter box and the sandbox, and I rushed out of bed and into the bathroom, because E has a way of being awake at the most inconvenient times.

I should have trusted Ben. The box—or what I presumed was the box—sat inside a grayish tent. A little cat head poked, distractedly, through the opening in the tent and gave me that "Do you mind?" look cats give in such circumstances.

"Oh, sorry," I mumbled, and retreated to the bedroom, where I found I was too awake to go back to sleep. I came back to the bathroom, where Pythagoras was now standing outside the tent looking in, while the tent made some distinct mechanical noises. My parents had always talked of getting a mechanical, self-cleaning box for Fluffy. It would be like Ben to be that practical. Even if he was the most annoying creature who had ever drawn breath since the beginning of human history. I frowned remembering his treatment of the Secondary, Auxiliary Officer Hotstuff, Gay Division. Annoying man. Not his type!

Humphing under my breath, I turned on the water and took a quick shower, then dressed in my working jeans and T-shirt. I fully intended to wake Ben and tell him to keep an eye out for E, but found it wasn't needed.

He was in the kitchen and he looked exactly as if I was sure I had looked the first week of E's life—like someone had dragged him through Hell by his heels, taking care to hit the spiniest places and the roughest ground. His hair stood on end. His eyes had dark circles. And I had to point out he was presenting the eyedropper to the wrong end of the rat he held.

The look he gave me seemed to imply that I had somehow rotated the little rat on him. He muttered something from which the words *insatiable* and *glad I'll never have kids* emerged. I felt somewhat mollified. I mean, he was still an unholy pain, but he was an unholy pain who'd foregone sleep to look after baby rats. "I'll go work on the piano for a couple of hours," I said. "And then I'll take rat duty for a while so you can sleep, okay?"

I thought he said yes, though frankly, when people growl like that it's very hard to tell. So, I went out back and stripped the top of the piano, and then started on the sides. I would need, I realized, to figure out how the heck one applied French polish.

Asking Cas to look it up on his computer was out of the question. If he looked it up, he would know I didn't know how to do it, and then he'd go all weird about it. So . . .

So, I thought, as I finished all the work I could hope to do without leaving the poor rats at the mercy of a man who was as likely to give them breakfast as a formula enema, I would have to go to the library. Around noon, perhaps, once Ben had slept some. I'd go to the library and look up French polishing on their computer. And then I could look up Jacinth Jones, too, I thought brightly. If I was going to be at the library, anyway . . .

With a song in my heart and virtue in my mind, I came back inside, where the little rats were screaming bloody murder. Ben was on the sofa. He slept like a mummy, all wrapped up and immobile, and that was exactly what he was doing, only this time the mummy had a look of serene stubbornness, like he was determined not to hear the crying of the rats, and no one could make him.

So I did what I had to do, going into the kitchen and feeding the rats, one by one, then rubbing their stomachs with moist cotton balls to make them pee and poop.

There were letters written in black marker on the rump of each of the little rats. The largest one had RTL, then the chubbiest one had RTS, the next one, which was almost black, had FNK written on his tail, the only place it could be seen because there was no black fur. The next rat, all white, had FAC on his rounded rump. The next rat was

completely black, so you had to squint to make out darker
black letters YDR. The next one had written on his rump
NEST. And the next one said TAIL, which was funny because it had a slightly bent tail as though it had been caught
in something and kinked.

I considered waking Ben to ask him about the writing on
the rats, which seemed like the sort of thing no one should
do while sober. But I remembered his growling at me, and I
thought better of it. Instead, I spent the time making a pile
of pancakes for breakfast, then feeding Pythagoras—who
by then was looking somewhat hopefully at the baby rats.
Ben had bought a load of cat food and put it in the pantry
cabinet. Alphabetized, of course. I upended a can of tuna
into a tea saucer and left Pythagoras to it, while I returned
to feeding baby rats.

I was finishing this when E came dragging into the
kitchen, looking like he, too, had been up all night. His
pajamas were askew and his little fluffy golden hair stood
on end. He looked at me out of bleary eyes, crept up to the
table, climbed on a chair, and put his head on his arms on
the table.

"What's wrong, baby bunny? What do you need?" I
asked brightly, as I finished wiping up the rat with TAIL
on his rump, and setting him back in the aquarium, being careful to set the lid back on it.

E opened an eye and glared at me. "Need coffee anna
cigarette."

He sounded like he meant it, too, though I had no idea
where he might have learned it. And though I might often
give him less than organic, home-cooked food—which he
got at All-ex's house—I was not about to try for the Worst
Mother In The World competition.

"How about a glass of milk and a pancake with chocolate syrup?" I asked.

The offer was graciously accepted, and I heard Ben get up from the sofa. I looked at the clock, amazed it was only nine o'clock. Mind you, most of the time, even when he stayed over, Ben was long gone by this time of day. He worked as a financial planner for a local firm and took his job very seriously, which probably accounted for his doing very well at it—but the whole company had closed down for Christmas week and Ben had decided to take the two weeks after as vacation, perhaps because all of us had been telling him he was more wound up than a slinky in a tourniquet.

Of course, we—or at least I—had expected him to actually do something with his vacation, instead of hanging out at my house, desperately trying to impose some sort of order on my arrangements. However, Ben was who he was, which I supposed also accounted for his behavior the night before. . . . not that much accounted for that, actually. Because while I didn't expect Ben to fall madly in love with the first decent-looking gay man who crossed his path, I did expect him to at least be polite. And he'd been skating the edge there yesterday. I wondered what exactly had caused that.

Meanwhile, I poured myself coffee, and grabbed a pancake, and was feeling almost human by the time Ben came into the kitchen looking like a new man, or at least one who had slept and put on a nice clean shirt and pants, and tied his tie to a degree of exactness that pleased him.

I let him grab a coffee and pancakes, before I asked, "Why did you write on the rats?"

He blinked at me, as if I had asked him why he had a nose on his face. "Eh?" he said. And then with a shrug. "To tell them apart."

"Ben . . . they all have different patches of color!" I said.

"Do they?" He looked genuinely surprised. "I don't know. In the middle of the night they all looked the same. I wrote on them to make sure I fed them all." He looked around on the counter and gave me a notepad with a name line: Ratley, Ratso, Rat Fink, Rat Face, You Dirty Rat, Nestor, and Rat Tail. Each of the names had three neat check marks in front of them. "The rats now have names?" I asked

Ben nodded. "I used your laundry marker," he said.

It was both so strange and so absolutely Ben with his mania for organization that I started giggling.

"What? It was perfectly logical," he said.

"They're lucky you didn't put a little arrow by their heads, with *This End Up*. Or perhaps not."

He grinned ruefully. "I would have figured it out," he said. "Eventually."

In the best of humors, he agreed to keep an eye on Pythagoras and feed the never-satisfied rats while I went to the library. I stuck the old letter from the piano in my purse, but let Ben assume I was just going to browse for refinishing materials or look in at the flea market, or the other things I did when I had time. As a peace offering—and because I was afraid he would either run over Pythagoras, topple the aquarium, or maim Ben with the electrical motorcycle, I took E with me.

I first bathed him in the bathroom, which between Pythagoras's little tent and Ben's case of beauty products—the man had a moisturizer for each time of day, I swear—was getting pretty cramped. Then I dressed him in his little jeans, blue sweatshirt, and the jacket Mom had brought him from the Inspector Maigret Fest she had attended in Paris last summer. I assumed she hadn't bought it at the convention itself, since it wasn't even vaguely murder related. It was a lambskin jacket, with a hood with little rounded ears sewn on it. The back read *Douce Comme un Agneau*. It made old ladies say, "aww," and everyone else smile when they saw E. It also ranked up there with the most brazen lie in the history of the universe.

Still, perhaps because a toddler in possession of an electric motorcycle, a cat, and seven rats—even if his mother isn't kind enough to give him cigarettes and coffee for breakfast—has very little more mischief he needs to make. E was quiet except for the sort of remarks he makes when he's strapped into his car seat at the back of the car. These tend to consist of his pointing at things out the window and saying, "Car!" "Car!" "Dog!" "Red House." I don't know if he does this because he thinks I can't see them or if he wants to show his amazing ability to see and say. Impressively, he shouted, "Books!" as we pulled into the parking lot of the library—one of the old Carnegie libraries, in golden stone, set in the middle of a garden all the more surprisingly luscious with old green trees and grass, as it was the middle of winter in Colorado, where the only way to keep a green lawn was to have a plastic one, or to have sold your soul to the devil.

Being the heartless woman I was, I couldn't care less which librarian had condemned herself to eternal hellfire to bring about this result. I reveled in the tall evergreens surrounding the library and the carpet of grass that extended from the parking lot all around the building.

Inside, the library was very well kept and though I had heard of this strange trend where libraries were eschewing actual books in favor of audio books, programs, and even movies, the Goldport Library devoted itself to books almost exclusively. The meager collection of audio books huddled by the door, on a ratty bookcase, looking like at any minute it might be banished to the eternal darkness, or at least the eternal evergreen lawn outside.

The book area, on the other hand, was well lit, and contained comfy chairs arrayed around large, well-polished tables. I had a dream where I became a great scholar or a writer or something and came to work here every morning, in the quiet and the clean. I knew it was just a dream and also that it would last about five hours of my being there before all hell broke loose, an effect I had on most places I frequented.

However, for the time being we were safe. I took E to the children's area—lower bookcases and vast, washable cushions—and left him there under the benevolent eye of a volunteer manning, or at least "girling,"the area.

For a kid who could, and often did, make the religious minded cross themselves or look up elaborate exorcisms, E was fairly safe around books. I credited—or blamed— Ben who, not having the slightest idea what to do with kids, spent a lot of the time reading to him. Ben swore up and down the block that E had a particular predilection for Ray Bradbury's science fiction and a fine appreciation of the poetry of Jorge Luis Borges.

I thought that sooner or later Ben would end up needing intensive therapy, and could only hope he would wait long enough he could get a group discount with E who, raised by All-ex and myself couldn't possibly escape it.

But it couldn't be denied that E would remain quiet and happy as long as there were books around that he hadn't looked at. The problem around the house was that I simply could not afford enough picture books.

Freed for the moment, I went to the computer area and

looked up French polishing. It sounded absolutely daunting, but I printed the article, nonetheless, and folded it to stick in my purse. Then I found the letter and did a quick Web search for Jacinth Jones, but found nothing.

So I went over to the research desk—*wo*manned by a tall, dignified lady in a red and yellow pullover that looked exactly like she'd run down some poor creature on the way to work and was now wearing it, in all its blood and fat—and asked about a previous resident of Goldport, by the name of Jacinth Jones.

"Oh, you want area history. There's a special wing for that."

"There is?" I asked, as I imagined them strapping a pair of wings on me, so that I could access the unattainable heights of local history.

It turned out to be nothing so exciting. It was just a part of the library I'd never known existed, behind the children's area. There was an oak door that looked like it came from a castle. Above the door I expected it to say *Abandon All Hope Ye Who Enter Here*, but instead it said *Donated to the City Of Goldport by the Family of Abihu Martin*.

Inside the clean and quiet atmosphere of the rest of the library turned to clean and upscale. The wing was all polished mosaic floors and oak trim. There were massive file cabinets and flat files like my artist friends used. There were polished-oak bookcases and tables that looked like they were real antiques—possibly French polished.

And there was another tall and imposing woman, this one dressed all in white—a white skirt suit—and with her white hair firmly pinned back. I couldn't get rid of the impression she'd come in here as a young woman and then become bleached by never going out in the sun again.

She answered my queries with a lot of polite murmurs, consulting a computer that I assumed wasn't linked to the Internet. Then she led me amid the flat files and pulled out a drawer. From the drawer, with almost reverent care, she pulled out . . . laminated sheets of newspaper.

On the whole she ended up going through three drawers and getting me three different pages from three different editions of the *Goldport Conspirator*. It was—appropriately from what I knew of its present-day edition—yellowed and the date on top declared it to be from 1929.

The first one had a headline proclaiming "Owner of Local House of Ill Repute Vanishes. Creditors Enraged." And right in the first paragraph was the name of Jacinth Jones.

I asked the lady to photocopy the pages, and she looked like I had asked her to kill her newborn children and tender me their blood in a cup. I was treated to a lecture on the Proper Treatment Of Archival Materials, with all the capitals clearly audible. It turned out, though, that the papers were available on microfiche and that those could be printed. I paid the price for them, stuffed them in my purse with the printouts on French polishing, and rushed out.

To find that pod people had replaced E. The lady in charge of the children's library told me he was the sweetest little boy she'd ever seen and also that she'd been reading him some books, which he would like to borrow. Did I have a library card?

I refrained from pointing out that, as the daughter of bookstore owners, not only did I have a library card but it was probably the same age as my birth certificate. I also refrained from asking her what she had done with my son and who this smiling-faced little boy holding a stack of six books could be.

The books turned out to be a children's series called The Lab Rats Adventures. They were predicated on the concept of lab rats who accidentally acquire intelligence and live in the walls of the lab. I half expected it to plead the line that experimentation was wrong, but it didn't—I checked by skimming. Not that I like hurting little rats or bunnies, or worse, cats or dogs, but I did understand it was better than hurting humans—instead the rats had adventures, helped the scientists, and generally got in trouble with the help of their great cat friend Euclid.

At least it made sense for E to be fascinated with rats just now.

When I got back home, there was a police car in the driveway. Or rather, there was a car no one would identify as a police car, but that I had seen Cas drive before.

I opened the door, half expecting to find Cas in the house. I was, of course, wrong.

"I came by to see how the rats are doing," Nick said, looking more than a little embarrassed. "I used to have rats when I was little . . . And I had some time at lunch and I thought . . ."

"Not a problem," I said. I noted that Ben didn't offer to give him all the rats right then. I also noted that Ben was at the stove doing something. I refused to guess why he'd been such a pain the day before and was being so nice now. Instead, I took E to the bathroom, washed both his hands and mine, set the books down in his room, and came back to the kitchen to find that E was petting a bewildered Pythagoras. I contemplated whether to wash his hands again, but Ben pointed him at the table and told him to sit down. For a miracle, E did. So did Nick, who apparently interpreted Ben's stern expression as a command to everyone around. I didn't, because given half a chance, Ben would set up as the evil dictator of the world. Or at least as the extremely organized ruler of the known world and the rest of the universe as soon as he got to it.

"I couldn't make omelets," Ben told me, with a hint of censure. "Because you didn't call me to tell me you were coming back, and I had no intention of making shoe leather."

He pointed at the table again, and this time I went, because there was no use fighting it. Nick and E, I noticed, had taken up the two central seats. Since the table was against the wall, that left me with the option of sitting next to one of them. I sat next to E. If Ben didn't like that, let him stew.

Ben set a pot of soup in the middle of the table, then went back, opened the oven and, moments later, set down a basket of savory cheese muffins, covered with a kitchen cloth that looked like it was trying to be extra prim to avoid serving as a rat receiving blanket.

Ben sat down in the remaining available chair, without so much as a frown at me. "It's just vegetable soup with bought broth," he said. "Sorry. I didn't have time for anything more complex. But the muffins are savory cheese and should be good."

I didn't ask why he was apologizing to the woman whose main culinary accomplishment was pancakes. It was clear he wasn't apologizing to any woman at all. I just wished he would decide whether he wanted to fish, cut bait, or reel the fish in and let it go very fast until the fish had concussion.

Poor Nick was already looking like someone had hit him on the back of his head, hard, with a baseball bat. Only that would account for the way his smile went all wobbly.

CHAPTER 5

Old News

"**I just thought you were right**," Ben said. "And I'd been a bit of an ass yesterday, okay? There's nothing else going on! He came by to look at the rats, and I thought it was fair to offer him lunch. I mean, he wanted to go out to lunch, but I couldn't leave the rats."

"Right," I said.

"In fact . . ." Red climbed up his face in waves. Watching Ben blush has always been one of my favorite things, because he usually doesn't allow anyone to see his emotions, but he has the type of clear, translucent skin that shows blushes like a neon sign. "If you could take over rat duty . . . this evening . . ."

"Yes?" I said.

"Well . . . He asked me if I wanted to go out to dinner, and I didn't want to be rude again, so . . ."

"Oh, very good. About time you had a date."

"It's not a date! We're only going to dinner. He wants to talk about the animal killings. He thinks I have a good mind."

Ben had, of course, an excellent mind. And I was absolutely sure that was not what Nick was interested in. Oh, perhaps that, too, but I thought his interests were more . . . material. I didn't say anything. Look, Ben is quite capable of cutting off his nose to spite his face, and if he thought I was hoping he'd actually get in a relationship with a guy who—for once—seemed to be decent, then he would go out of his way to avoid and snub Nick.

"Okay," I said. Then I added, since I was feeling a little guilty, "You know you don't need to stay here with the rats. I mean at night. I can manage, I think. I mean Pythagoras is a really good cat."

"Yeah, but, Dyce, I'd never forgive myself if something happened to them. I'll stay. At least a couple more days. They should start walking around by then."

"All right," I told him. "And of course I'll look after them tonight."

While we talked, he was picking up stuff from the table. He's always much better than I about washing up after meals. I said, "I'll help."

He said, "No, go work on the piano. I'll keep an eye on E and the animals. That way, tonight, you don't have to worry about not having done anything."

"Oh, okay," I said. I grabbed the printouts from my purse, and went to my shed. But it wasn't the French-polishing instructions I was most interested in.

Out in the workshop, I separated the sheets on French polishing from the printouts of the old newspaper. There were far more than three sheets of printouts, because the librarian had printed all three articles and the things around them, too.

I remembered going to restaurants, when I was in high school, where they reprinted old-time ads as decoration on the tables and paper place mats. Ads for corsets and indoor plumbing and such. They were entertaining, though there had been only a dozen or so of them printed over and over again.

These ads—or rather, the half ads you could read around some of the articles—were just as interesting. A lot of them, given the difference in technology and culture were the same as today's: feel younger, buy this patent tonic; enrich yourself by reading this book; visit our store for amazing bargains.

The articles themselves . . . I put them in order and started reading, gathering facts as I went. To begin with, apparently, a house of ill repute was not a brothel, which, of course, was what I had initially thought. It seemed that Mr. Jacinth Jones had come from parts unknown—heavily hinted to be back East, in that undertone that my grandmother would use to say that no good will come of this. Apparently no good *had* come of it. He'd first lodged in a boarding house, then he'd bought premises on Fairfax—about three blocks from where I lived and one of the city's largest east-west arteries, which he'd turned into the White Horse Saloon.

There were complaints associated with these premises. In fact, despite the newspaper's restrained tone, I got the strong impression that there were at least three a night and that, had there been telephones, they would have rung off the hook with complaints about the goings on at the White Horse.

The paper hinted darkly at drunk and disorderly, brawls, dancing, loud music. It said that there had been rumors of gambling and even stories of adulterated liquor.

It was hard to tell at this distance whether Mr. Jacinth Jones had been a good man doing the best he could to provide a service that, obviously, would be needed—or at least wanted—by the hard-drinking miners and rootless settlers who filled the city in those days, or whether he'd been a shady character, profiting from vice and ruined lives. If people were the way they'd always been, I imagined he had been a little of both.

The article said that he had been seen with the wife of a well-known local politician but—and I supposed that was the difference between the press then and now—the woman was not named.

But most of all what the articles detailed was Mr. Jones's sudden and inexplicable disappearance. Oh, sure his saloon had been under scrutiny because of the many complaints. But Mr. Jones had stayed on, managing to save his business, if not his reputation.

Then one night, between nightfall and morning, he'd vanished, never to be seen again. The first article detailed his disappearance, the second and third dealt with the fallout—the White Horse going into bankruptcy, then being purchased by a consortium of locals. I wondered what the White Horse was now—what stood at the site of its erstwhile premises.

But two other things captured my interest. One was a picture of Mr. Jones. It caught my attention because his features were at once familiar and attractive. If the bad printout of a sepia photograph meant anything, he'd been a broad-shouldered man, with curly hair and light eyes. More important, though, in a time when a person had to sit perfectly still for a photo, a time in which most people stared out at the camera with all the ebullient animation of a zombie, Mr. Jones looked at the camera as if he were sizing up a potential friend, or perhaps a potential date. And his lips were set in just the slightest hint of a smile.

I felt that, if I had met him, we'd have gotten along. Even if he were—and, of course, there was no way to know he wasn't—an operator, taking advantage of lawless times. I guessed there would be humor there, and perhaps warmth.

The other item, missing the end, was one of those odd notices that people put (or used to put. I wasn't sure how it was done now. Maybe through a posting or perhaps Craig's List) in the paper about no longer being responsible for other people's debts.

I remembered first seeing a batch of those on the back of the Sunday paper when I was hanging out at Grandma's and asking her what they were. She'd explained they were notices people published when they got divorced or dissolved a partnership or perhaps when a child was emancipated before his or her majority.

Nowadays, I supposed, credit companies took care of it and all that happened was that a person had one of those embarrassing moments when a card did not go through and everyone stared. I'd had my share of those after the divorce with All-ex, when instead of paying the credit cards the court had allotted to him, he'd chosen to either max them out or cancel them. Which was why he was All-ex. Because he might not care about me—and no one would blame him if he didn't. Our marriage had been mutually unpleasant—but he also didn't seem to care if I had money to buy diapers and baby food for his only child. I'd survived, but I still had cringing memories of those times at the cashier.

Back in the Old West, of course, credit cards didn't exist. I'm sure they had notes of credit or whatever, but they weren't commonplace, and they didn't have any history with them. Instead, in the small communities people lived in, credit and worthiness were judged by what people knew about you, which could be that you were married to someone rich, in partnership with someone with bottomless pockets, or else the child of someone who could cover any debt.

Which made these announcements necessary. Also, I thought as I read the one that had been captured at the bottom of the article, probably a great deal more cringeworthy than my embarrassing moments at the cash register.

This one started with, "To Whom It May Concern," and went on to charmingly declare that, "I, Abihu Martin, of 1523 North Waterfall Street, am no longer responsible for the debts incurred by my wife, Almeria Martin, nee Almeria Richards. She has left our domicile on the night of the twenty-fourth of June, and neither her whereabouts nor her financial welfare are of my concern or legal responsibility any longer."

I cringed, in fact, on behalf of the unknown Almeria. What would it be like to have this splashed all over your hometown newspaper? What could you do? Hide? Change your looks?

It depended, I guessed, on how well known you were. If you were just someone in the town and your picture had never been published, you could change your name and start being Mrs. Smith, or Mrs. Jones and no one the wiser.

Mrs. Jones. I looked above. Almeria had disappeared on the same date as Jacinth Jones.

My neck prickled, at the back, just under the hair, and I sighed. Of course. The Almeria who was forever his. So, what had it been? A hired carriage at midnight? Horseback, headed East?

I realized I was thinking in terms of cowboy movies, and of two horses headed into the sunset (or sunrise if they were going back East). It wouldn't have been like that, particularly since Almeria had said she was bringing "baby." Besides, I had some vague idea that horses really couldn't travel that far without having to stop and rest. That seemed like a very inefficient way to run away from a husband.

No. She'd probably taken the train to . . . wherever. With Mr. Jones. Perhaps back East, if that was really where he came from. I wondered if she'd been happy.

I set the papers aside, and considered the French-polishing sheets, but was in no mood to concentrate.

Instead, I turned my attention to the piano, once more. I had to be very careful stripping it over any area that might drip into the inside, since Cas would be dealing with that later. It occurred to me, not for the first time, that it would have been easier to remove the mechanism from the case and work on them separately.

But having spent the last several months looking for and at pianos with Cas, I knew my brilliant idea was not as easy as it sounded. Apparently it took more than a bit of effort to unbolt frames and remove the innards of pianos. And while it was being done, it was all too easy to crack the soundboard, which seemed more fragile than an addled egg, considering the number of them that we'd found.

So I sighed—put on my protective suit: chemical resistant—or at least thick enough not to let chemicals through—fabric, heavy gloves, and goggles. The goggles were important because splattering some of the chemicals I was using in my eye would mean at the very least an emergency trip to the hospital and at worst blindness. I didn't put on the ear protectors because I was not going to use the heavy sander. Also because should Ben scream for help and tell me Pythagoras was eating the rats, or that E had run over Pythagoras, I wouldn't hear him with the ear protectors on.

My hair was already tied back, and I thought I could avoid splashing the paint remover around wildly enough to splatter it.

I grabbed one of those expensive refinishers I rarely used and spread it, carefully, in a corner of the keyboard cover. It was the sort of refinisher that was thickened with starch, so that it clung to nearly vertical surfaces and didn't run. The not-running being the important part in this case.

I waited till the paint started bubbling and scraped it with my five-point painter's tool, being careful to throw the shavings into a can, so that they wouldn't fall inside.

Because I had to work in little, no-more-than-palm-sized patches, it was deadly slow, and not exactly cerebrally engaging, so I let my mind wander as I scraped. Right. So, there it was—my mystery letter resolved. And it was nothing as exciting as a long-ago murder.

Just a tawdry romance between the wife of Mr. Abihu Martin—whose descendants, I remembered, had donated the historical wing of the library—and the disreputable Mr. Jones from down the road. I wondered again if she'd been happy with him. So many women seemed to suffer a fatal attraction to bad boys. And so often the attraction turned out to be fatal in the most literal of senses.

But wasn't it weird that Mr. Jones had left, without trying to get money from his assets? Almeria had said she'd meet him at the fruit stand. I'd actually heard of this, growing up in Goldport. There were half a dozen attractions that our teachers would take us to, when spring was in full force and our little butts wouldn't stay still on the desk chairs.

There was the old jail in what had been the center of town, complete with the very large tree where people used to be hanged.

I think I felt the frisson and horror of death once. Maybe. Considering the first time I'd seen that tree was kindergarten, it's unlikely I realized it was the same tree. But I could still recite—with my eyes closed, and in the exact same voice as my teacher in third grade had used, how people were brought to the tree mounted on horses, and then horse shooed away, so they dropped. She always lowered her voice on the last part, and tried to make it sound spooky, while we stood around in the little park and enjoyed the grass and the trees and tried not to yawn too obviously.

The other place they took us to was the house that was all that remained of the fruit stand. It was now a small blue and white bungalow with nothing special about it. It just shows how desperate our teachers were for something of supposedly redeeming educational value they could do outside the classroom, that they'd take us there, and stand outside the neat picket fence, telling us it used to be a fruit stand, and that behind it, the building that was now a hardware store, had been the terminus station for trains headed from the East into Goldport. These trains often brought consumptives West, to clear their lungs or whatever, and the fruit stand was their first chance to buy food in probably a day.

So if Almeria and Jacinth had met at the fruit stand, I was probably right: they'd meant to go somewhere by train.

But that meant, didn't it, that Jacinth had had some time to prepare. He'd have gotten her letter . . . what? A week before? I vaguely remembered a date somewhere around the fourteenth, and tried to imagine an elopement in slow motion. Nowadays she'd e-mail him and they'd be on their way the same day.

But that was the whole point, wasn't it? Nowadays he would also be able to handle his affairs through representatives, or long distance, over the Net. In those days . . .

I was almost sure he would have had time to talk to his lawyers, and leave instructions. I remembered the paper said the law firm of Fenris, Fenris, and Nefer had been in charge of the dissolution of his property and satisfying his creditors. So, why hadn't he left instructions? And why hadn't he written letters, afterward—even if he sent them from some city other than where he was—giving instructions on how to dispose of property? Surely it was not that hard? Even if he and Almeria were hiding from her husband, surely good ol' Jacinth was smart enough to send the letter to a friend of his to mail from across the country. There was just no reason whatsoever to let the business go, like that, as it would.

I set the five-point painter's tool down. I'd cleaned off all of the keyboard cover, and now had only the final, fine sanding to do, before I had to figure out how to do French polish.

And meanwhile, I found, I wasn't at all happy with the solution to the little mystery started by the letter.

Which meant that I would have to do some more poking around. I didn't even know why, but the story needled at me. Perhaps it was the parallels between Almeria leaving with "*baby*" just as I had left in the middle of the night, with E only one year old. These days, it was easier, but all the same . . . And then there was that credit thing. And the feeling something just wasn't right.

When I was about to be born, my parents had had the worst—possibly the only—big argument of their marriage, over what they should name me. Dad wanted to name me Sherlockia. Mother wanted to name me Agatha.

Unable to reconcile their differences, they had separated for months. Mom had taken a job somewhere—no one ever said exactly where—and lived in a boarding house.

My father's mother, who would live to raise me, had felt her son was distraught over this. I won't even guess how she detected this, since my father was not known to talk much at the best of times, unless he talked to his books, which he often did. To Father, at least left to his own devices, not eating, not bathing, and walking around in a bathrobe all day with his nose in a book weren't symptoms of clinical depression. They were what he called normal life, unless Mom was around to make him act like a functioning adult human.

But either Grandma had seen or imagined signs of depression in my father, or perhaps she had simply seen the store closed day after day—since my father hated selling books. Grandma knew that the prospect of my father becoming a mad recluse loomed, a prospect Mom had banished by molding him into a merely eccentric bookseller. (The difference was small, but the recluse might die under an avalanche of books and not be found for months, while the eccentric bookseller would live to a ripe old age, admittedly getting more and more eccentric.)

Besides which, no doubt Grandma had some understandable interest in knowing her grandchild. At any rate, she'd searched high and low till she found where my mother was staying, and she'd convinced Mother and Father to meet in the neutral ground of a candy shop.

By then, so much time had gone by that Mom was ready to pop. Which she did. Right in the candy store. Which was why my name was Candyce Chocolat. Mom had wanted to make it Candy, but Dad had mercifully added the two extra letters.

Now, as I finished cleaning my tools, and hung up my protective clothing, I considered the possibility that both my parents had been right to begin with. Given how much the old mystery the letter hinted at wouldn't let me quit it, perhaps I should have been called Sherlockia Agatha. Or Agatha Sherlock.

CHAPTER 6

A Cheating Heart

By the time I got into the house, I had my entire story prepared, and was moving too fast for Ben to ask too much about it. As it was, it might have been unnecessary effort, since Ben was deep in a book, his brow furrowed in confusion. Judging by the title the book was about surviving depression, and he had a notebook open and was making notes.

I would have been worried and imagined he was on the verge of wandering about in a robe, reading books and not bathing, only I could see dollar signs on the cover, too, so I guessed the depression they were talking about wasn't psychological. And since Ben was a financial planner, it made perfect sense.

"Working?" I asked him.

He had the aquarium with the rats, a supply of kitchen towels, the dropper, a thermos I'd bet would contain formula, and a wad of cotton balls all on one side of him, and Pythagoras on the other. From the sounds of wood blocks being tossed around his bedroom, E was doing what passed for quiet play for him. Ben had given him a set of Thomas the Tank Engine wooden tracks and trains, and E delighted in creating and destroying railroads. Over and over again.

Ben looked up. "What? Not exactly. But yeah . . . some of our clients have left, and I didn't get nearly the bonuses I expected. Not that I'm not doing what I should, but . . ."

"Yeah, times are tough all over," I said. I didn't add that it might be the right time to shack up with a good man with a steady income because, despite all appearances to the contrary, I do not, in fact, have a death wish. "I need to buy some supplies for the French polishing," I added, before he could do more than nod assent to my platitude. "I'll be gone about an hour, maybe two. Is that okay?"

"Oh, sure," he said. "I'll just stay here with the animals."

I didn't ask about E. I had a feeling he had been included in that description. Instead, I got out fast before Ben asked me exactly what kind of supplies I was buying.

North Waterfall Avenue was five blocks west of me. It was the richest area of downtown and, it had never gone to the dogs, even during the hard times and fast suburbanization of the seventies. Even the part of town where Mom and Dad lived, which was now a gentrified upscale area of brick houses with shops downstairs and lofts on the upper stories, had become a bit seedy in the seventies, when most of the houses had been apartments or flop houses. But North Waterfall had remained as it had been since it was built by the founder of our city, Major Goldport, and his cronies:

dignified mansions, set a long way back from the street on immaculate lawns that could only be maintained in Colorado if a homeowner was willing to pour money out the water spigot and all over them twice a day, pretty much year-round unless there was snow on the ground.

Looking at the houses, you wouldn't know there was any depression for Ben to be worried about, although there were a few more for sale signs than usual. The funny thing is that on this street even for sale signs were more upscale and discreet than in the rest of the city. Instead of screaming bright colors proclaiming, "price reduced," or the garish metal signs showing pictures of smiling realtors saying you could trust them, these were wooden, easily confused for business signs, had this not been an aggressively residential area of town. One of the signs even had realistic-looking grape bunches suspended from its frame. The name of the realtor was Toscania Properties, which I supposed made sense, in that Colorado was absolutely nothing like any part of Italy and was not exactly a major grape growing region.

The house I was interested in didn't have a for sale sign. Which, of course, gave me less of an excuse to ring the doorbell. But I was fairly sure I could think of something on the fly. So I walked down the walkway amid the trees. It was done in mosaic, in the roman style, with little colored pebbles making out designs—in this case the designs seemed to be infinitely curling dark spirals on a white background.

It seemed to me if you were going to spend a lot of money to make a design on your walkway, you would want something more imaginative. At least fauns or something. But I guessed the rich were truly different than the rest of us. For one, they had more money.

The doorbell, too, was impressive. When I pulled the hand ring next to the polished door, what sounded inside was like the carillon of a thousand abbey bells. Frankly, it was such a big and important sound, it almost scared me into leaving. Surely a house like this had a service entrance, and perhaps I was supposed to go around to it, and ring the bell that was sure to sound much less churchy and more practical. But then again, I wouldn't bet on it, and besides, the one quality I got from both of my parents was tri-plated stubbornness.

So I stood my ground till at length the door was opened by a lady in a white apron. The fact that she was wearing a white apron didn't make her any less of a lady. Beneath it she wore a dove gray blouse, and a tailored black skirt. She had a string of pearls around her neck. Probably fake, but nice-looking. Every one of her white hairs was in place, and her blue eyes shone down on me— she was taller than I—with benevolent enquiry. "Yes? How may I help you?"

I gave her a smile that would have made Nick's seem pale. "Hello, my name is Dyce Dare. I run Daring Finds, a furniture recovery business. It's been my experience in homes like this, furniture can be stored and forgotten in various states of disrepair." I saw the look behind her eyes, and knew if I used the economic motive and pointed out I could pay for such old pieces, I would lose her completely and she would shut the door in my face. But I had another angle. "These days a lot of people who are ecologically minded view it as their duty to recirculate those pieces, thus allowing people to buy them once more, instead of purchasing new furniture, which would deplete our old growth resources, as well as pollute the world further with factory effluvia." I could see her waver, so I put the pressure on. "I will of course pay for anything I think is recoverable, but the payment is purely nominal. The money should be of very little account, of course, compared to saving the environment."

She blinked. Then sniffed. Then cleared her throat. "If you'll wait a moment, Ms. . . ."

"Dare," I supplied. And waited. She didn't close the door completely, which I guess counted for something. So I got a view of sparkling hallway marble tiles, a glimmer of a very clean, elaborately framed mirror to the side, and heard her distant footsteps and echoes of her voice, though not actually the words.

When she came back she nodded to me. It was the nod of an aristocrat to a young and upcoming servant. Or something. "Mr. Martin says you might look at what's stored in the carriage house," she said. "We have recently sold some of the better furniture, but the trash pieces have been lingering, and one doesn't quite know what to do with them."

I wasn't sure what had prompted the furniture sell-off, but I could never leave well enough alone. So, as I followed her out back, I said, in a casual voice. "You don't have any idea how much they mean to list it for?" She could think I was talking about the furniture, of course. Or she could think anything she wanted, including that she had misunderstood me.

But she didn't seem to give it a second thought. She nodded and said, "No, I'm afraid that's quite out of my provenance. In the low two millions or thereabouts, I'd expect. But it's more a matter of moving out into the country, as they've always wanted to. The ranch . . ." She shrugged. "With Miss Martin entering the hospice, there's no longer any reason they shouldn't, is there?"

It didn't seem to occur to her there was no logical reason that anyone coming out of the blue to ring the door-bell would know anything about the Martins or their cir-cumstances. But maybe I was the one who was delusional here. The family had lived in the public eye since at least the early twentieth century. Perhaps everyone in town knew everything about them, except me.

I made noncommittal noises and followed her out back. I was, of course, less than interested in whatever I might find—but I ended up surprising myself. What these people considered trash pieces made me start. They were of a better quality than what I was used to buying, fixing up, and reselling.

To be honest, my business was on the low rung of the ladder, and often, when I needed to sell but had little money to invest in materials or new pieces, I'd gone Dumpster diving or driving by expensive areas on trash day.

My bottom category of acceptability was low enough: the piece had to be real wood, not some unholy conglom-erate, and it had to be reasonably well built, preferably with dowels, though I'd take screws.

My top, when I could get it, was antique. The contents of the carriage house—a vast, dusty expanse that still had, on the floor, a giant daisy-wheel type of contraption, which had at one time been used to turn carriages around in the available space, fell somewhere between the two. I would guess most of it was somewhere between fifty and seventy years old—too young to be a bona fide antique, but quite good enough for vintage furniture.

All of it was wood. In the dim light, I could see nearby a vast modern desk in what looked like cherry. The finish was dusty and crazed, but it might yet be recoverable. Against the wall was a china cabinet balanced on thin, spindly legs, its glass-front doors so dusty they were opaque. But the wood looked like mahogany. My mouth went dry. The business was doing better lately. Much better. A small antique table that had come my way six months ago had sold for enough profit to allow me to attend an estate sale, and that in turn had allowed me to turn an even handsomer profit. I had money in the bank. I cleared my throat. "What . . . what would be for sale, and what not?"

She gave a fine aristocratic shrug. "Oh, Mr. Martin said everything here is to be got rid of." She inclined her head. "It will show better if it's empty."

Knowing I was insane, I tried to calculate how much I could afford to pay for it all, and how much would be too much. "Uh . . . how much for the lot?" I asked.

She looked disdainful. "Mr. Martin said five hundred would be fine."

Right. For a token payment, five hundred was stiff. But not for the contents of this carriage house. I would guess there were at least twenty pieces here, large and small. I didn't know what amount of fix-up they'd require, but I was fairly sure that when I was done, the smallest table would easily sell for a hundred. And I actually had about four times five hundred in the bank, for once. Of course, I'd been saving to replace the car. But then again, if I pulled this off, I would be able to get a better car.

Only there was no way in hell I would be able to put everything in my shed. And paying for storage might completely destroy any profit.

Giving the woman a polite smile, I said, "If you'll excuse me," then stepped away and toward the dust-caked window on the left, which didn't exactly give me privacy but gave me that polite distance that allowed both of us to pretend that I was in private.

I dialed my parents' number and was answered by my mother's voice, "Remembered Murder!"

"Mom!" I said. And immediately repented it. Mom lives in the expectation that I'll call them to tell them I'm about to do something that fits their ideas for me—go back to school, marry, or perhaps write a mystery. They had just about given up on the idea that I would marry Ben, though not because they accepted for a moment that Ben was gay—despite the fact that Ben was not particularly in the closet—but because I was dating a policeman. Mind you, they would much rather I was dating a mystery writer but a policeman was almost as good. It gave them access to the details of crime investigation. And Cas humored them—he read the books they recommended and discussed them afterward with great solemnity.

I realized that what I was hearing from the other side of the line was my mother's expectation I'd called to announce that Cas and I were getting married. I plunged ahead, hastily, "I was wondering if I could borrow your garage for a month or so."

"Borrow?" Mom asked. She was clearly thrown by the fact that the subject was not marriage.

"Well, you see, I'm about to buy a whole lot of furniture," I said. "And it won't fit in the shed, so I was hoping I could store it in your garage, until I had time to work on it."

I could hear—in the silence—my mother considering her options. She could tell me that my line of work was unseemly for a lady. She could tell me I needed to get married and start acting like an adult. But she had told me all this before, and I hadn't seemed to care. And there was the hope, of course, that if I was buying a lot of furniture, it meant that Cas and I were about to furnish a house together.

"All right," she said. "You can put what you buy in the half of the garage where the business van goes. We can park on the street for a while."

"Thank you, Mom. I'll have someone pick it up and deliver it, and I'll be there when it's supposed to come in."

Mom sounded less than convinced this was a good thing, but accepted my thanks gracefully, and I turned to look at the lady in the shadows. "Five hundred," I said. "We have a deal."

I pulled my checkbook from my purse, made out a check and handed it to her.

"I'll have someone pick up everything," I said. Probably Starving Students, since they looked like they'd work for twenty bucks and a can of beer.

"Of course," she said, as though that were a given. This time she showed me out of the carriage house through the garden, not through the gleaming, antique-appointed house.

The garden was perfectly fine, mind you. There were benches and statuary and such. Things I hadn't seen outside the most upscale catalogues. But it seemed to me like I was being given a firm snub being shown out this way. As though the dust from my feet might pollute their upscale interior. Or as though they were afraid I would steal the antique knickknacks on the tables and credenzas.

As we walked, she said, "When your employees come, if you would be so kind as to tell them to come to the side entrance, by the driveway. I really should not be admitting tradesmen through the main entrance."

I was left in no doubt that I was being included in those less than worthy tradesmen.

I felt as if I had entered an Agatha Christie novel, and though I enjoyed Agatha Christie, I didn't like the rigid class structure in her novels. However, the fact was that even though I now worked with my hands, my maternal grandmother had been one of the grandames of society—such as it was—in Goldport, and on the sheer strength of that, my peculiar ex-hippie mother, with her obsession with mysteries and her vague ways, was admitted to the ranks of ladies who did lunch.

Remembering this was what made me go a little mad. Of course, those who know me and love me would probably say I've always been a little mad.

All I know is that I straightened my back and looked up at this ladylike housekeeper person and fired the most impertinent question I could think of. "It took quite a long while for the family to recover from the scandal surrounding Almeria Martin's disappearance, didn't it?"

When I got in my car, she was still standing at the garden gate, looking quite pale, opening and closing her mouth like a fish out of water. I'd rarely scored a truer hit.

CHAPTER 7

The Weird Get Pro

I got home to find Ben sitting on the sofa with E, reading him the adventures of the lab rats. I was fairly sure that he was adding lines to the books, too, because I would bet no children's book author would write, "And Ratty was very calm and happy because he took Prozac by the bucketful." However, E seemed content and it had been a long time since I'd tried to put the brakes on Ben's weirdness. Because if I tried, he was likely to retaliate.

Instead, I called Cas to find the number for Starving Students and, incidentally, to let him know that Ben had plans for the night and we couldn't plan to unload E on him. I needed to let him know, since Cas had got in the very bad habit of assuming we had a babysitter, unless otherwise stated.

"Too bad," he said, when I told him Ben would be un-available. "I was planning to bring you to my place and cook. Best we can do till Alex returns from his extended vacation. We're sure he'll return, right, and hasn't left for good? I mean . . ."

"Yeah, I'm sure he'll return," I said.

"Good. Oh, wait, you said Ben will be busy . . . not with Nick?"

"Yeah," I said, lowering my voice, and walking from the kitchen to the powder room. After I'd shut the door, I continued. "With Nick, why?"

Cas made a sound that was probably a cackle, but might also have been a cackle crossed with a "yes!"

"Castor Wolfe! Have you been playing matchmaker?"

"Uh? Of course I have. Nick's ex left him when Nick lost his job, and if I get Ben to date him, he'll leave you alone more often. More Dyce time for me."

"You are a bad man," I told him.

"Because I want time with you?" he said. I could hear him smile over the phone. "And why would that be bad? I call it eminently sensible."

"Yeah, yeah," I told him. "Prove you mean it by helping me babysit rats tonight."

"Sure, and you'll tell me all about your great buy, of course."

Which I did, but it wasn't as easy as that. First we had to face the fact that Ben was doing as good an imitation of crazy as I'd seen in a long time. He drove to his place. He returned with five outfits. He proceeded to model them for me.

Which, considering that I was a woman known for forgetting what color blouse she was wearing, should give you an idea of how completely far from sanity he had gone. I also had been known to not notice when Cas was wearing a suit instead of his ubiquitous jeans and polos, and therefore miss the fact that he intended to take me to an upscale restaurant. Needless to say, in those situations, I went right ahead and made the most inappropriate clothing choice possible for myself.

If you add to this the fact that Ben was either going through a beige phase or had decided that Nick would like beige, you'll understand how I sat, in horrified silence, as my friend modeled first beige pants with a beige shirt, then another pair of beige pants with a different beige shirt. Then yet a third beige pants with beige shirt combo.

"Ben," I said. "You're putting me on. Those last three outfits were exactly the same."

"No," he said. "Can't you tell they're completely different tones of beige?"

"No, Ben, I can't. Looks the same to me."

"But the cut on the pants is completely different!"

I bit my tongue before telling my best childhood friend that I refused to look below his waist and tell him which pair of pants was most flattering. Instead, I looked up at his eyes and spoke to the sheer confusion there. "Listen to me, Benedict Colm. The man has seen you feeding rats. I think you could show up for the date naked, and he wouldn't care."

This got me a smirk, and I revised hastily, "Okay, okay, he'd care if you were naked. But you probably could show up in tie-dye and he wouldn't notice."

Blood left Ben's face. "Tie-dye!" he said. "Why would I wear tie-dye?"

"You wouldn't," I said quickly, trying to remember how to give first aid, in case Ben should require it. "It was just an example."

Ben vanished into the bedroom grumbling, "If I showed up in tie-dye, I would hope that he'd notice and be appropriately horrified."

Then he started the dance of the seven neckties. Seven ties, all in tones of muted green. He wanted to know which one looked best with beige. While I could see the differences in the ties—one was slightly warmer than the other, one had a little pin-dot effect, etc.—I could no more tell how each coordinated with beige tones that were only different from each other in Ben's fevered imagination.

Refusing to point out that, if anything, this mad confusion over clothes was giving away the fact he wasn't going out with Nick to be polite, I picked a tie at random, shoved him into the bathroom where he had hung all his outfits, and closed the door, telling him not to come out till he was dressed.

As luck would have it this happened just as Cas came in the door, using the key I'd given him some months ago, because when All-ex had E, Cas often had to work late into the night and his having a key was better than his ringing my doorbell and getting me awake enough to figure locks in the middle of the night.

"Does Ben often wander around naked?" he asked. "Or is he threatening to go out naked? Is Nick taking him to a nudist restaurant or something?"

I shook my head, though I knew Cas was joking. "He wants me to decide which tone of beige he should be wearing."

Cas had time to roll his eyes, before Ben emerged, looking perfectly attired, in beige shirt, beige pants, and a nicely coordinating tie. And then—to further prove he had gone completely off the deep end—he asked Cas's opinion of his outfit. Even as Cas stood there in faded jeans and a white polo.

The love of my life had just managed to say, "Uh . . . it's very . . . uh . . . beige," when the doorbell rang.

Nick was wearing not just jeans, but jeans that had tears I couldn't help thinking were strategic at various points in the leg and possibly other places I didn't look. The jeans themselves looked worn, but not in the way any person would have worn them. More like they'd been pre-worn for the customer's convenience. At any rate, the fabric had thinned enough to mold like a second skin, even though I was doing my level best not to stare. With the jeans, Nick wore a plain white T-shirt that stretched across a well-developed chest. And I would have thought he was seriously underdressed, except the effect that came across was that he'd probably spent more time on his attire than Ben. Though I'd bet he hadn't bothered a childhood friend to ask if his white T-shirt was nicer than his other white T-shirt.

Ben stared for a moment, said, "Hi," then wheeled around, and grabbed my shoulder en passant. I was very much afraid he was going to say the date was off, since Nick had shown up in a T-shirt, and that I'd have to explain to him that a T-shirt was not the same as tie-dye. However, before I could get the words out, Ben said, "Come on. I need to show you the rat system!"

"Excuse me?" I said. Cas and Nick followed behind, all the way to the kitchen, where Ben had set the aquarium back on the counter. The rats were starting to stir, and there was a notebook pinned to my fridge with a magnet, seriously disturbing the panorama of E's art.

"See, there're their names," Ben said. "Make sure you match the names to the initials, and mark them with an *X* so I know how many feedings you've done on each of them. Don't forget to rub their tummies. And—"

"Go," I said, trying very hard not to laugh. "I promise to look after the rats properly."

"I'll supervise her," Cas said.

Ben looked doubtfully at both of us. "E is in his room," he said, as if he must make sure that we remembered all our obligations. "He was drawing the rats last I saw him. But he's been quiet awhile, so you might want to check. And I put the motorcycle in your shed, Dyce, so that he wouldn't, you know, take off without your noticing."

I realized my childless friend was now lecturing me on the care and upkeep of my toddler. Okay, granted, Ben had often been the adult in our association, but all the same, I suspected that, having known E since before he was born, I had some idea what to do.

Looking at Cas, I read the same thoughts in his eyes, but he was doing his best not to say anything. Except for clearing his throat and saying, "Ben, we'll take care, you may go." He was exhibiting great forbearance.

I looked back at Nick, expecting him to be horrified, but he looked more amused, which was a good sign. Actually all of it was a good sign, considering what had pushed Ben's last partner over the edge had been the fact that he'd perceived Ben as emotionless and uncaring.

"You know my cell number, if something happens that you need my help with," Ben said.

"And we're going to be at the Branding Iron," Nick said. "If you can't get him on his phone."

"Right," I said, as we actually managed to get them out the door. After they left, Cas turned to me and asked, "The Branding Iron? I've known Nick since we were kids. I wonder if there is something I missed? Will Ben be safe with him?"

I laughed. "Uh . . . How much does Nick talk about his private life with you?"

Something like a shadow passed behind Cas's eyes.

"Not much, since I offered to beat up his ex for him. The offer seemed to horrify him for some reason. Mostly we work on his car together and we watch sports. Why?"

"Ah . . . His car?" I said. I had an idea of some horribly beat up clunker that Nick was trying to rehabilitate.

"Uh . . . I should say his hobby car. Nick likes to buy old muscle cars and fix them. He has like three of them, but the current project is a 1955 Chevy Bel Air convertible. It was . . . uh . . . horrible when he got it. He keeps it over at my parents' garage. He rented out his place when he went to Denver to study, so now he needs to wait till the lease expires to move back in. So he has all his equipment and stuff at my parents', and that's what we do in our free time." He grinned. "When I'm not with you." He grinned again. "I confess most of our emotional sharing refers to the damn wrench that can't be found or what in hell he thinks he's doing to the radiator. Why?"

"Very . . . guy," I said. I was trying to figure out how this motor-head thing would play with Ben. I was never very clear on what were Ben's "ew" or "hot" buttons. Though then again, even if we didn't work on classic cars together, we, by agreement, said very little about our love lives to each other. An arrangement that had seen us through since middle school. "At any rate, the Branding Iron is not anything fringy. It's just one of the local gay bars. . . . It's like a restaurant with a dance floor. I mean, the purpose is less cruising and more nice meals in friendly surroundings. They have white tablecloths and all." I noticed Cas was looking at me very weirdly, and said, "Ben had a birthday party. His friend Peter from the Philharmonic threw it for him. Surprise. Peter invited me. They don't actually prevent women coming in, you know."

Cas grinned. "No, I was just . . . if Ben and Nick frequent the same places, it's a miracle they didn't already know each other."

I waggled my hand. "Not really. The Branding Iron has only been open a year. Nick was away at school, right? I'm going to guess he's either never been there, or never at the same time that Ben was . . . Or they just never noticed each other. There are . . ." I coughed at having to explain this to Cas. "You know, Goldport is a population center for this area and there are ranches and . . . small towns, and . . ."

"Yeah, yeah, yeah. Now we can stop discussing the ins and outs of gay dating, right? They're gone. We're alone." He cornered me against the wall and was kissing me very thoroughly, when I heard, "Ew. Peegrass chewed up a rat."

I think we beat all possible speeds between the living room and E's room. It turned out my son was absolutely accurate. In a weird way. Though the rat that had gotten—apparently—chewed up then spit out in a pulpy mess was one of E's drawings.

"Pythagoras," I said. "Honestly!"

"Mee-ooo?" he asked, which probably translated as, "I'm sorry, kind stranger, isn't the ritual chewing up and spitting up of paper a custom of your land? I promise to endeavor to practice more appropriate behavior in the future."

I looked up to read frustration and amusement in Cas's eyes. "That cat," he said, "is seriously insane." He disappeared into the bathroom and returned with a wad of toilet paper, which he used to pick up the paper pulp and dispose of it in the bathroom trash.

"Right," I said. "I'm going to go cook something."

"No way," Cas said. "I've ordered pizza. It should arrive any minute."

"Pizza!" E said.

"You didn't have to," I said.

Cas slipped his arm around me and kissed my forehead in an almost chaste way. "Babe," he said, "I've seen you cook. The way you get all confused, we'd end up with baby rat soufflé, and then Ben would kill you, and then I'd have to arrest Ben, and then, likely as not, Nick would be mad at me. See pizza saves us all that."

"Pizza!" E said, as he started to draw a round pizza with green pepperoni on black cheese.

So we'd had pizza and beer, except for E who had fruit juice, and then we'd fed the rats and helped them poop. And then we'd fed Pythagoras who was starting to eye the rats with a speculative look.

We installed E in a chair at the table, to pursue his newfound artistic enthusiasm, I washed dishes, and Cas dried them and put them away, in a sweetly domestic way.

He caught me looking at him and must have seen something in my eyes, because he smiled back at me. "You know, I've been thinking. There is a way to avoid all this you know . . . having to abstain from unseemly behavior while Alex is away."

"There is?" I asked, since though I hated to admit it I was frankly missing the unseemly behavior and everything that went with it.

"Well, you know, I got this place. It's not in the best area, but it's better than this." He'd bought a working-man's Victorian a few blocks from me, in the other direction from Waterfall Avenue. "And it has two bedrooms, and a big garage. You could take over one side of it for the refinishing and, you know, there would be a yard for Peegrass and the rats."

I had to blink away an image of Pythagoras chained next to the rats, each of them with their own little dog—or cat and rat—houses, each one with the name written on top in Ben's exact handwriting. "His name is Pythagoras," I said. I looked over at E who was completely absorbed in his drawing. "Cats and rats aren't yard sort of animals. And besides, I thought we'd agreed we weren't going to do that."

"We did? Agreed we weren't going to put the cat and the rats in the yard?" He was smiling teasingly, but it was entirely possible he was also confused. I seemed to have that effect on people.

"Well, we did agree we weren't going to have you stay over so that we wouldn't confuse him." I gestured toward E. "I mean, it's bad enough that he has three parents, I don't want to subject him to a revolving door of step fathers or . . . something."

"Revolving door?" Cas asked, sounding somewhat incredulous.

His surprise was justified since, of course, he had probably gathered there hadn't been any dating between the breakup of my marriage and his not taking no for an answer about becoming a part of my life. "Okay," I said. "Probably a bad analogy, but I just wanted to point out that we've only been dating six months, and what if you move on, and then he wonders where you went and . . . you know. This sort of extra-legal relationship is fine for adults, but when the adults have kids, one has to—"

"Silly," Cas said, sounding affectionately amused. "I wasn't asking for extra-legal anything. What I was trying to say—"

The phone rang. There followed an intense moment of hunting for the phone, and the answering machine had already picked up with my mom's dry voice saying, "Candy, I know you're there," when I found the phone and said, "Mom!"

"Oh," she said. "Are you screening calls? You didn't break up with Cas, did you?" I made a face at Cas, who had heard that—Mom has a loud phone voice—and was grinning at me.

"No, Mother. Cas is right here. We were just washing the dishes and had to find the phone."

"Oh."

E chose this moment to be excited by his grandmother's phone call. Normally his level of excitement for anything relating to my parents hits somewhere between watching paint dry and yawning, far lower than his interest in a small rock, since small rocks were collectors' objects for E, who carried them in his pockets by the dozen. Possibly to provide ballast. In which case they failed. He continued to move at a speed just below that of light.

Not that I blamed him for being indifferent to two people who either read him murder mysteries or tried to convince him he wanted to change his name to Sherlock.

"Gamma!" E said, pulling at my shirt with one hand and reaching for the phone with the other. "Gamma, we have rats! And Peegrass."

"Candy, did the child just say you had rats? Do you need me to give you the name of a good exterminator? When we had mice in the store—"

"No, Mom. Pet rats. Seven of them." And then, with utter mendaciousness, I added, "They're Ben's. We're helping him raise them." If Ben was going to write names on their little rumps, he could damn well own them as far as my mom was concerned.

"Oh," Mom said. She paused then sighed. "That man," she said, decisively, "must get married."

I mumbled something, and Cas grinned and mouthed at me, "legal in some states," which I chose to ignore. Instead I said, "You did not call to ask about Ben's love life." At least I hoped she hadn't, although knowing Ben it was entirely possible he had chosen to take Nick by the store, and that my mother, being my mother, had decided to call me to discuss the matter.

But it turned out I was lucky. "No," my mother said. "I was going to ask you if all that furniture you bought was from the Martin estate."

"Why?" I asked. "It was, but why do you ask?"

"Ah. Thought so. John called me. John Martin. He said you'd given his housekeeper a check and he didn't know there was anyone else but my daughter in town by that name."

I refused to ask whether it was my first or my last name he recognized. At a bet the first, but I wondered if Mom actually admitted to her friends that she had named her daughter Candyce. "You . . . know John Martin?"

Mom sounded surprised. "What? He and your father went to school together. And he's just married the sweetest woman. She works as a curator in the Martin area of the public library. You might have met her."

"Does she look . . . colorless?" I asked.

"Oh, that." Mom could be heard—I swear—to smile condescendingly on the other end of the phone. "Well, Asia was always a very pale girl. You know, pale and blonde, despite her name. So . . . you know, they fade early."

I understood the smile, since my mother was a blonde who hadn't faded early. I'd found that the older my mother got, the more she was gratified by evidence that her friends were aging worse than she was.

"Mommy! Peegrass."

"Oh, your grandson would also like to tell you we have a cat named Pythagoras," I said, forestalling my mother concluding something completely different.

"What an odd name for a cat," my mother said.

"Ben named him."

"Oh . . ." Mom sounded dubious. The truly sad part of my relationship with my parents was that, though I was an only child, I was not their favorite child. No, that honor was reserved for Ben who was not—not even slightly—gay and who was absolutely and completely the best son anyone could want. "Well, Ben was always so erudite. I must ask him which story he got the name from."

I refused to be baited. It was like Mom to think that if someone had named a cat an unusual name, it must be in honor of some fictional detective, and it would take too long to correct her. "I hope you're not upset I bought the Martins' furniture?"

"Oh? No, of course not. I explained about your little business." The way Mom said it, it made it sound like Daring Finds was a hobby that I played between sunbathing at the Cote D'Azur and attending concerts in Vienna. "Of course, they have to get rid of almost the entire contents of the house, now that old Diane is going into the hospice or the old age home, or whatever it is. At ninety-seven, an old age home is functionally a hospice, I suppose."

"She could live to be a hundred and twenty," I said.

"Really unlikely," my mother said. "Frankly, I know it has surprised the entire family that she has lived as long as she has. She was a very frail little girl, I understand. Quite her mother's darling. So sad."

"Her mother . . ." I said, noting that Cas had detached E from my legs and was carrying him to the living room from where, in short order, I heard the reading of the adventures of the lab rats, done in voices.

If Cas meant something more than just moving in together, was I ready for it? Was it something I could consider after knowing him for only six months? He was kind, considerate, and quite indecently good-looking. And he hadn't run as he'd got to know E. Hell, he seemed to like E.

I shook my head and returned to the conversation at hand, "Her mother was Almeria Martin?"

"Yes." Mom sounded surprised. "How did you hear of her?"

I was about to tell my mother about the old letter, but thought better of it. "I've been considering writing a book about local stories. I'd heard some mention of her, but it wouldn't be a mystery," I said emphatically, as I heard Mom draw breath in preparation to gush. "Not even a true crime. Just a collection of events that occurred in Goldport."

Mom sighed. "Well, you could write a book on the unexplained mysteries of Goldport. Almeria was one of them. Your grandmother's generation, you know . . ." She hesitated. "Your grandmother didn't seem to think Almeria was very happy with Abihu, though. You know, these great men . . ." She sighed again. "At any rate, your grandmother refused to listen to rumors that involved that bar owner, whoever he was. But the thing is, Almeria did disappear one night, and was never heard from again. Your grandmother was very hurt that she didn't at least get in touch with her and their other friends. It was a great grief to her."

I bit my tongue, trying to avoid asking Mom whether

Almeria might have been killed. Suddenly the letter I'd found seemed sinister again. Maybe she had been killed. By her husband with whom she didn't get along? Or by the bad boy she'd run to? There was no telling.

"I don't suppose," I said, "you could introduce me to John Martin and Asia?"

There was a silence from the other end. "Well . . ." she said, "I suppose . . . depends exactly what you want from them. I mean, they're divesting themselves of most of their good furniture, but I don't think you could afford . . ."

"No, no, not that. For research, you know?" I hastened to appease her. "Not that I have any intention of asking them bluntly, to their faces. I just want to know, you know, if there're any family legends of what might have happened to Almeria. It might come up in conversation . . ."

"Well . . ." Mother said, "as a matter of fact I'm hosting a tea for the historical mystery society tomorrow, and both John and Asia are attending, since they are such history buffs. It's at the country club. I can take you as my guest. If you promise to wear something decent."

"Sure," I said.

"Your ex's wife will be there."

"Michelle?" I think my voice squeaked. Not that I had anything against the woman, except that she always made me feel ill dressed—or worse. "They're back in town then?"

"I don't think so," Mom said. "She said something about getting into town before lunch, then coming to the tea, and how she'd probably be all shopworn when we saw her."

Right. Shopworn. She'd still look about ten times more elegant than I'd manage at my most fixed up. I tried to concentrate on the good news, instead, and hung up the phone, and went to the living room where Cas was still reading to the mostly asleep E.

"All-ex will be back tomorrow," I said.

"Daddy?" E asked. Then shook his head. "Don't wanna Daddy. No Peegrass. Or rats."

The idea of my ex allowing either Peegrass or rats into his immaculate McMansion made me want to laugh, but I said, "Only for a few days, baby. Then you can come home to me again." I'd almost said to us, and bit my tongue at the thought, though Cas was looking incredibly domestic, as he rose from the sofa, holding E. "Come on, now, kiddo," he said. "Let's get you to bed, okay?"

We got him into his pajamas and into bed, an effort only slightly hampered by the fact that he had gone all heavy and limp, like a very large rag doll. Pythagoras got into bed, by his side. As I leaned over and kissed E, he said, "Kiss Peegrass, too!"

So I did, and Cas patted them both as if they were dogs, which both of them seemed to be all right with. We left E asleep and Pythagoras stretched out by his side in the faithful-guardian position, and went back to the living room.

"I was saying," Cas said, as soon as we were sitting on the sofa, "I wasn't proposing any sort of temporary arrangement."

I noted he didn't mention marriage, either, and I sighed, but was glad, because that might be the one offer I couldn't refuse. Instead, I said, "I don't know, Cas. I still say we've only known each other six months . . ."

"Okay," he said. "I realize it's different for you, because you've been married before and all, and you're not sure if this will work out. I just want you know where I stand. So . . . when you're ready . . . you know . . . let me know."

Right. I'd let him know. If I was ever ready. The problem was that, having had a marriage blow up in my face, I should—at least if I were a feminist heroine—have sworn off marriage for good and decided that from now on only casual relationships of the most transitory and carnal kind would do.

The problem was that I was not a feminist heroine. In fact, it was quite possible I wasn't any sort of heroine. I was almost sure I wasn't the main character in a book, either. But if I were, it wouldn't be one of those deeply philosophical tomes on the six-thousand-year home oppression of female kind. It was my considered opinion that both female kind and male kind were oppressed in completely different ways, and though they did occasionally oppress each other—and the Victorian age, other than its houses—had been one of those periods, most of what did the oppressing of both men and women was biology. A biology that came from a certain evolutionary history and that, therefore, was quite different for the hunter side of the species and the gatherer side of the species. Not to mention the one for whom spreading seed far and wide on as broad a dispersion setting as possible was a viable evolutionary strategy, versus the one who would pay in energy and vitality for each cub.

What was amazing, given the differences between men and women, was that we ended up being more alike than not and being able to understand each other on an intellectual level. Though I still said Ben was making up that thing about different tones of beige.

So, if I were a character in a book, it would probably be a cozy or perhaps a book on a woman who had an unhealthy relationship with discarded furniture. This left me with the ability to realize it wasn't marriage itself I had a problem with, but marriage when the other half didn't take it seriously.

Which meant, of course, that jumping into a relationship that most people took even less seriously than marriage was quite out of the question. I sighed as I snuggled into Cas, "I'll let you know," I repeated.

He leaned over and kissed me. "I hope so," he said. "And I hope it's soon." And then he kissed me again.

Let me make it very clear that any woman being kissed by Cas shouldn't be able to think of anything else. So I must have been really worried about that letter in the piano, because as we broke off kiss number two and Cas started descending for number three, I said, "Can I consult old files, at the police station?"

This, predictably, caused him to recoil, which was a pity, and say, "What?"

"Do you still keep records of cases in the twenties?" I asked. "And would I be allowed to look at them?"

He was frowning at me, slightly, as though he weren't absolutely sure I hadn't been taken over by pod people from Saturn. Frankly, I was starting to suspect it myself. After all, the words at the back of my mind were *what were you thinking? We were about to be kissed.*

But the front of my mind was in full command. "The thing about that letter? Remember?"

"Oh, the woman? The star-crossed lovers? Dyce . . . why would that be a police report?"

"No, not the star crossing or lovering." I proceeded to tell him about my research at the library and what Mom had said. I abstained from mentioning that I was going to a tea with the family tomorrow because, after all, it was none of his business. Also, Cas got worried about the stupidest things.

In fact, I could already tell he was getting worried,

from the way he was frowning as he looked at me, with his forehead all wrinkled and his eyes squinched.

"Would you mind terribly not looking into it any more?" he asked. "I mean, I might be an idiot, but the whole thing feels off to me. And you know, you really shouldn't disturb this old stuff."

"What are you afraid of?" I asked. "That the ghosts of Almeria and Jacinth will come back after me?"

He shook his head. "No. More . . . you know . . . people have friends and descendants and . . ." He shrugged. "Look, Almeria and Jacinth have to be dead. Okay, her husband might have made their lives miserable, or they might have ruined all his happiness, but the thing is . . . you know . . . they're all dead. What does it matter?"

But to me the idea seemed rather like saying that in a hundred years we'd all be dead, so what did it matter how we lived? Human life might be brief and all, but it should count for something. Otherwise, what was the point?

"I'm curious about it, is all. I just want to know if there was a disappearance claim over Jacinth, and what it says. Do you have reports that old?"

He sighed like he meant it. "Some. The building of the police station is still the same, and we have some stuff."

"Could I look at it?"

He made a face. "Maybe. Some reports are public, or I can get permission for you to look at them—you know, local history and all. I can ask my boss. If he says you can look . . ." He perked up. "I'll call you tomorrow, if he says you can come and take a look. And then if you come before lunchtime, we can have lunch together. That way you can satisfy your curiosity, and I get to spend time with you."

I avoided groaning. So tomorrow there would be lunch and tea. Such were the dangers of criminal investigation "Sounds fun," I said.

"Good. So now we can resume what we were doing when we were so rudely interrupted by your prurient curiosity about past loves."

We resumed. And it was a very good resumption. So good, in fact, that though we heard a car pull up in the driveway and saw the lights being turned off, I wasn't in the least alarmed when Ben didn't come in immediately. In fact, though I didn't pay much attention, it was quite a bit of time before Ben came in.

"Oh, for the love of Bob," he said, as he came in the door. "Don't you two hear the rats squealing? Have you fed them at all?"

"Once," I said, as I looked up and noted that Ben's hair was rumpled and he'd somehow lost his tie.

"Isn't Nick coming in?" Cas asked, in the most casual of ways, though I was sure he too had noticed the lack of tie.

"No. He . . . had to leave." The blush came like a tide up Ben's face, and I wondered what in hell it all meant. Not that I had time to ask, as he more or less fled to the kitchen. Even if it was the most casual-seeming retreat I'd ever seen him beat.

When I went to check on him, he was feeding one of the rats, and looked at me accusingly. "You didn't mark the feeding on the notebook!"

CHAPTER 8

Of Rats and Dates

I had a night of disturbed dreams, where the piano kept appearing in my mind again and again, in what I presumed was its glory. A woman in a Victorian gown, her face invisible, and the handsome Jacinth Jones from the newspaper picture stood cornered in front of it, while an ax came down, and her letter fell inside the piano.

I woke up feeling so strange that I actually went out to the shed, in my T-shirt and shorts—what I slept in when Cas wasn't spending the night—to see if there were any ax marks on the piano. Needless to say, there weren't.

When I came back in, Ben was in the bathroom. I didn't hear the shower. This was generally a bad thing, since it meant that Ben was having quality time with his beauty products. By their quantity alone, they required the sort of attention that Solomon must have reserved for his harem.

I could have pounded on the door, but I didn't feel

awake enough to, so I went back to the kitchen and started coffee going, while I checked on the rats. There was a little sticky note taped to their aquarium, in Ben's handwriting. "Just fed them, leave them alone."

With nothing more to do I turned my hand to pancakes, at which I was amazingly accomplished because E and I had lived on them for most of a year.

When Ben emerged, fully dressed, I had dished up pancakes, scrambled eggs, and bacon and was feeling rather pleased with myself. The fact that he gave me a worried frown as he sat down and helped himself was weird, but not as weird as the hesitation in his voice as he said, "Uh . . . you don't have plans for lunch, do you?"

I started to open my mouth to tell him that I might have a date with Cas when the phone rang. It was Cas and he sounded altogether too cheerful. "Hello, beautiful," he said. "So, are you ready to come and keep me company for a while?"

"Uh . . ." I said. "Does this mean that you found . . ."

"It means that you should come and spend some time with me, in about two hours or so. And then I'll take you to lunch. How does that sound?"

"Great," I said. "See you for lunch, then."

Ben's fork clattered down on his plate. "You didn't just make a date for lunch!" he said, sounding about two years old.

"Um . . . I did, why?"

He glared at me. "I suppose we can feed the rats, and lock Pythagoras up to make sure he doesn't get in trouble, but you'd better be planning to take E."

The idea of taking E to the police station while I was trying to do research didn't exactly make my hair stand on end, but it didn't fill me with warm fuzzies, either. Frankly, the few times I'd taken him by there—usually when we were picking up Cas for dinner or meeting him for some other reason—E's sell-by date went to about five minutes.

You simply can't ask an active toddler to stay sedate and quiet in a place of business. And in E's case you couldn't expect him to stay sedate and quiet anywhere. Not that E was hyperactive, exactly. I'd asked the pediatrician— mostly because All-Ex worried—and the pediatrician told me that a child could only be considered hyperactive if he wouldn't settle down and work at any task for any length of time. This did not describe E who could sit down and be absorbed in something for hours. Of course, that some- thing, in the past, had involved such interesting projects as melting his entire box of crayons on the radiator or remov- ing all the screws from my bed frame. In fact, it was a good bet that if E was quiet and seemingly behaving, it was time to investigate. It might not be completely amiss to call the police and the fire department, either, just in case.

"I'm sorry, Dyce," Ben said. "But you didn't ask. And I did make a date with Nick."

"Oh, did you?" I asked. "To talk about the animal poi- sonings?"

He glared at me. "There have been two more, since we found Pythagoras. Nick is very worried."

"Yes, I imagine he would be," I said. "You didn't get in a big argument or anything?"

He stared. "No, why?"

"Well, he wouldn't come in."

Again the blush came in waves, and I wondered if he knew how obvious it was. "Uh . . . he had to go home. He had to be in early this morning."

"I see," I said.

He threw a pancake at me. I ducked, and the pancake

hung, art-installation-like from the knob of the cupboard. "Benedict!" I said. "I can't believe you are wasting good food."

He did his best to glare, but grinned. "Don't, Dyce."

"Well, considering how much you teased me . . ."

"Yeah, yeah. But . . . don't. It's very early still. I don't know anything yet. If . . . if it turns out to be right, you'll be the first to know."

I picked up the pancake and threw it in the trash. "The problem," I told him, "is that I was going to go early and hang out with Cas a bit before going to lunch."

"And it has to be today?"

I had a strong feeling it did, so I nodded.

"I don't suppose your mother would look after E?" he asked. "I mean Fluffy is gone. Maybe E can take Pythagoras with him."

"Pythagoras," I said. "Chews paper. I don't think it's a good idea to leave him in a bookstore. And as for E . . . Remember the last time? They forgot he was there and he left, and it took hours to find him down the block."

"Oh, yeah," Ben said. "Your son made the mistake of not being a book."

"Besides, Mom is going to a tea . . ." I stopped, as I remembered what she had said about All-ex's wife. I grabbed the phone and dialed Mr. All-ex Mahr's residence. One ring, two, and I started praying.

Who says faith counts for nothing. Right on cue, the phone was picked up, and the new Mrs. Mahr's supercilious voice answered, "Hello, Mahr residence."

The little bitch didn't sound in the least tired. I got a strong feeling that she and All-ex had actually been back for at least a week and hadn't told me, so they wouldn't need to take care of E. Yeah. The mills of Dyce ground slowly but they ground exceedingly fine. "Michelle!" I said, probably giving the woman a near heart attack, since I'd never called her by her first name to her face, and what I called her behind her back tended to be less than complimentary. "I'm so glad you're home. I have an emergency this morning, and I must have E stay with you. Would that be acceptable?"

"But—" she stammered. "Uh . . . we have something this afternoon at the country club, and I—"

Yes, indeed, she was a female dog of unknown provenance. The two of them thought nothing of leaving me alone with E—and incidentally taking up Ben's time—for a whole two weeks, but they would not tell me they were home because they wanted to go to a tea at the country club. Yeah. I glared at the phone and my voice became so saccharinely sweet that if anyone were exposed to it without warning, they would die of diabetic shock. Smart people who had known me for more than an hour knew what that tone in my voice meant,. But the current Mrs. Mahr wasn't smart. "Oh, don't worry about that. If you pick him up in the next hour and just keep him till one o'clock, I'll get him then." I neglected to mention that I, too, was going to the country-club thing. Let her be surprised!

She hemmed and hawed. She covered the phone and I heard her talk behind it, probably consulting All-ex. After a while, she said, "Hello. Yes, I can pick him up. No need to pack a bag since he'll be returning to you. No need for you to come get him, either. I'll bring him back."

I smiled beatifically. Indeed. I was quite willing to have E return to me. In fact, I was fairly sure that to take him away from Peegrass and the rats right now would require physical violence—particularly in view of the fact that his new obsession was great enough to make him forget the bike. However, the time for payback would come. And come soon enough. All-ex had a large yard after all. And the next time E went for an extended stay, the motorcycle could visit, too.

"Stop that," Ben said, as soon as I hung up.

"Stop what?" I asked, looking at him. He was calmly finishing his pancakes.

"Stop smiling like that," he said. "It scares me."

I patted him on the head, on my way out of the room. "Relax, my child," I said. "My plans are not for you."

He mumbled something, and I went out of the room to get E up and ready to go. Bathing him was easy, though the bathroom space was much reduced, and Pythagoras kept walking back and forth along the edge of the tub meowing little inquiries concerning this strange torture of putting small humans in water.

By the time E had been dressed and had eaten his breakfast, he'd registered several times the fact that he didn't want to go to Daddy. He was sulking in the kitchen, glaring at both of us in turn.

Ben was feeding the rats and looking guilty. "If he—" he said.

I shook my head. If Ben wasn't going to break his date for me, he sure as hell wasn't going to break it for my bratty child. "I'm sure he'll live, Ben. It's just a few hours. If you don't mind staying with him a couple of hours later this afternoon, while I go to a tea at the country club."

At that moment, the doorbell rang, so I left Ben to take E to the front door and into the arms of his equally sulky stepmother.

E wailed as a parting shot, "I want Peegrass." Gratifyingly, Michelle's eyes went huge and round and she said,

"Uh . . . honey, we use the bathroom at Daddy's house," while giving me a reproachful look.

Ben was settling the rats back in the aquarium, as I came back to the kitchen and started washing dishes. "You know," I told him. "I think sooner or later that woman will die."

"Your ex's wife?" he asked.

"Yes."

"Uh . . . Dyce. Murder is still—"

"I didn't say anything about murder," I said. "I figure she's completely brainless, and there's only so long residual brain-stem activity can last."

"Yes, but . . . Dyce!"

"Yes?"

"What are you going to do at the country club? I mean, it's not . . . you've never had . . ."

I considered telling him the truth—I was going to see the Martins to try to get more information about the letter. On the other hand, I remembered all too well that the only thing worse than an upset Ben was a Ben in full protective mode. "Oh, nothing," I said. "It's a tea for the fans of historical mysteries Mother is giving and the current Mrs. Mahr has annoyed me, so I figure I'd discomfit her a little."

Ben frowned. "You haven't fought with Cas, right?"

"Right. Remember, I'm going to have lunch with him."

But Ben didn't look convinced.

CHAPTER 9

A Minor Rebellion

Dating a policeman hadn't put paid to all my romantic notions. Well, obviously not, since he brought me chocolates and flowers and took me out dancing. However, it had forever destroyed any mystique associated with police stations.

What the downtown police station in Goldport looked like was . . . a nineteenth-century bank. This was not exactly strange, since most of the commercial buildings downtown looked like banks. It was as if everyone back in the late eighteen hundreds had used the same architect, someone who had never been out of Goldport. All he knew about what commercial buildings were supposed to look like came from a picture of a bank in Denver that he'd seen in a newspaper.

So, except for two buildings that had gone up sometime in the late nineties, which were the usual very tall, blank glass-faced monstrosities, every other commercial building was a squat stone square.

Some of them, like the police station, were at least pretty, since they were made of mellow gold-bearing rock. On a clear afternoon, you could see the sun glint on the stone façades of Goldport's commercial district. It made the town sparkle. When I was little, I used to imagine mining the walls for gold, but let's just say that the one time I'd tried that with a chisel on the wall of the medical building it didn't end well. It was just as well I'd never put my more elaborate plan—involving dynamite—in motion since later on, when I supposedly grew up, I was told that the gold remaining in the rocks was too little to justify the trouble of extracting it and that the rocks were in fact wastage from gold mining.

I parked my car at the back of the police station and came around the front, where a broad staircase led to double doors, flanked by white globe lights. The doorway said, *Police* over it, in carved letters and I'll assure you that so far it looked very impressive, particularly with all the police cars parked up front.

But once through the double doors, it was completely different. There was a floor in what I was fairly sure was linoleum old enough to contain asbestos, colored an indifferent pink with darker reddish and white occlusions. It would have made me feel as if I were walking on pepperoni, except that it was rather dirty, so I would have to imagine it was gray, dingy pepperoni.

On this unattractive surface, two unattractive battered metal desks stood, and at each of the metal desks sat a woman. They had those little headsets on that people use who talk on the phone all day, and both of them seemed to carry on various simultaneous conversations composed of a lot of "Would you hold, please?"

It was all, "I don't know, I will check, will you hold, please?" and then "Well, he was released yesterday, will you hold, please?" and then "The mother would have to be present as well, will you hold, please?" and then "As soon as bail is posted, will you hold, please?"

The women, one matronly and probably just a little short of my mother's age, the other about my age, very thin and harassed-looking, used to stop me when I came in the door. But now I was a familiar face, so they merely waved me through as they continued their conversations.

There was one of those doors with hammered glass at the back of the entrance room. Well, actually there were a series of them, looking exactly like refugees from a film noir set. But only one door interested me, and I'd only ever been through the one door. I presumed the others led to various other operations the police carried on, operations that had nothing to do with Cas.

The door I went through was labeled *Serious Crimes Department*.

Once past it, I entered the mid-twentieth century—all polished-oak floors, a broad hallway lined with file cabinets on the right, and a row of more of the doors with glass and names and titles on it on the left.

I went past the one that said *Rafiel Trall*, and I swear I heard a snuffling, as if Rafiel had a very large dog at the office. But that was none of my business. Cas's door was past his. They were the only senior investigators and the only ones meriting offices. Beyond that stretched a vast, cavernous room, lit by broad windows and cut up by the sort of ubiquitous cubes that seemed to be part of every business these days.

I noted Nick at a near cube—if for no other reason because he was taller than most of the other people—but he was staring at his computer screen, so I didn't say anything. Instead, I knocked at the door to Cas's office.

And the time machine leaped another fifty years—at least—forward. The inside of Cas's office was furnished mostly with things he'd bought from me over the last six months. He had a nice Persian-looking rug on a polished floor, a wall of dark mahogany bookcases containing not just process folders but the occasional—nicely—disguised file box made to look like a decorative wooden container. His desk was equally broad and a light oak color. The clean lines had attracted him when he'd first seen it.

There were two large armchairs facing the desk, his office chair was the sort that's incredibly expensive but supposedly good for your back as well as decorative, and on the lower bookcase against the wall—piled neatly with papers, which pertained to his current work, and hosting the printer on the highest left-hand shelf—was a reproduction of Rodin's *The Kiss*, which I had bought in a horribly rusted condition and spent weeks polishing, painting with an undercoat, and finally gold-leafing. It had been my Christmas gift to him.

Cas was working on a laptop and looked somewhere between bewildered and tired, but grinned as he saw me. "Hello, Dyce," he said. He got up and came toward me at the same time I closed the door. "I'm so glad to see you."

In the next second, he showed me how glad he was, with only the thin door and its hammered glass protecting us from the most glaring violation of the public displays of affection ban in the history of Goldport Police Department.

When we'd both come down to earth and recovered our breath, I asked, "The file, on Jacinth Jones's disappearance? Do you have it?"

He nodded. "Actually," he said, dropping his voice, "I brought it in here this morning, after a conference . . ."

"A conference?" I asked.

"My captain called Rafiel and me in this morning." He frowned slightly. "It was very strange. He said that he'd been told someone was writing a book about cases that had never been solved, in Goldport, and that he had been asked for us to keep those files away from any curious eyes. Now, mind you, he wasn't exactly stopping us from showing them to someone. Just giving us a heads-up that from what he had heard the book might disparage the police department and we were to make things difficult for this writer."

My mind spun. I'd given the writer story to my mother. To the person at the library, too, I supposed. Either of them could have talked, but who would they have reached that would have led to the two senior investigators in the Goldport Police Department being told to make my life difficult.

"But—" I said.

"I talked to Rafiel and we both agreed that we were not going to sit on an old file just because some big brass is all upset at having to admit we fail sometimes." He gave me a tentative smile. "Rafiel has a rebel streak a mile wide, you know."

I shook my head. "I have no idea what can have brought– "

"Attention to this?" Cas sighed. "I wish I could believe it was someone else poking around, but I don't think so. I told you, Dyce, that it could become dangerous."

I bit the tip of my tongue before I told him that, of course, it was dangerous, but once I had started down this sort of path, I could no more stop myself than I could grow wings and fly. That letter had rung too many emotional bells for me to ignore. Yeah, the writer and the man she'd written it to might long be dust in the dust, but the thing was—we'd all be dust, someday. It didn't make us stop mattering. It didn't make who we'd been and what we'd done stop existing.

"Gosh," Cas said, putting on his best aw-shucks intonation. "Stop looking at me like that." He gave me a nervous smile. "Somehow you always look years older and wiser when you do that. I get the impression that I've been tested and found wanting. I'll talk to you about it at lunch, okay? I still think there are dangers, and you need to at least be aware of them. But meanwhile, the file is here, if you want to read it."

He motioned me toward one of the oversized armchairs, and reached into his desk drawer, to pull out a very yellowed envelope. So yellowed that I didn't know if it had been yellowish to begin with. He set it down in front of me, and pulled out pages.

I was surprised they were typewritten then told myself I was an idiot. Of course they had typewriters in the twenties.

He handed the whole mess to me and went back to his desk and his laptop.

The first thing that surprised me was the thoroughness of the investigation, considering the time period. There were, for instance, pictures. Poor quality and sepia-colored, of course, but pictures, which I never expected. Pictures of the front of the house where Jacinth had lived. I looked at it avidly. It should have been a familiar place.

Only blocks from me, I must have driven or walked past it dozens of times.

When E was smaller, the only way of making him fall asleep was to take him for a drive or for a long ride in his baby carriage. Mind you, nine times out of ten, when we got home he'd wake up again, but sometimes, particularly when he was fussy right after All-ex and I separated, I'd taken him on long walks all over the neighborhood. So that house should have been as familiar to me as the outside of my own apartment building.

Only it wasn't. To begin with, it sat on a bare yard, without a hint of grass, much less trees. And though grass is notoriously hard to grow in Colorado, my neighborhood had trees everywhere. Big, shallow-root conifers sat next to the houses, climbing ever taller, posing a danger to power lines, passing vehicles and, in wind storms, sometimes the houses themselves. On the devil strips and sometimes in front yards, huge old maples grew, lifting sidewalks and dipping their roots into sewer lines and enriching Roto-Rooter.

The thing was that I knew houses with their accompanying greenery and never without, so looking at this isolated house, standing there, with no greenery of any sort seemed odd. It threw me off. Of course, it was sepia, too. But more than that—the house itself looked so bare. All of the other houses in the neighborhood sported porches, upper-story verandas, and what not.

This was simply a saltbox, square and tall, with nothing about it to say that any personal thought had gone into the building. Just a shelter in what was still, back then, in many ways the Wild, Wild West.

At least, I thought, squinting at the brown expanse of the picture, the yard wasn't totally bare. To the right of the house there were two tiny trees that had just been planted. Saplings, maybe all of five and a half feet tall. I couldn't tell whether they were maple, but presumed so.

I set the picture aside and turned to the next three. These showed the inside of the house. That truly impressed me, since the idea of photographing the inside of a potential crime scene couldn't have been normal at the time. I smiled, imagining that I should credit some ancestor of Cas's who had a friend who was a photographer.

I concentrated on the pictures, the first one of which showed a kitchen arrangement. There was one of those square sinks with a water pump on it and next to the sink, a Franklin stove.

On the other side of the sink was a small table that had clearly been the focus of the photographer's attention. It showed two coffee cups turned upside down as if to dry, on a smudgy bit that I thought was a tea towel or the equivalent.

I turned to the next picture, of what looked like a Victorian living room with a wooden-framed sofa. On the sofa were two piles of paper, looking like someone might have been in the middle of a job and set a few on either side of him. A pile for "looked at" and "not" perhaps.

The last picture was of a wardrobe, the doors flung open to show an array of neatly hanging clothes, and a suitcase on the shelf above them.

I went on to the report to look for indications of what the pictures meant. The main investigator was a policeman glorying in the unlikely name of Domingo Dunkirk. Well, Goldport had always attracted odd balls, and in my mind the gentleman's image formed. A sad Mexican face with dark blue eyes. He would, of course, be half Mexican and half Anglo Saxon and would have taken refuge in our little eccentric mountain fastness to escape the prejudice of the larger world.

However, since I wasn't writing a work of fiction—or even nonfiction—I had to pass on thinking about Domingo Dunkirk any further and turn to what Domingo Dunkirk had to say.

The report was dated almost a month after the date the letter gave for the rendezvous. The first paragraph detailed how: *since Mr. Jacinth Jones has been missing from his usual haunts and business for the last month, without having given anyone reason to believe he had absented himself on travel or voluntarily, his friends, associates, and creditors had asked the police department of Goldport to look into his effects and his domicile and determine whether he might have been the victim of foul play.*

I squirmed in the seat and made myself comfortable by shoving a leg under my own behind, the position I used to sit in when listening to Grandma's stories. As far as narration went, I had to admit the style of the nineteenth and early twentieth century was far more pleasant to read than current dry reportage.

Plunging into the flowery narration with gusto, I found that the pictures were meant to show that the house looked as though Mr. Jones had left the premises in some hurry, surely intending to return. Nothing appeared to be missing but the clothes he was last seen wearing. Even his business papers, some of which the report pointed out, were letters of credit, which could be exchanged for assets, had been left on the love seat in what the report quaintly called the parlor.

However, no signs of violence or blood were found in the house. But behind a chair in the kitchen, a hairpin, such as a lady might wear was discovered.

The report made no speculation at all on who the lady might be, though that long-ago investigator had included two newspaper clippings, dated six and three years before, respectively, each intimating that Mr. Jacinth Jones had been seen in the company of a local lady whose name started with *M*. The later clip intimated that the lady was the mayor's wife.

I made notes to check out later, all the while wondering what I hoped to gain by this. The conclusion of the investigator was that Mr. Jones had left the house in a hurry, fully intending to come back.

Was it not possible that it had happened just that way? He thought, perhaps, that Almeria was exaggerating their danger, and that they didn't have to go away. Or perhaps he'd thought he could calm her down. But then she'd come to him and said, "We must run, my husband is after me," and he'd left, without thinking twice, because he loved her that much.

I realized I was chewing on my lower lip, something I only did if I was deep in thought. And I also realized I didn't believe the pretty story I'd just told myself.

Yeah, he might have been deeply in love with her. That was the first thing a person would think, of course, when reading about things like this—that the man must have been madly in love with the upper-class politically connected wife. Otherwise, why would he take the risk of getting involved with her and invoking the wrath of her powerful husband?

The problem was that it didn't always—or perhaps not even most of the time—work out that way. After all, the powerful husband would have many gifts in his giving. And if the man could manage to manipulate the wife behind his back, so that she made sure some of those gifts fell your way, then you were golden.

This might be particularly useful if a person was running a saloon—and I made a note of it, because I was almost sure that at the time Prohibition had still been in effect. I'd need to look it up. If that were the case, did Jacinth serve just root beer, in his saloon, or did he perhaps serve things that were stronger in the back? At any rate the place had gambling, by all accounts, and at the time running a saloon was at best straddling the law. That meant having connections with powerful people would be essential.

I stared at the yellowed pages in my lap and wondered about the man the report was about. Perhaps he had been a smooth operator, on the take, and his bets had finally gone wrong. Heck, if Prohibition was still in effect, he had to know some bootleggers, and that immediately brought up the prospect of his having been killed or "disappeared" by them. On the other hand . . . On the other hand what if Jacinth was truly in love with Almeria. Willing to risk all for her. She was clearly in the upper echelons of society in Goldport. Now, that might not have meant as much as it does now. Western society, in particular, was more permeable. People would come from menial jobs or from the lower middle class in the East, arrive in Colorado, give themselves airs, and either become bigtime financiers—mostly men—or married rich people—mostly women.

Still, born to it or not, Almeria would have been used to a luxurious existence. More important, back then, because the gap—not so much in the earnings, but in the manner of living—between rich and poor was so much broader. Surely if he loved her, Jacinth Jones wouldn't hare off into the blue, taking nothing with him to support them, would he? Even the money orders that could easily have been converted into money in almost no time, before or after he left?

And where had Mr. Jones come from after all? Who was he?

It seemed to me the entire mystery revolved around his character—whether he was decent or not. I looked through all the papers again, and found a reference buried almost at the end. Something about making inquiries to Chicago, from which Mr. Jones was said to have come, and getting no conclusive answer.

"Cas," I said, and he jumped in a way that told me that he'd completely forgotten I was present. Which in the normal way of things should, I suppose, have annoyed me, only I knew Cas so well, and I knew that he forgot just about everything while he was working. He looked up. "Yes?"

"Is there any way you can check with Chicago and find out about Jacinth Jones, after all this time?"

"Where in Chicago?" Cas asked. "They do have more than one police station, you know. . . . Even in those days, they probably had more than a dozen."

"It has a number here, of the precinct the detective, Domingo Dunkirk, called," I said. "I don't know if he called it because Jones came from there or because he knew someone there."

"Could be either," Cas said, and shrugged, as he noted down the number in the papers I held out to him. "And I have some people back there that I know from past cases, but you know . . . It's been a long time."

I nodded. "Of course, you probably won't find anything, but I'd like to know as much as I can about where Jones came from and what he was doing in Colorado." ·

Cas grinned at me. "He was running a saloon during Prohibition . . ."

"So it was during Prohibition?" I said.

He nodded. "I doubt it made much difference," he said. "Those miners who came down after months alone on the mountains probably weren't dying for a root beer and a nice little game of pinochle." He made a face. "I suspect there was both liquor and women available, you know, discreetly. We know about the gambling."

"But you realize that doesn't make him a bad man. He was serving a need."

He frowned. "Babe, drug dealers serve a need. It's still illegal and probably immoral."

"Yeah, yeah, but . . ." I shook my head. "But it doesn't mean he was a cad, or that he was doing something underhanded with a woman who loved him. I mean . . . In those days . . ."

"It was harder to get somewhere, and sometimes people resorted to illegal stuff?" He shrugged. "Possibly. Possibly still. It is always very hard for a policeman not to judge a criminal, but I try. I try to understand what I might have done in their position. It doesn't make much difference in how I apply the law, but I feel the rest is none of my business."

I nodded. "So I think we need to know who Jacinth Jones was and where he came from. Because he might have gone back there."

Cas looked up at me. "Probably."

"Or he might not," I said.

CHAPTER 10

Sandwiches and Violin Cases

We finally left to go to lunch. By pure coincidence, we did so at the same time that Ben pulled into the police lot and Nick came out. Ben got out of his car and joined Nick who was standing by a magnificent bicolor vehicle with a convertible top. It was beautifully finished in creamy white and glossy red, and as the two of them got in it, and Nick put the convertible top down—a ridiculous thing to do in weather that was good for January, meaning it verged on the low forties—I could see the leather of the inside seats was just as creamy and white.

I resisted a ridiculous impulse to shout out that Ben should wear earmuffs—he was older than I and certainly able to look after himself—as we waved at them and they drove out of the lot.

" Nick's car is very nice," I said to Cas.

"Isn't it? It's the one he's using now. The most recent project," he said, and grinned at me. "Usually he finishes one and uses it for a while, then sells it and uses the new one. It's a hobby as much as a means of transportation. I keep telling him if the price of gas goes up much higher, he'll have to buy a hybrid." His grin turned wicked. "He shudders."

"I imagine," I said. And because it had been nagging at me I said, "How come his last name is Nikopoulous?" I asked.

"Uh. It was his father's name. What do you mean?"

"Well, he's your cousin. Shouldn't he be a Wolfe?"

"Nah. We're cousins on the maternal side. My mother and his mother are twin sisters. My mother was adventurous and married outside the Greek community. His was more traditional. But they stayed close, so Nick and I were brought up somewhere between cousins and brothers." He shrugged. "And I get to help him with his ridiculous hobby. Hey, maybe I should get a car of my own to fix up. Do you like those cars, Dyce?"

"That one was very pretty," I said.

"Nineteen sixty-one Corvette Roadster. We found it in a barn, out in the country. Chickens had been nesting in it."

He drove for less than five minutes and pulled up in front of a one-story, glassed-front building, just outside the main commercial strip. It looked, from the outside, like a supermarket. The hand-painted sign above the door proclaimed, *Deli-Cioso*.

Inside, it turned out to be an Italian deli, with a large grocery-selling component. There were shelves with imported foodstuffs and a large counter with two scales on it, and a line of people clearly buying cold cuts and such. But in the corner were five tables, and clearly Cas was known there, because the lady behind the counter waved at him and said, "I'll be with you in a minute, honey."

And in a minute, she was, giving us just enough time to read the menus on the table. We each—not of common accord—ordered a Milanese sandwich and, on my being told the Caesar salad was huge (or in Cas's words, could feed large Italian families) a Caesar salad to share.

"The food is wonderful," I told Cas, as I dug into the salad, which tasted like homemade Caesar is supposed to and like restaurant salads so rarely do.

"Isn't it?" he said. "I discovered this place two months ago. Save room for dessert. They make the best cannoli." He looked around, while chewing his salad. "The best thing about it, though, is that these tables are away from the counter and that very few people come here for lunch. I think it's a new thing they're doing, serving lunch, so people haven't got used to it yet. I bring files to work on while I eat. I get things done and it beats eating at my desk."

"And you brought me here to have privacy to talk?" I asked with a smile.

He winked. "I see that nothing escapes you, Ms. Dare. Perhaps they really should have named you Sherlockia."

"Don't make me throw something at you," I said. "The only things on hand are food and I like my food."

"No, but seriously," he said. "I did bring you to talk, because I think you're not taking some things into account."

"What? Oh, I know. They're both dead, yadda yadda, and all that. Letting sleeping dogs lie, which somehow always leads to mad dogs and Englishmen, making me wonder if Englishmen were known for lying down with mad dogs, or . . ." I noticed the corners of his mouth twitching and stopped.

"Those are good points, Dyce," he said, then frowned. "Except for your very strange notions of Englishmen." The corners of his mouth twitched further. "The expression you're referring to has nothing to do with letting sleeping dogs lie, except perhaps to imply that Englishmen don't. The full expression is 'Mad dogs and Englishmen go about in the noonday sun.'"

"I suppose it's very colonial, from when the English were in all these tropical and subtropical climates where people sensibly took siestas and they didn't. None of which," he said, with a sigh, "has anything to do with what I was about to tell you. It's not some vague, undefined disturbing the bones of the dead that worries me."

He ate a mouthful of salad and then resumed. "It's the fact that Jacinth Jones's disappearance was never solved, and the fact that he was almost for sure involved with organized crime."

"What, because he came from Chicago?"

Cas shook his head. "No. Oh, that might have something to do with it. For all I know, he was one of the mob's advance guys, sent down to start a center of operations here, but that . . . well, I'd worry about it when we got there, if that were all the issue. But Dyce, you already know that someone got hold of my captain and told him to tamp down any investigations into this. Pardon me if I feel it's less than safe for you to pursue it."

"But . . ." I said. In my mind there was an image of men getting out of a big black sedan carrying violin cases. "Surely you don't mean the mob? I mean, Al Capone and all that." I waved my hand. "Aren't those all things like from the thirties?"

He frowned at me. "Various mobs are still heavily involved in illegal businesses probably practically every drug, gambling, and prostitution transaction in the U.S."

"Are you trying to tell me," I asked him. "That you

think your captain is involved with the mob—the same mob that Jacinth Jones might have been involved in?"

He shook his head. "Not my captain, but the other business the mob is and has always been heavily involved in is politics. They finance political campaigns you know." He smiled. "Don't look so shocked. It's a well-known fact. Most of the mobs operating now—or at any time—have the underhanded branch and the above-reproach legitimate businessman branch. These days I think they keep them more obviously separated than in the twenties and thirties, is all."

He took another forkful of salad and ate it thoughtfully while our sandwiches, with piles and piles of cold cuts and melted cheese were delivered. "The thing is," he said, once the server had gone a little way away. "That someone in city government clearly talked to my captain . . ." He shrugged. "Well, government or society, you know, those people who donate heavily to the benevolent organization and attend the dinners. So, it's someone with power, and if they're connected . . . well . . . you could be in danger."

"But why would I be in danger?" I asked. "I mean, what could anyone be afraid of? Surely whoever killed Jacinth, if he was killed, must be as dead as he would be, even if he lived a long and full life?"

Cas nodded. "To be honest." He took a bite of his sandwich, set it down, and mopped sandwich juice off his chin with the napkin. "To be honest, the fact that someone wants to shut you down is my main reason for assuming that Jacinth may have been murdered, and that whoever did it was connected. Because otherwise who would care now. Unless there's some mob secret involved that no one wants brought to light."

I thought about it, while I ate my sandwich. "I hear what you're saying," I said. "But somehow, instead of making me want to back down, being warned makes me want to pursue things further. I mean, if Jacinth Jones was killed by people more powerful than he was, and who took advantage of their power and connections to keep it secret . . ." I looked into my boyfriend's uncomprehending eyes. "Look, it's like this. In a way Jacinth Jones's character was defamed." I saw Cas open his mouth and I went on. "I'm not talking about whether or not he was involved with liquor runners, or what else might have been going on in his saloon. I mean, until that point, rumors and complaints swirling around his establishment notwithstanding, he was assumed to be a responsible businessmen. And then in the middle of the night, he just skips town, leaving bills and creditors and commitments he didn't honor.

"And don't forget, we still don't know what happened to Almeria. If he left of his own free will, perhaps she left with him. If not . . . Well, what happened to her? Was she killed, too? And before you say anything, let me point out that we don't even know if she was breaking the law, as we assume he was. Adultery it might have been, but that's not illegal. Or at least, even if it was back then," I added as I thought about some of the strange laws still on the books, like how you couldn't park your giraffe in downtown Goldport. "it wasn't enforced."

"Calm down," Cas said. "I'm not impugning the moral purity of the missing Almeria, adulteress or not." He shook his head. "I can even understand why you would feel obligated to her in a way, since we bought her piano. Not to change the subject," he said, clearly wanting to change the subject. "How's that coming along by the way? I'll have to plan to come over and deal with the innards, once you're done fixing the shell."

We had the cannoli, which were indeed excellent, for dessert, went back to the station, and parted in the parking lot. The convertible was already parked, and Ben's car nowhere in sight.

"He probably went home to feed the rats," I told Cas.

"What will you do when he goes back to work in a couple of days?"

"No idea," I said. "I'd better put an ad in the paper, or call the Humane Society or something."

I worried about it all the way home where I found not only Ben, but E just being returned by the current Mrs. Mahr. Looking at the clock, I realized they were right on time and I was the one who was late.

E was all smiles, as he ran up to the house and yelled, "Peegrass!" The cat gave him his usual, neurotic, slightly cross-eyed "I'm not bothering you, am I?" look.

I walked past them to the kitchen, where Ben was feeding rats. I think we both spoke at the same time. It had occurred to me that Ben probably would want to go out again tonight with Nick, too, since whatever their relationship was, it seemed to be on a fast track.

So as I came into the kitchen, I said, "I should be home at about five thirty, if you have—"

At the same time he started, "If you could be home before six, I have—"

We stopped and smiled at each other, and I said, "Cas is worried about the rats."

"Oh?" Ben said, looking up from rubbing a ratty tummy. The rats, I noticed, were getting short white fur. They also looked more alert.

"About what we're going to do with them when they grow up."

He sighed. "I'll probably keep one or two," he said.

"Rats?" I said. "In your place?"

He chuckled. "They're white, Dyce. Like lab rats. Who knows where they came from? It isn't so bad, if you think about it. Most of the time they'll be confined to their little aquarium. If I go on vacation, I can either buy some fancy food dispenser that will allow them to eat what they need every day, or you can come over and feed them once a day. It's not like they'll chew my shoes because they're lonely or something."

"Uh . . . but the rest? That leaves us with five rats. I would give them to the Humane Society but—"

"You're afraid they'll let people take them who would use them for snake fodder?" he asked.

I nodded. He sighed. "That leaves us in the business of adopting them out. I think they'll be ready in about a week. I'll put a note on a list or two online if you don't mind."

"I don't mind. We need to do something. You're going to work what, in two days? I don't want you to feel you're abandoning the rats. But I can't stay in front of the aquarium, protecting them from Peegrass."

"Now, don't you call the poor cat that. Yeah. Locking him in the bathroom even for two hours was really not good. He looked so upset when I let him out."

"E is petting him," I said. "Can you handle E and the rats till I come back?"

He assured me he could. All right, he might have laughed at the idea that he couldn't. Frankly, I thought the only reason he laughed was that he had completely forgotten that E might at any minute jump on his motorcycle and terrorize the house or, heaven forbid, the neighborhood. On the other hand, he had now developed symp-toms, including but not limited to talking to baby rats, so I was seriously worried for his sanity.

But I wanted to go to this tea, find out what the Martins had to say for themselves. What Cas had said about politicians controlled by the mob made me shudder. I'd much rather have kept thinking such things ended with the era of fedora hats and empty violin cases.

In my bedroom, I looked through the clothes hanging in my closet, selecting a white blouse and a salmon-pink, knee-length skirt, under the theory that I needed to look feminine and like I belonged in country club circles. Besides, both colors looked wonderful with my olive complexion and dark, curly hair.

I tied my hair back, put on that modicum of makeup—blush, eyeliner, a touch of loose powder, a bit of lipstick—I allowed myself in these situations, and made a face in the mirror. I slipped on one of my two pairs of good shoes—black pumps—but I still didn't feel dressy enough for a tea. I wished I had one of those big flower hats that old ladies wore to church.

In a fit of creativity, I grabbed a pink scarf from my drawer, and tied it around my head.

The outfit seemed to make Ben lose the ability to talk for about a second. He was sitting with E on his lap reading from the lab rats books when I came in. He looked up, and his jaw dropped. He had to swallow before he could speak. "Dyce, unless you're actually dressing as a character from Agatha Christie, I'd lose the scarf. And, really, honestly, with ice still on the ground, should you go out wearing a pink skirt?"

"It's a tea," I said helplessly. I always feel helpless when Ben starts talking about the clothes I'm wearing.

He sighed and herded me ahead of him to the bedroom. "You can leave the blouse on," he said, and threw on the bed, in rapid succession, a black skirt and my black blazer. "There, let's go for decent and presentable, instead of romantic fantasy, shall we?"

Like the gentleman he is, he left the room to allow me to change, but shouted back through the half-open door, "And don't even think about the bead earrings and necklace. Wear the pearl ones your grandmother gave you for high school graduation."

I withdrew my hand from the beads, mentally protesting against whomever it was who had given Ben the power to read minds.

"No, I can't read your mind," he said from the living room. "I just know your taste."

Right. And he expected me to believe that?

CHAPTER 11

The Other Half

The country club in Goldport is located on Country Club Drive, which, strangely, is not in the most expensive area of town, but out toward the middle-class suburbs, most of them built in the fifties and tidy enough, if hardly the homes the wealthy would want.

I suspected—knowing how planning worked around these parts, that there had been some sort of development planned for that part of town, which the country club was going to anchor, only the development had never happened. So the country club was in the southern part of town, while the upscale and ever growing suburbs were on the other side. Not that it mattered, since the people who belonged to it could afford the gas and the time to drive across town.

I drove into the parking lot in front of an unassuming low-slung, one-story building that could have been an artsy design for a ranch—all rough stone and low-slung timbers.

Behind that was a stand of trees, and I knew—from previous visits, back in my married days—that there were actually paths running through the tall conifers to the various other buildings of the club. Farther behind them were the horse stables, which had never meant much to me. Until I was ten, I had thought that horses were carnivorous, and, to this day, I still wasn't sure my instinct hadn't been right.

I noted that my mother's ancient Volvo with the *I Brake for Good Books* bumper sticker was parked near the door, but I saw no signs of All-ex's all white, babied Hummer. Not that this meant anything, as—this being Colorado— the parking lot was filled with various SUVs and I wasn't willing to go row after row, looking for All-ex's particular vehicle. I didn't even have that much interest in seeing him, except that I knew whenever he met me anywhere he didn't expect to, it ruined his day. Yeah, I'm petty and small, but I enjoyed making All-ex's life difficult, provided it didn't affect E. After all, he made my life difficult in so many small ways.

I went into the country club head high, half expecting to be tossed out because of the stains of refinishing fluid under my nails, but of course that didn't happen. Instead, when I asked about the tea for the historical mystery society, I was directed to one of the buildings at the back. The reception hall was large and decorated on massive lines, with a huge fireplace, where logs seemed to burn summer and winter—in summer, with great help from the air-conditioning system, I assumed—a massive desk, and the sort of chairs that gave the impression of having been built for giants and then accidentally dropped into an ordinary room.

The actual room where the meeting was being held— on the other hand—looked Victorian in appointments.

Wainscot paneling in a damn good imitation of red mahogany, walls painted in various pastel shades, hung with decorative plates and tapestries and hunting-scene pictures.

I don't know what I expected, but I suppose it was something like people sitting down at little tables, and servers circulating amongst them. That was how things had been when I'd been here before, during the time I was Mrs. Mahr. For this affair, on the other hand, there was only occasional seating. What I suspected were actually folding chairs had been swathed in a profusion of pink fabric—to match the walls—and bows. These chairs were then set out in random groupings. Amid the groupings, here and there, though not necessarily near the chairs were dainty tables with multitiered plates on them. On the plates was pastry, or fruit, or sandwiches with their crusts cut off.

At slightly larger tables were tea services, the teapots, rounded and huge, gleaming silver, and the creamers either silver or china. These stations were attended by white-gloved, suited young men. A few of them gave me nervous looks as I walked by, and I couldn't imagine why. It wasn't as if any of them was old enough to remember the things I'd done at this place, when I was a child before Mom had decided to stop bringing me with her.

Mind you, it had all had been purely accidental and, sometimes though rarely, the result of my having been really bored. I would then think up things I thought might amuse me. One afternoon, I found out that removing the white tablecloth from under the warming plates at a buffet was not considered amusing. It just hadn't gone as I'd planned. I hadn't removed only the tablecloth. Chafing dishes and little warming candles and all had come tumbling to the floor, but honestly, was that my fault? The book of magic I'd found at Grandma's house assured me it was all in the speed of the hand, and heaven knows I was fast enough, since neither Mom nor any of the attendants had managed to stop me.

In fact, Mom had ended with one of the candles on her lap—fortunately the glass of water that she'd been drinking had dropped from her nerveless fingers, too, so there had been no fire.

But all that had happened a good twenty years ago, and none of these young men looked old enough to remember it. Circling around the crowd, trying to identify familiar faces, I blushed as I thought I might have become a legend at the country club, the memory of my exploits passed on to each new employee, like the stories of the ghost on the tennis courts.

Surely not! Unless they also showed a picture of me at the same time, how would these young men know me? And I'd been about six then. They'd never recognize the adult me. Would they? I caught a suspicious glare from one waiter who should have been looking at the tea he was pouring, and hurried the other way . . . smack into my mother who—ah, Ben should see this!—was wearing a lilac skirt suit and a massive hat in the same color. With flowers.

"Mom!" I said, half startled by her getup.

"Candy," she said, as though I were the long-lost prodigal daughter finally returning to the land of crustless sandwiches. "I'm so glad you're here. The Martins were asking about you."

I froze in place. "The Martins?" I said. "Because I bought their furniture?"

"No, no. And by the way, the truck made the delivery, so you must come by and see if everything is there."

"Of course," I said, mechanically. "But why would the Martins want to talk to me?"

"I told them of your little project," Mom said. "Oh, don't look so stricken. It's not a bad thing. They don't mind talking about the disappearances. In fact, John was positively eager to speak to you."

"Uh . . . he was?" I felt very odd. All of a sudden it hit me that it was indecent to pry into these people's lives, under the excuse of a book that I had no intention of writing. Somehow, from Mom's shining eyes, I deduced she had been waiting all along for me to show a talent for anything more than turpentine and a way with a five-point scraper.

I would have registered my objections, too, I swear, except that Mom was dragging me through the crowd like an ocean cruiser at full steam dragging a small tugboat. I could no more escape her than I could grow a second set of arms. In fact, growing a second set of arms might be easier.

We passed more perfumed, well-dressed people than I cared to mention, including—I was sure of it, though I couldn't stop to take a close look—All-ex and Mrs. All-ex, she attired in what looked uncommonly like a blue wedding cake. I made a note that I must check out that dress, even as Mom brought me to a halt in front of a couple.

The woman I recognized almost immediately from the library. She was the colorless, white haired librarian, but something had happened like that old movie cliché, where a woman shakes out her hair and becomes someone completely different. She had let down her white hair from what must have been a fairly tight bun and masses of it flowed around her shoulders.

While she was probably the most conservatively dressed

woman there, after me—thank you, Ben!—in a gray suit, both the jacket and the skirt cut loosely, giving the impression of being merely separate pieces of cloth that happened to fall in an incredibly becoming way on her spare figure, she managed to look beautiful and very feminine.

Her husband, on the other hand, looked about as out of place at a country club as I felt. To begin with, unlike all the other men around, he wasn't wearing a suit, or even a proper button-down shirt with a tie. Instead, he wore an unbuttoned-at-the-neck white shirt, under a pullover the same color as his wife's suit. Over that, he wore an unzipped black leather jacket. His pants were also black and, I realized as I looked down, he was wearing black cowboy boots with incrustations that looked awfully like he'd been walking in the stable yard just before attending the tea. I hoped not, otherwise the waiters would probably start showing pictures of him around to new hirees, too.

They both greeted me like a long-lost friend, smiling over my buying their used furniture and pretending to be awfully interested in my work as a furniture refinisher. I could tell that their housekeeper had talked to them, too, because Mrs. Martin gave me this great approving glance and started talking about how she wished more young ladies were as environmentally conscious in their choices of small business.

I answered their questions and tried not to appear unfriendly but also tried to keep my imagination under control, because I had a strong feeling I could tell them I removed the paint from old furniture by squeezing the tail of a fire-breathing lizard and pointing it the right way, and they wouldn't have known any better or thought it at all unlikely.

Not that they were stupid. As my mother shoved—daintily—a saucer and cup of weak tea and a small plate of sandwiches into my hands, and they started to talk, (I pondered the age-old dilemma of how one eats when both one's hands are taken up just holding the food—that extra set of arms would have come in really handy right about then) I realized they were intelligent and interested in their particular fields. Her's seemed to be the conservation of historical documents and also the uses to which such archival treasures could be put. His was horse breeding. I had no idea what this very strange couple talked about when they were home alone of an evening. I sort of imagined them sitting there, their twin monologues crossing in the air as they periodically took notice of each other.

"It really would have been much better," she would say, "if newspapers were printed on acid-free paper."

"That new stud at the ranch. Man, you ought to see the colts he sires. I swear they come out running. I was wondering if I should start breeding him to—"

"Why, today we found a rare issue of the *Conspirator*, must have been the first that was printed, and—"

"Did it say anything about horses?"

"My dear?"

"Never mind."

I pulled myself back from that little fantasy, as Mrs. Martin said. "I heard you were interested in the mystery of Grandmama's disappearance."

"My grandmama," John interrupted. "Almeria Martin."

"His father was her son," his wife said. "Her older son, you know. He was about ten when she disappeared."

"My father never fully recovered from it, I think," he said. "But of course, Auntie Diane had it much worse."

"She was only eight and very frail, you understand. A

sickly little girl. She was her mother's best friend, you know, and she—"

"—was never the same after her mother disappeared," he finished.

I was fascinated by this distributive method of speaking. Ben's ex had complained that we finished each other's sentences, but never like this. This was like something they had learned, perhaps rehearsed. I kept expecting them to break into song along the lines of "auntie never recovered, poor little thing."

So vivid was this impression that I must have stared at them for a minute before realizing they were no longer talking. Then I cleared my throat. "She . . . do you have any idea where she might have gone?"

This time, they started both at the same time. "You must understand, Grandpapa, he was a great man and he did a lot for Goldport—"

He stopped suddenly and made a vague gesture with his hand, then backed up and disappeared into the crowd. I wondered if I was supposed to follow him, but his wife put out a hand and touched my coat. "John just went in search of something to drink," she said. "He so hates this many people and this confined a space. You know how men are."

I made a vague comment that might mean that yes, indeedy, I was acquainted with a male or two. While I was doing so, John came back, bearing a delicate rose-figured cup of tea. The smell coming from it, though, was nowhere near tea and I almost said something, but even I am not that completely stupid.

"What you have to understand about my grandfather, Ms. Dare," he said. "Is that he was a very odd man. A great man, but like all great men as capable of evil as of good, you know. His heart . . ." He spread his hands and swung some of the liquid around onto the carpet. I could already imagine some of the servers taking snap shots to warn newcomers about him. *He's worse than the tablecloth chick,* they'd say. *It's cow shit and whiskey as far as the eye can see, and it just won't come off the carpets.*

I gave him my blandest smile. "Uh-huh."

"Well, great men are like that," he said, and seemed disposed to sulk. With his buzz cut, pale eyes, and broad features, he could have been a rancher who'd never been to the city, rather than the scion of one of the richest families in Goldport. "They have their right points and their flaws. And you see, my grandmother, she was a very kind, well-disposed woman, and she took it to her heart to try to improve the social standing of Mr. Jacinth Jones. He was, you see, very raw, as my mother would say. Just arrived from the East, and probably not from any family that counted back there, if you know what I mean, and he was . . . well . . . *nouveau riche.* His saloon was doing so well that people around were jealous of him and complained. And then, you know . . . He didn't have the graces so he could keep those criticisms at bay.

"So my grandmother undertook to help him. Nothing . . ." He sipped the whiskey. "Nothing underhanded, you know, or even remotely scandalous. Just, telling him what he should wear, what establishments to patronize. But in those days behavior standards were a lot more rigid, you know?" He swigged again, and must have emptied the cup. "So, you know, she was . . . well the local papers talked about it." He started moving away again.

His wife put out a hand to stop me from following him, not that I'd made any attempt to, and said, "The thing is, you know, though the papers never named her, my husband's grandfather figured out what it was all about and he was not a man to take such a thing kindly. He was then the mayor. I don't know if you realize, but it was during his term and largely with contributions made by him or projects procured for him that most of the downtown was built. You must come to the Martin wing again, I'll give you all the relevant documents, since you'll want at least a brief introduction to his career, you know, for . . . for balance."

I nodded and mumbled something about balance, although right then the only balance that concerned me was my ability to hold tea and a plate of sandwiches, and what did my mom expect me to eat it with, my toe or my ear?

Then Mr. Martin was back, with a freshly filled tea cup. He continued his story as though there had been no interruption. "Well, my grandmother was . . . er . . . with child, and he told her, he said if the child didn't look like the two children that she'd already had with him, then he was going to kill both her and Mr. Jones, with his wood chopping ax."

I almost dropped the sandwich plate, which might have solved my dilemma but would certainly get me on that most-wanted list that the waiters were keeping. "Excuse me?" I was thinking of that lovely mansion with all its antiques. It had been the home of a man who had threatened to kill his wife with an ax.

John Martin took a swing of his whiskey, which clearly conferred telepathic abilities, because he then turned to me and said, "Well, those were much . . . rawer times, you know, much rawer. People were still very close to survival and they . . . they had to eat or be eaten, metaphorically. And my grandfather was a big man, yes, sir, a great man, but choleric." He took another drink. "My father always thought Grandma Almeria, his mother that is, was . . . innocent, you know? That the child she was carrying was his father's, but . . . who can guarantee what their next child will look like, I ask you? So, we think, she . . . that is . . ." He took another swig. "We think to save her life, you know, and Mr. Jones's—I mean, certainly you couldn't expect her to just wait and allow herself to be killed, could you?—so, in self-defense, and in defense of this man she'd been trying to er . . . mentor . . . yes, mentor, she—we think—ran with him."

"Ran?"

"Yeah, left, ran, eloped. Somewhere. We never knew where. To his dying day, my father—he died last year—wondered if he had a sibling out there, the baby his mother was carrying, you know, that he never got to see. It weighed on him to his dying day. He left me instructions that if this person or his descendants were to surface, I was to do something for them, you know, whatever they needed and I could help with."

"Has anyone surfaced?"

He shook his head. "No, we think . . . she . . . they . . . er . . . must have left the country. Gone somewhere else."

"Any indication of this? I mean, is there a reason you think it? Did she ever send a letter or a postcard or . . ."

He shrugged and finished his second teacup of whiskey. "I don't think so, leastwise not that anyone ever said, certainly not my father. But my father had private investigators look for her high and low, you know, all over the country, and he never found a sign of her. Mr. Jones, it is said, was swarthy, though blue eyed, so my father always said that they might have gone to Mexico or South America and changed their names."

"It is a very romantic story, isn't it?" Mrs. Martin asked.

I agreed. It was very romantic, and I had no doubt at all that it was a story, as in something fictional designed to provoke a certain reaction. I was not sure what the reaction was supposed to be, but my first feeling was that this had been shared with me to keep me from asking any more questions.

"It's very strange," I said. "A lot of people are very protective of Mr. Jones's past apparently. I had asked my friend, Castor Wolfe—he's a police officer—if he could get me some information on it, and he said he could not. He said that his captain had asked him not to give information to anyone writing a book on Mr. Jones. Very odd, don't you think?"

"Very," the woman said, and blushed as badly as Ben tended to.

Her husband didn't say anything, but left once more to return shortly with yet more whiskey. It soon became obvious that there I was, holding a plate of crustless sandwiches and a cup of now very cold tea, and they didn't have anything else to tell me. which only reinforced my impression that I'd been told a well-rehearsed tale. Why, I didn't know. But at least they didn't seem to be Mafiosi, and had nary a violin case between the two of them. I apologized and explained I needed to get home to babysit rats so my best friend could go on a date.

As I made my way through the crowd, I did notice that the current Mrs. Mahr was indeed attired in a dress that defied description, though I'll do my best to try. Imagine a dress that starts as a tank top in blue satin that shades to white in horizontal stripes. Right at the crest of her breasts, which were more inconsequential than mine, she had . . .

a hoop, sewn into the fabric, so that it stood stiff and proud, well away from her breasts. So far so good, right? I mean, no one has circular boobs, but it could give her a slightly more imposing figure. However . . .

However, she could not let a good thing go. So farther down, just above her waist, there was another hoop just slightly bigger, and so on all the way to her mid-thighs where the dress stopped on a ball-end fringe much like the ones that had been used in lampshades in the seventies.

Since there was a sort of inverted-bucket thing in the same color as the dress and with the same fringe perched on her bleached blond hair, I considered, momentarily, the possibility that she was, in fact, trying to imitate a lamp-shade, but it seemed so unlikely. Besides, if that were her intention, surely she could at the very least have put a little flashlight inside the hat or something, so we knew what she meant.

The second hypothesis was that she was trying to look like a wedding cake, an impression reinforced by the fact that she was wearing popular—if artificial looking—frosting colors.

What was worse, I thought, as I realized that, yes, I was going to go talk to them, was that this . . . confection . . . had probably cost her as much as my entire wardrobe combined. Had to. There was no way a normal seamstress, no matter how much fabric glue she might have inhaled, would come up with such a design. Heck, even the so-called designer lines available in our stores were not so crazy or ugly. To achieve such a level of awful—just as to achieve the casu-ally elegant—it took massive amounts of money. That dress had probably been purchased right off a runway show, and I wouldn't be surprised if the show had taken place in Paris or Milan or some other capital of fashion.

"I'm sorry, Michelle," I said, as I approached with a terribly bright and happy smile on my face. "I didn't recognize you at first. I must compliment you on your installation."

The effect was immediate and beyond my wildest dreams. Both of them turned and exclaimed at the same time, "Candyce!" If they had pointed fingers, turned pale or clutched hands to chest, it would have given a good impression of the worst Shakespearean acting possible.

As it was they came close. "What are you doing here?" All-ex asked. "I thought you were supposed to be watching Enoch?"

Michelle looked at me and said, in a slow, puzzled voice, "Installation?"

I smiled brightly first at All-ex. In fact, I smiled so brightly that you could have lit entire towns with the wattage. "Oh, don't worry," I said. "Ben is babysitting him for a few hours."

"Ben! Do you mean Benedict Colm?" The problem All-ex has with Ben is, I think, that he can't decide why he disapproves of him. On the one hand, he badly wants to disapprove because Ben is gay, but is slightly held back by the political correctness and common politeness of the circles he aspires to run in. On the other hand, he is convinced that Ben, as well as any other male who comes within three yards of me, must be having an affair with me.

This leaves him in a horribly painful position, where he isn't sure why he disapproves of Ben, but is fairly sure he does. "You cannot leave him alone with Benedict!"

"Well, it's a good thing, then, that I am going to go home right away." Then I turned to his wife, and my smile expanded. "Of course, I get that it's an installation," I told her. "I mean, no woman would actually wear as a dress something that gives her the shape of a wedding cake. I would guess you are performing interstitial art by reminding everyone present at the historical mysteries society tea that marriage and the bonds of matrimony were so very important in both birth and death in times previous to our own. My hat—metaphorically—is off to you." I gestured toward her with the cup and cake plate in such a way that, being normal and possessed of normal reflexes, she couldn't help but reach out her hands for them. At which point, I deposited them in her hands and walked away free as a bird.

I was feeling so bouncy that it wasn't till I was in the car that I had time to think about the story of Almeria and Jacinth. What part was true, and what part fable? The part of her just—to quote her grandson—er . . . mentoring Jacinth was almost certainly a lie. A woman running away with a man who is at best a friend, just to save both their lives, doesn't sign a letter the way she had.

I mean, there were many things I could imagine telling Ben, but none of them would be that I was his always. This left . . . the bulk of the story untouched.

On the way home I took a detour and went by the address where Jacinth Jones had lived. No wonder I hadn't recognized it. Instead of the spartan, lean saltbox shape, there was now a weird, jutting construction. It was obvious that the property was owned by a rental company—and not just because it had a for rent sign on the front lawn, but also because it had had two enclosed porches added on the bottom floor and one on the top floor. This was the sort of thing companies that rented to students did, in order to increase their number of units.

In addition, it was a bright, fluorescent purple, that almost glowed. As for the two little saplings in the front yard, they'd grown quite a lot. They'd been planted, I realized, less than six feet from each other, so that they had grown entwined, like two lovers taking a parting embrace.

How odd, I thought. *Perhaps they are possessed by the spirits of Almeria and Jacinth.* It gave me the oddest feeling, thinking of that and looking at the two maples, their branches growing entwined.

I am not normally given to poetic thoughts, but in that time, in that place it seemed . . . almost inevitable.

CHAPTER 12

Please Open Up

When I got home, I reached in my purse for my key, and it wasn't where I normally left it, in a little pouch just inside the zipper.

Sometimes it fell into the greater inside of the purse, so I rustled about in there, but found nothing. On the verge of panic, I checked all my pockets, then decided I must have left it in the pocket of the jeans I had been wearing earlier.

I knocked at the door and Ben let me in. And I went to look through my jeans, but both pockets were empty.

Ben, already fully dressed for his date, this time in a slightly more colorful, darkish green pullover over a white shirt—for a miracle without a tie—and dark brown pants, seemed absolutely baffled by what I was doing. He followed me around, as I looked through the clothes in the hamper, on top, then looked in the pockets of my leather jacket hanging from a peg in my bedroom and then in despair looked through the pockets of my robe, thinking perhaps I'd considered going out in the morning.

"What are you looking for?" he asked me.

"My house key," I said.

He frowned. "Your . . . key?"

"Yeah, I swear I had it in my purse when I went out, but it's not there now, and I wonder if I forgot it in here, somewhere."

"Dyce, you have to have it. You drove home. Isn't it with your car key?"

"No. It wouldn't be lost if it was." He stared at me and I sighed. "Ben, you're the one who told me not to have all my keys on the same key ring, in case someone stole my car while the key was in it. Besides, you know how much I hate it when the keys jingle on the ring in the car."

"All right. And you're sure you had it before you left for the tea?" He frowned at me. "Dyce . . . I have to ask— why did you go to that tea?"

"Oh, to see what I could find out about the people who wrote the letter. I mean, the woman who wrote it and the man it was written to." I said it as if he should have known this, and perhaps he should, the man had known me for so long. As if to confirm it, he didn't show any surprise.

"Let's think through this," he said. "There were people at that party who were relatives of a woman who disappeared almost a hundred years ago, right? So . . ."

I shook my head. "I hadn't thought of that. I mean, that they might have taken my key. And I don't think they could have anyway, Ben. There was a crowd, and even though the place was . . . well . . . packed, people were wearing nice clothes. They wouldn't want to jostle each other. No one touched me. Besides, the couple, the Martins, were always in front of me, unless he was off in search of whiskey."

"Um," Ben said. "Do you want me to cancel my date? Or are you going out with Cas tonight? Under the circumstances I don't like leaving you and the E Monkey here alone while I'm gone."

I shook my head. I was fairly sure there were worse sins in the world than raining on Ben's potential dating life when he was just starting to acquire one again, but I did not plan to go out and kill puppies with blunt scissors, anyway. "No, Cas isn't coming over tonight, but it's okay. I'm sure I just put the key somewhere stupid. I've been known to do that, and then, of course, I knew you'd be here, so subconsciously, I was sure of being let in the house. I'm sure that's all. There is nothing to worry about."

Ben crossed his arms on his chest. Ben's father was a high school teacher, a rather massive sort of man. His mom taught piano, but she was not exactly a small woman, though not by any means fat. I had always had the impression that somewhere in Ben's ancestry there sailed a never-ending number of Vikings standing at the prow of their longships, looking for new things to conquer and pillage.

Of course, if they were Ben's ancestors, they had probably worn fur ties with their impeccably polished horned helmets, but I was sure, judging from the way my friend glowered when he got mad, that they had committed their fair share of mayhem. Right now, with his arms crossed, Ben looked like he was contemplating committing some of his own. "Dyce, it's not safe. I can picture you and E going to bed, all confident, and someone coming in with your own key."

"Okay, then . . . I won't go to bed," I said. And at that moment, from the way Ben frowned, I realized I'd said the wrong thing and started apologizing. "Oh, I'm sorry," I said. "I didn't realize. Were you planning on . . . I mean, did you intend to—maybe not come back here tonight?"

He opened his mouth, then closed it, then said, with a sort of forced cheerfulness. "No, no. It's fine. I mean, no. It's too early for that, isn't it? We'll just go to dinner and a show or something and . . . I'll be home by twelve. How does that sound?"

"Sounds fine. I can stay awake later than that. Don't hurry home because of me. I've been known to stay up till two."

He hesitated. "Are you sure Cas can't come and stay with you?"

I shook my head. "No, he's working on a case. Something about a body being found in the amusement park."

"I think I read a piece in the paper about that," he said.

"Yeah, well, he expects to be busy for a while." I gave a thought to the fact that recent possible murders were no doubt more important to the Goldport police than century-old possible murders.

"Hey, E," I said. "You can come and draw at the kitchen table, while mommy cooks, all right?"

"What is mommy cooking?" My unmotivated son asked without looking up.

"Mac and cheese!" I said. "With Vienna sausages."

Ben muttered, "The dinner of champions!" but E's eyes lit up and he said, "Yay!"

Ben followed me and E to the kitchen. "Shouldn't Nick be here?" I asked.

Ben shook his head. "No, he said between five and six. He's also very busy, see, with the animal cruelty case."

"How is that going?" I asked.

"They've found dead animals all over this neighborhood," he said. "Another one today. Poisoned. Same way Pythagoras would have gone if we hadn't saved him. But whoever is doing it is being very smart. He or she is using industrial fertilizer, and in a region with ranches and farms . . . it's almost impossible to focus in on a suspect. Nick is sure it wasn't anyone downtown, but that's it."

He played with the metallic band of his watch, something he did when he was worried or thinking deeply. Finally, he said, "It's obvious that you've been holding back on this entire investigation thing you're doing. I thought you knew better than that. Are you going to tell me what you've been up to, or do I have to cancel my date?"

I made a face at him. But part of me wanted to tell him. Oh, yeah, sure, Ben is overprotective and so methodical that OCD cases are envious. Also, he can be a bit of a stick in the mud. Okay. More than a bit.

The thing was, though, that when it came right down to it, if you needed someone to stand by you in good times and bad, Ben would be your very best choice. And I was feeling confused and upset about this entire almost hundred-year-old murder. I needed someone to talk to other than Cas who had already warned me off.

I told Ben the entire story, starting with my research at the library, which for some reason made him smile and ask me if I'd even attempted to take the first step to find out how to French polish the piano and if I didn't think Cas was likely to notice it hadn't so much as been varnished.

I made a face. "I'll get around to it," I said. And cleared my throat. "Eventually."

"Uh-huh."

I was afraid he'd cross his arms again, so before he could, I continued with my story, while I boiled the mac. I finished with the two trees, interlaced.

"I don't know," I told him. "It gave me the shivers. Those two trees just newly planted—I mean, you could still see the ground disturbed under them in the picture—when Almeria and Jacinth disappeared, and now they're grown all entwined. Like they're possessed by the ghosts of the lovers."

"Maybe you should write the book," he said. "You do know that it's entirely possible it wasn't an affair. Her grandson said—"

"Her grandson told me a well-rehearsed story," I said. "I'm sure of it."

"Why," Ben asked, and smiled infuriatingly. "Because it's not romantic enough?"

I shook my head. "No, Ben, because she signed the letter 'Yours always.' That's not what a woman writes to just a friend."

"Maybe not these days," he said. "But it's quite possible people of that time did. They had different modes of conduct. It's also possible that, having made a pact with him—a pact that saved both their lives—this was her way of reassuring him she wouldn't back out."

I mumbled something. It seemed to me in that case she'd have written, "I won't back out" or "My mind is quite made up" not "Yours always."

"I think you're making a storm in a teacup," Ben said. "It's entirely possible they simply left in a big hurry and that they didn't dare come back or contact anyone. Hell, if I had some maniac after me with an ax, I might decide the climate was a little uncongenial. Wouldn't you?"

I shrugged. "I don't know, Ben . . ."

He smiled, that infuriating way he smiles when he thinks he knows better than I do. He gave me that stupid smile all the time when I was taking pre-calc and got stuck on a problem, because he was an advanced math student and was, at the time, studying calculus. "I see," he said. "You still need to convince yourself, or perhaps come down from the high of investigating what you're sure must be a murder, haunted trees and all . . . Tell you what," he said, as the doorbell sounded. "You can use my laptop to research whatever you want. It's right by the sofa."

"Thanks," I said, because I knew he hated to have anyone play with his electronics. "But if you think it wasn't murder," I called after him, "why are you so worried about what happened to my key?"

"Simple," he said, as the doorbell sounded again. "Theft, home invasion, rape, and the fact that there's a nut bar around this neighborhood poisoning innocent cats and dogs."

"Oh," I said, as I heard him open the front door and greet Nick. Then he called out, "I'll be home before two. Keep the door locked."

And he was gone. I made mac and cheese, and E and I enjoyed it thoroughly. Then I read to him an exciting lab rats book—about gold-plating objects, it turned out—and put him to bed. For a wonder, he went to sleep, perhaps because he had Pythagoras right there along with him, snoring up a storm. How a cat that small could have such a huge snore was something I couldn't understand.

I went back to the kitchen and fed the rats that were now very playful and jumping all over each other. They no longer had their paws splayed to the side, doing the ratty shuffle, but had them firmly under them and were doing the things toddlers do while playing, including chasing each other all over the aquarium, mock fights, and tumbling about. I thought we should get them some play structures, of some sort, and for once I was very glad that

Ben had laundry markered their fat little butts, otherwise I'd have fed some of them—Rat Fink—at least twice, and left others—Rat Face—completely unfed.

I had to wipe down You Dirty Rat who had somehow managed to get himself all sticky, but after an hour or so they were all fed. I checked on E again. He was asleep. I checked on the bolts both on the front and the back door. And suddenly, for no logical reason, considering how many nights I had spent alone with E in this apartment, I felt very nervous.

It was the damn key, which I was sure would show up under—I did a perfunctory look under the sofa cushions—or behind something. Maybe Pythagoras had taken it for a toy. I gave up on that idea, because Pythagoras wasn't, after all, the sort of cat who played. In fact, other than eating paper, I hadn't seen him do anything but eat and sleep and look like he was afraid we would shove him out into the cold, cruel world, or perhaps like we would at any minute force him to write, direct, or act in psychologically profound movies.

This was not good, because it meant I had, at the very least, lost the key outside the house.

Feeling discomfited, I grabbed Ben's laptop. My first thought was that it wasn't a real laptop—just a little thing that looked like the lead in a movie called *Honey, I Shrunk the Electronics*. Then I remembered what Ben had told me about having acquired a Netbook, which at the time had sounded very odd—and sighed. Oh, well. Keeping up with the Ben in electronics would mean I wouldn't even have money for my daily pancakes.

Instead, I concentrated on my research. To be exact, I concentrated on finding what there was online about the Martins. It seemed like the least I could do.

I figured if I typed in John Martin I would get a never ending number of pages, even if I added Goldport. So instead I typed in *Abihu Martin* and waited.

The first link to come up surprised me so much that I felt like I was waking from a deep dream as the phone rang.

I leaped up to get it partly because I was afraid it would wake E—and I'd trained myself through my years of motherhood to do *anything* rather than wake E. Partly because I felt like talking to someone else—anyone else— would be an improvement on dealing with what was on my screen.

It wasn't.

As I picked up the phone and said, "Hello," a raspy, low voice answered me. It sounded less like a voice and more like the entire malice of the world distilled into vocal signals.

"What do you think you're doing?" it asked. And before I could recover from the shock, it added, "Stop it. Or we'll make you stop."

The words by themselves didn't seem all that threatening. But the voice in which they were delivered added a dimension of malevolence and terror that left me standing by my kitchen counter, shaking.

To be honest, it was so horrible that it was almost a relief going back to the unbelievable stuff on the computer screen. Even if the top headline running across the page was "Abihu Martin, KKK Mayor of Goldport."

The article itself made fascinating reading, of the sort they don't tell you about in school—on how the KKK had once been a force to reckon with in Colorado politics, even placing their candidates for governor in office. Goldport had been at the tail end of this influence, but apparently the original lockers in Goldport's North Elementary—long gone by the time I attended—had born inscriptions thanking the KKK for their gift.

It was hard to credit. Like most people of my generation, I had grown up believing that the KKK were always a fringe movement—crazy people who walked down the center of town in their hoods and sheets, only if the town would allow them. Nothing, I thought, that could reach for the levers of power, much less touch them.

Mr. Martin's term as mayor—other than his detestation of anyone with dark skin, Jews, Catholics, and immigrants—seemed to have been almost admirable. By modern standards, the fact that he had decided Goldport needed a downtown and commercial buildings and had undertaken to tax and bully the businesses and citizenry into creating his vision might seem autocratic, but I had read enough books set at that time to know that the strong leader who made decisions and got things done was the kind of man people looked up to.

They had a picture of the man, at the end, done in the same sepia tones, then a picture of him again, near his death in the seventies. Both showed a pale, fair-haired, almost colorless man with a high-bridged nose.

I wondered how he looked when he talked about axing people to death. That kind of anger didn't seem to go with his almost aristocratic features.

Had John Martin and his wife sold me a load of goods? Or was there fury hidden beneath Abihu Martin's bland countenance? That would almost have to be true, wouldn't it? After all, he was supported by the KKK, a group hardly representative of kindness and light.

The phone rang again. This time, I was prepared, and

hit the record button on the answering machine right after I pressed the answer button.

The lunatic had taken balloon juice. At least what came out of my phone was squeaky and high and almost incomprehensible. "Ratty, ratty, rats," it said. And then what sounded like, "I bet you're planning on eating them!"

This so shocked me I forgot to be scared. *"What?"* I asked.

He repeated what he'd said before. Or she. At the range the person was speaking it was impossible to tell, but this time I could hear the words, which were, "I bet you if you sell them, someone will eat them. Snakes, snakes, snakes. They eat rats."

"Excuse me? Who are you?"

"Let them go free. Release them in the wild. Nature will take care of them, Gaia the all loving."

By this time I had pulled the phone away from my ear so it wouldn't hurt me, and was staring at it as if it were in danger of growing tentacles. The thought that the phone had gone insane was ever so much more comforting than the thought that I had gone insane. I have nothing against the environment, and even—if understood as an interlacing of systems—nothing against calling Earth Gaia, but this idea that nature would take care of anyone, that nature was personified, a goddess of sorts and benevolent to boot, that struck me as the most bizarre nonsense. Anyone who believed in the benevolence of nature never watched a boy go through adolescence or a woman go through menopause.

"Rats were born to be free!" said whoever was at the other end of the phone. "Rats and raccoons. Not to be pets and slaves of men. Not like cats and dogs."

And they hung up. I stared at the machine, wondering what I should do. It occurred to me that the calls might be related to the case Nick was investigating.

Well, hopefully he would come in with Ben, and I could tell him.

Meanwhile, I went back to my Web search, but other than more articles about the infamous—or sainted, depending on what you read—Abihu, the Martin family was unexceptional.

There were pictures of John Martin's father—a surprisingly swarthy man who must have taken after his mother's side—and his wife who had the same broad face as his son. The wedding announcement of John and Asia showed a sturdy boy and a frail, blond girl who, even back then, seemed to have an interest in library science, which she was studying at the UCG down the street from where I currently lived.

John's horses had won prizes at horse shows. He seemed never to have had another interest in life. He was involved in charities, but they were all about horses. Homes for aged horses, medical care for horses whose owners were in strained circumstances, horses for the third world. It was a little daunting, as if he thought horses were a more worthy species than man. And perhaps he did.

His mother and father had been involved in some local charities, but were neither great philanthropists, nor great socialites. They seemed to have raised John between the ranch and the city, and it was clear he loved the ranch better.

Asia Martin, besides her library, was devoted to charities for children at risk, and seemed to donate a lot of money to things involving foster care.

Well. Good for her.

Absent from all these reports on the family were mentions of Diane Martin, John Martin's aunt. Oh, there was a mention of her now and then. She'd been present at the funeral for her father. She sometimes attended the symphony.

When she was mentioned, her name was always prefaced with the "frail" Miss Martin—no one ever called her Ms.—or there were references to her ill health not allowing her to take place in this or that.

Reading between the lines, it was easy to realize that Diane Martin was the only reason her nephew had ever bothered to divide his time between country and city, instead of living near his beloved horses. Further proof of this was the fact that now that she was going into an assisted-living facility, the Martins were moving to the country once and for all. I wondered how the old lady, who'd lived her whole life in that house, felt about letting it go.

I was feeling vaguely melancholy as the phone rang again. I marched to it, this time hissing under my breath and wondering what version of the voice would greet me. I picked up the phone and almost yelled into it. "Listen, I don't give a damn what you think about the rats. If you wake my son up, I'll stew you and the rats together in ginger sauce."

There was a deep drawing in of breath from the other side, and I expected the click of a slammed phone. Instead, I got a "Dyce?" in Cas's voice.

"Cas!" I said. "I'm sorry. I thought it was—"

"Someone who wants stewed rats?"

"No," I said. "No. It's a . . . uh . . . I've had two anonymous phone calls, and I expected this to be the third."

"Oh," he said, sounding somewhat worried. "Are you alone?"

"With E. Ben is out on a date."

"Oh," he said again. "I was wondering if I could come by."

"I have E," I said.

"Yes, I realize that. But I just want to come by and talk to you for a few minutes."

"Oh," I said. "All right. I'd love to see you, even if only for a few minutes."

And at that moment, I heard E, from the dining room, "Mommy?"

Wonderful. Once the E was up, it would be almost impossible to get him to sleep again. I put my best face on. "Yes, Bunny?"

"Peegrass can't sleep," he said. He stood in the middle of the dining room, rubbing his eyes, Pythagoras beside him.

"I can see that," I said. I looked toward the aquarium. Apparently the rats couldn't sleep, either—they were playing a version of ratty leapfrog. I wondered about the lunatic who was so concerned with them.

"Rats play?" E said.

"Oh, yeah," I said. "They're little boys, like E."

"Rats need motorcycle," E said firmly, putting paid to my notions that he'd forgotten the accursed toy.

"Oh, yes," I agreed. "We'll ask Ben to buy them one, okay?"

"Yeah! Then they can ride around the 'quarium."

"Right," I said and, casting about for something that might make E go to sleep. "Would you like some nice milk?" I asked.

He looked at me like I'd offered him Pythagoras's head on a platter. "No!"

Similar offers for reading to him and/or a blow to the head failed, and by the time Cas came in, E had regained his second wind, and was running in circles in the living room, while I sat on the sofa watching him.

"Uh . . ." Cas said, looking aghast.

"Well, the phone woke him. I doubt I'll be able to make him go to sleep again tonight."

"Uh." Cas said, again. I fully expected him to bolt out the door saying something like, "Kind lady, I didn't realize that the son you had was a complete lunatic. I will now be taking my affections to ladies less burdened."

But instead, what he said was, "Would taking him out for a ride help?"

"Taking him out for a ride is almost the only thing that helps, but I didn't particularly want to go driving around in my car, on roads that ice at night. I don't have snow tires."

He grinned. "Ah, but I do." Catching E midrun, he picked him up and took him to his bedroom, "Come on, kiddo, we'll go get you a blanket and a nice stuffed animal, and we can go for a ride in my car, how's about that?"

"I want ice cream," E said, always one for pushing his luck. I don't know where he gets it.

Cas should have said that with the temperature outside edging into single digits the idea of ice cream was at best insane, and at worse criminal. He didn't. Instead, as he came back with E wrapped in his big blue blanket, snuggling his platypus, he said, "Why not? Jor and Jas gives extra points for buying ice cream in cold weather."

I grinned, as I put my jacket and boots on. Jor and Jas were college boys who had made good, starting an organic ice cream company in downtown Goldport. I imagined they'd had more trepidation and fears than not, but the company had grown, heavily patronized by college students.

Now it was one of the biggest establishments in downtown Goldport and did a brisk business summer and winter.

To encourage business in winter, though, they had a point system, by which they gave you extra points for a free cone if you came in during a snowstorm or when the temperature was below a certain level.

I didn't mind. I locked Pythagoras in the bathroom, despite his apologetic meows, and we were off. It was warm in Cas's truck and the trip downtown took less than five minutes.

But when we got there, as he was parking, he said, "Dyce, do you mind if we don't go in? Just get cups and eat in the truck? I'll take us to a scenic overlook, if you want . . ."

I looked at him. "Why?"

"I want to talk to you, and I'd rather not do it in an ice-cream shop."

I took a look at E in the backseat. "What is so important that requires sacrificing your upholstery to E and chocolate ice cream?"

He grinned. "Ah, well. That's what upholstery cleaners are for, isn't it?"

Then he grew serious. "I want to talk to you about Jacinth Jones."

"You had an answer to your query about him?"

"Yeah." He didn't sound particularly happy about it.

CHAPTER 13

The Top of the World

It turned out Cas's upholstery was in much worse trouble than I thought. E picked raspberry and chocolate ice cream in a cone. While Cas drove away from the store, E kept making little comments from the backseat, about "Ice cream" and "Num num."

"I'm sorry," I whispered to my patient love. "Your seat is going to be a mess."

He smiled at me and managed to look almost bashful. "Ah, it doesn't matter. I'll have it cleaned. He's kind of cute all happy over ice cream."

I was holding my cup—Rocky Mountain Road—and Cas's cup of Daring Climber Cherry, a name that I thought was trying to sound regional but only managed to sound creepy. Still, I abstained from making jokes about it all the way over mountain roads, to one of the relatively larger foothills overlooking the entire city.

Cas drove us right up to a ledge—though not so near
that we could fall over with an incautious move or an un-
expected trembler—parked the car and shoved the parking
break home. "My parents used to call this the top of the
world," he said, as he took the ice cream from me. "When
we were being brats and everyone needed to get away for
a bit, they'd get us burgers at one of the fast-food places
and drive up here. They convinced us it was the greatest
treat ever."

"Us?"

"Nick stayed with my family a lot even then. His parents used to have a restaurant here in town, and they were
trying to get it off the ground, so he would stay with us
during the busiest times, usually the weekend. Then his
parents realized they could do much better in Denver, so
they sold and moved there, and he ended up living with us
for our senior year. Though . . ." He grinned. "By that time,
we were a little past being appeased by going to the top of
the world."

I smiled at him. "I should hope so." Then, suddenly curious, as I looked out at the magnificent panorama of
twinkling lights and the lighted ribbon of the highway in
the distance. "Not even as a necking spot?"

"Are you trying to find out about my past love life, Ms.
Dare?"

"Well?" A man like Cas couldn't have been celibate or
even single most of his life. I knew he had never been
married but that his one high school girlfriend had left
him for someone who was going into law school and not
just law enforcement.

"Not here," he said. "I mean, yeah, I had my share of
girlfriends, though none particularly permanent, and my

even higher share of one-date-type of things, but I didn't bring them here. This place is special to me. It's something, you know . . . I did with my family, which made me feel important and connected to them. Can't answer for Nick, but I don't think so. I used to joke if I ever got married, it would be up here, in a car, with the minister in the front seat."

"How quaint," I said, as I marked the *if I ever*, which seemed to be irrevocably in the past and in the negative.

"Isn't it?" he asked, and leaned in and kissed me. "Of course, I'd need to find a woman crazy enough to agree to it." He looked all dreamy. "We could bring burgers from Cy's. Hell, I'd even pay for the minister's."

I cleared my throat. "Yeah, okay. So, what did you find out about Jacinth Jones."

His playful mood vanished. He looked forward and stabbed viciously at his mound of ice cream with his little plastic spoon. "My colleague in Chicago found some stuff. Not, you know, criminal, but a couple of complaints Jones made about someone who was harassing him. He worked for some sort of accounting firm there, apparently that's what he was actually trained for. Which, yeah, meant he came in contact with the mob now and then. Impossible not to, in Chicago, at the time. But my friend says that Jones himself seemed to be above board and squeaky clean, particularly when the times are taken into account. But . . . here's the thing . . ."

"Yes?"

"You know at the time anything legal took race into account, right?"

"Uh . . ."

"Yeah. Well . . . Jones was registered in Chicago as Negro. He came, apparently, from New Orleans, where his mother was the mistress of some rich white guy, who was presumably his father."

"The police records said this?" I asked.

"He did some work for his father's firm, and it brushed on mob-connected liquor running, though of itself it seemed to be clean."

"Uh," I said. "The West must have been more integrated than I expected then, because none of the newspapers said anything about this race."

He looked at me as though he were about to tell me something I didn't like, "No, hon. I'm afraid the West wasn't any more integrated, except where it ignored laws, but what it was was a land of opportunity, where any man was what he said he was."

"Uh—"

"Jones clearly looked white enough to pass. Hell, his mother might have looked white enough to pass. Coming out West and dropping the racial classification from his description opened new horizons for him. He wouldn't be the first, nor the last to do so. As far as I can tell, he worked in Chicago, as a bookkeeper, long enough to save enough money to start a business out here. He was smart enough, too, not to try some harebrained business like prospecting. I mean, there was so much more money in catering to the miners than in trying to be one."

I looked at Cas, as I remembered what I had been reading before I left. My stomach felt cold and the ice cream fell into it like a hundred-pound weight. I set it atop the dashboard, and looked at Cas. "Cas, oh, this is so not good."

"The ice cream? I'm sorry," he said, suddenly solicitous. "Is it spoiled or something?"

I shook my head. "No, no. Not that. It's . . . what you

said. You see, Ben told me I could use his laptop, and I was looking through the Net for stuff. (No, I don't have wireless access, but the upstairs neighbor lets Ben hook into his whenever he's around, and I thought it didn't matter if I did, too.) Anyway . . . when I was interrupted by prank phone calls, I was looking up Abihu Martin."

"Yes?" Cas said. "The husband of the missing woman? Mayor of Goldport or something, wasn't he?"

"Yeah. And he ran on the KKK ticket."

Cas whistled under his breath. "Well, that would justify . . . uh . . . that would certainly justify her—and Jacinth, too—being afraid enough of him to take off without delay and without leaving a forwarding address. If she knew . . ."

"Yes, but . . ." I told him what the Martins had told me and the threats of murder with the ax. "I'd looked online, you know, and thought Martin was such a bloodless wasp that there was no possible way that he could have done something like that, but now I'm not so sure."

Cas took a deep breath. "Dyce, I'm going to tell you again . . . Abihu Martin might have blighted their lives, made them run madly some place, leaving no trace behind. But he's dead, and so are they. If people took it into our heads to punish everyone's wrongdoing going back hundreds of years, I'd be in a fine mess. I can barely cope with the crimes happening now."

I sighed. That was pretty much what I thought he would say. So I told him about the call I'd received. "Because Ben put an ad on an online list to give away the rats?" he asked.

"I presume," I said.

He made a face. "Sounds like the kind of loony Nick is looking for all right." He grabbed his phone from his pocket, and dialed. I started to ask what he was doing, but

someone must have picked up, because he said, "Nick.
Great. Is Ben— Right. Good. Did he bring his car or . . . I
see. So, you're bringing him back to Dyce's, right?" He
looked over at me and frowned slightly, though looking
amused. "Two a.m.? I see. Well, there's a message for you
to listen to and you probably should see if we can't trace
it with the phone company. No, I can't tell you exactly
what it said, but it was in response to the ad about giving
away the rats, and the caller seemed to have an odd pro-
rat anti-domesticated pet thing going, so . . . Yeah. Okay.
An hour or two then. Fine." He hung up and turned to me.
"They're at Ben's place, and they said they'll be an hour
or two, but he'll come in when he drops Ben off, so that
he can listen to the message, okay?"

I nodded. "Yeah," I said, looking back. Fortunately E
had consumed all of his ice cream and the cone before
falling asleep, but I couldn't swear the stains on his hands,
face, and blanket would ever come off. "We should
probably head back and put E to bed."

Cas looked back. "Shouldn't we wash him first?"

"What? And risk waking him up. My dear, you're
clearly not a parent!"

He opened his mouth, then nodded, and put the car in
reverse, getting us slowly off the ledge. "For the record,
Ms. Dare, when it comes to crazy women with unortho-
dox ideas, you're the only one I can ever imagine sharing
the top of the world with." He looked sideways at me, as
he stopped, poised between backing up and being on our
way. "What I must tell you, my love, is that if I ever really
reach the top of the world, I want you by my side."

I smiled at him. He deserved it. The man said such romantic things. I still wasn't sure about moving in with

him, though. It would take more than a honeyed tongue, I thought.

We pulled into the driveway and Cas carried E into the house. Which would have worked just fine if, as I opened the door, we hadn't found Pythagoras cowering against it, surrounded by rats. Two rats and Pythagoras tried to make a break through the open door, and I'm not exactly sure how, but I ended up holding two very irate baby rats by the tails, and a cat by the ear at the same time I shut the door using the back of my knee and my butt.

"Step carefully," I told Cas. "The rats are all over."

"You know this sounds like a line from a horror movie," he said, but tiptoed carefully through the rats darting madly around to put E in the bed. Then he came back and looked at Pythagoras whom I'd let go, with plain and open amusement. "Some ratter Pythagoras has turned out to be," he said.

"Well, it's a good thing. If we'd come back to rat remains, Ben would probably be very upset. He's gotten attached to them." As I spoke, I was collecting the rats and—lacking any other container—shoving them into the pockets of my coat. "Go get the aquarium," I said.

He tiptoed to the kitchen and yelled back, "The aquarium is on the floor in pieces. And there's a rat wobbling around amid the mess. He seems concussed."

But I'd kept track of the initials on the butts of the rats I'd picked up, so I could say confidently. "No, that's Rat Face. He always looks concussed. I don't think he's very bright. Maybe Ben fed him at the wrong end a couple of times in the middle of the night, or something."

"Creepy that you know which one it is," he shouted back.

"Nah, they're marked." I was holding the rats in my pockets with my hands and expecting E to wake and come running into the living room at any minute and try to help. "Just grab the big stock pot from the third cabinet to the right, would you?"

"Uh . . . Stock pot. There it is."

"Yeah," I said, as he brought it into the room. It was a huge pot, bought by Ben at a restaurant supply because— he tried to convince me—I could make stock from stuff like discounted turkeys around Thanksgiving, and at least inject some protein into mine and E's diet. "It has straight sides to keep them in. And I never use it for stock."

I dropped the rats in it, and we put some kitchen towels around them for warmth, though frankly now that they had fur they probably didn't need it. Then we sat the pot on the table and cleaned up the mess on the floor.

"I wonder if Pythagoras tried to jump on the counter," Cas said. "And caused the aquarium to fall."

"Impossible. We left him locked in the bathroom."

"Sometimes cats learn to open doors."

"Maybe," I said. But I had something else worrying at me. "But Pythagoras doesn't seem all that capable of guile, and learning." I frowned. "I wonder if it was someone with my stolen key."

As I spoke, Cas was squatting on the floor, patiently sweeping fragments of aquarium into the dustpan. He froze, dead still. "Your what?"

"My key was missing," I said. "When I came home from the tea."

"I'm still at a loss why you went to the tea in the first place. I know you delight in vexing your ex, but all the same, it seems like too much effort to that end."

"Well, yes. I wanted to meet the Martins. I still think

they might be politically connected enough to have caused your boss to upbraid you."

"Oh, you're probably right there," he said, resuming sweeping but in the slow, careful way that implied he could sweep me away too if I insisted on being weird. "But the thing is, why would you want to make these people feel upset or watched? If they're connected enough to get the chief to try to stop you from meddling with an old case, then they're connected enough to do things even more unpleasant indeed."

"Maybe," I said. "I hadn't thought of it that way."

"You also didn't think to tell me you'd lost your key," he said. "And why would Colm leave you alone in the house when you didn't know if someone might come in? I mean, I know he's infatuated, but—"

"Oh, he didn't want to, but I should point out I don't know that my key was stolen. I might have had it in my pocket and accidentally dropped it while getting a tissue or something."

"Um," he said. "Have you lost a key that way before?"

"No. I don't think I've lost a key since high school. I used to lose them very often then, but not since."

"Um. Look, Dyce, I don't like it. I'm not saying someone broke into your house. It's entirely possible no one did, and the aquarium just fell somehow. As slow as Pythagoras seems, he might have learned to get out of the bathroom, or the door might not have been closed as well as you think it was. All these door handles are rusty. It's a wonder this hasn't happened before. But all the same . . . Do you mind if we look around and see if anything is missing?"

We couldn't find anything missing in the house. Which, admittedly, isn't saying much. I once had a dream where someone broke into my house and felt so sorry about what he found that he'd given me money in the end and offered to steal furniture for me.

The most expensive thing in my house was the kitchen table and the matching chairs that Ben and Cas had provided. But people rarely take antique oak tables and matching chairs to be fenced. It's not exactly easily portable merchandise.

The appliances were only a fridge and a stove, both the property of the rental company who had outfitted the house.

While I owned a TV, it had been bought at a thrift shop, had a fourteen-inch screen, I stored it in the closet in the bedroom, and I rarely watched it. I kept it on the off chance there would be something I absolutely needed to know that was only available on TV. And for Ben, if it was some event so specialized that Ben couldn't find out about it hours earlier via the Internet and call me about it. I guess I kept it on the off chance that the revolution would be televised. And *only* televised.

The TV was there, as was my cheapo iPod knock-off. However, the deciding factor was that Ben's Netbook was also still there, sitting on the sofa, where I'd left it. "Okay," Cas said. "I think I can rule out a break-in, if Ben's Netbook was left," he said, and looked relieved. "So, not a problem. Now . . . I could bother Ben and Nick and ask them to buy an aquarium on their way here, but I think I'll go do it."

"Uh . . . where are you going to buy an aquarium at eleven p.m.?"

"All-night pet supply place!" he said, then grinned at me. "Twenty-four-hour superstore, hon, of course."

He was back in less than half an hour, with the aquarium, a new package of cottonlike nesting, a water bottle, a running wheel, and a play tunnel for the rats. "What can I say?" he said, when I teased him about it. "I don't have any kids to spoil."

"Oh, great," I said. "Next thing you know you'll get them a motorcycle."

"No, no. A drum set," he said.

I made tea and we sat on the sofa, drinking tea and talking. It was one of those rambling, intermittent conversations, having nothing much to do with anything. Recollections of our childhoods. The fact that he'd finally read the books my parents had given him for Christmas. He had sharp things to say about most of the police procedurals, but he liked Jill McGown and a lot of the cozies. Eventually our conversation degenerated into a Miss Marple versus Poirot point-by-point discussion and I was gratified to know that he, too, preferred Miss Marple.

We were still holding hands, interrupted by brief but intense episodes of making out, and I was leaning against his shoulder, more than half asleep when the door opened and Ben and Nick came in. I noted they were holding hands as they came in, though they let go almost immediately. However the hand holding made me quite happy, not the least because I'd dare Ben to deny they were dating now.

We took them to the kitchen and played the message for them, and then Nick called the police station and talked for quite a while, while I spoke to Ben about what had happened to the aquarium. "Yeah," he said. "We need to find them homes."

Nick looked up. "How about you take three and I take four?" he asked. "If we need two aquariums to keep males and females separated, that's okay. Frankly, I miss having pets, and the apartment I'm in doesn't allow cats and dogs."

"To be honest, they probably don't allow rats, either."

"Yeah, but who is going to tell them?"

"And you're a policeman," Ben said, in mock reproach and they gave each other a sappy smile.

"Well, sometimes you have to—" Whoever he was waiting for on the phone must have spoken again, because he said. "I see. Yes. I'd say so. I'll visit tomorrow and ask a few questions, and see if there's reason to ask for a warrant, shall I?"

They must have agreed because he closed the phone. "I hadn't thought of that angle," he said, looking up, with that intense expression that Cas got, too, when the gears were turning in his head. "I just realized that I should have been calling people who put adoption ads for animals other than cats and dogs, and asking if they've had these calls. Of course, I didn't realize our poisoner's abilities also extended to speaking on the phone.

"Or at least squeaking on the phone," he said.

"Sounds like he or she inhaled helium," Ben said. "To disguise the voice."

"Which you have to admit is an innovative technique," Nick said.

I made coffee—mostly because I wasn't about to have Ben make tea. I wasn't sure that Nick knew about Ben's weirdness about tea, and I wasn't about to expose him to it. You never knew. He might decide Ben was a bad investment before Ben was done reeling him in, and that would be just wrong.

So, instead, I made coffee. I had seen the standard of coffee at the police station. There was no way I could make it worse. However, that Ben didn't protest about coffee this late at night was a mark of how far gone he was. He and

Nick kept giving each other sappy looks that made me want an insulin injection.

Still, to give them credit, their conversation was perfectly normal, at least for a given definition of normal.

Perhaps it was inevitable that with two policemen sitting at the table we would end up talking about the letter and the star-crossed couple. I noted that no one was surprised with the idea of a KKK mayor. Considering that we'd all grown up in Colorado, I'd either have to assume I was naturally innocent and disposed to think the best of others or—and this accorded more closely with reality— that I'd happily zoned out through most of my history classes.

I think the last point of the night was made by Ben, pensively stirring his coffee. "I wonder," he said. "Why those trees were planted so close together. Wouldn't it be weird if they're planted over the bodies of the supposed runaway couple?"

CHAPTER 14

Uneasy Morning

With such a declaration before going to sleep, I should probably have expected to have nightmares all night, and I did. The oddest of them involved someone chopping the two trees for kindling.

I woke up at eight a.m. with the phone ringing. It was my cell phone, which I usually put on my bedside table before going to bed. However, it had clearly been taking instruction from the house phone, and decided to hide in my bed. I finally found it wedged between the mattress and the side of the bed, and fished it out. "Yeah," I rasped into the phone.

"Ms. Dare?" a very polite somewhat familiar voice asked from the other end.

"Yeah," I said, then managed to discipline both mind and lips to say, "May I ask who is calling?"

"This is Mr. Martin's housekeeper," the woman said, just

as her voice fell in place. "I was wondering if you would have a few minutes free around eleven? I very much doubt it will extend to an hour."

"May I ask for what purpose?"

"Of course. Miss Martin would like to meet you. She has heard you intend to write a book about her dear mama and of course she would like to give you all the help she can."

"Oh. I . . . I've already spoken to Mr. and Mrs. Martin," I said.

"Naturally," the housekeeper said. "And they've told Miss Martin how very nice and kind you are, and now she would like to speak to you. You see, no one has done anything with her mother's story, and she really feels it's such a poignant story. She wants to determine if you're . . . worthy of the task, I suppose I should say."

"Oh, but it wouldn't be a book about Almeria Martin, by itself," I protested. "It's supposed to be about a lot of unsolved Colorado mysteries."

"Miss Martin understands that," the housekeeper said. "However, she also believes that once you know the real story you might find that her mother's disappearance deserves a full book of its own. Who knows? She would like to tell you the story, and she's quite agitated, the poor dear. I can tell she's hardly slept a wink, and as she had a stroke just a year ago, I can't risk having her this excited. So, if you would . . . It would be a kindness."

"All right," I said, at last. I had about as much wish to go and meet the invalid Miss Martin as I had of pouring ice over my head or of getting up at eight a.m. for that matter. But it must have been my day for it, because the moment I hung up, the phone rang again, and this time was my mother, "Candy!" she said, in that way that always sounded like it was Halloween and we'd gotten one of the more militant trick-or-treaters.

"Yes, Mom?"

"I thought I'd best remind you the furniture has been delivered, and I'd like you to come over and take a look at it and make sure it's everything you expected. Not that I suspect the Martins of trying to cheat you, of course, but those men who delivered it weren't at all what I'd call trustworthy types."

I thought back to the Starving Students and nodded. No, my mother wouldn't like them. "All right, Mom," I said. "I tell you what. I have an appointment at eleven, but I'll come by before then, and see if everything is as I expected."

Groaning, since I'd gone to bed at close to three, I got up, and took my clothes into the bathroom with me so I could get decently dressed before coming out. It was a habit I had acquired when E was very small and had first seen me come out of the bathroom and commented, dismally, on my utter lack of penis.

The shower helped, like needles on my skin, waking me up, but I didn't feel like I was truly awake until I had got two cups of coffee into me. They were one of my typical compromises. Considering my very fancy coffee machine, I felt guilty as I poured the leftover coffee from the night before into cups and warmed those in the microwave. It was more than a little acid, and Ben would wax sarcastic if he saw me do it.

But I was in luck. Ben slept through my hasty breakfast of reheated coffee and cheese toast. In fact, he would have slept through my leaving all together, except that I thought I probably should tell him I was going to be away and he was left on his own with the cat, the rats, and E.

I wondered if I should feed the rats, but Ben had fed them just before going to bed, and they no longer seemed to need night feedings, or belly rubs. In fact, the Internet sites I consulted said that we should soon start trying them on Cheerios or other easily digestible cereal. So I contented myself with saying hello to them through the glass.

Then I checked on E who was still fully asleep, with berry stains all around his mouth and on his blanket, so that he looked like an alien murder victim with very oddly colored blood.

He also looked like an angel, a feat he only manages while sleeping. I kissed him, and went back to the living room. Where Ben didn't look like an angel, unless one's idea of an angel were someone rather large, with a face more handsome than pretty, almost twenty-four hours worth of reddish blond stubble, sleeping in what I called "the mummy position."

Ben slept face up, with his arms by his side, absolutely immobile. If he put a blanket over himself before falling asleep, the blanket would be in the same position and quite undisturbed when he woke up. I considered it unnatural and had several times mentioned that someday someone would mistake him for a vampire and drive a stake through his heart. His response to that wasn't printable anywhere children might read it.

The best way to wake Ben was to call his name repeatedly. Touching him didn't actually work, which was why, when we were seniors and he'd fallen asleep on the sofa during a party at a friend's house, we'd crossed his arms on his chest, put candles on either side of his head, and had a mock viewing. He'd woken up in the middle of it, and—in true Ben form—been puzzled and embarrassed in equal measures, though he laughed at it now, twelve years later.

So I called him repeatedly, until he opened his eyes and looked at me.

"Ben, are you awake enough to understand me?"

"Quite," he said, then blinked. "What is it? Six in the morning?"

"Almost nine."

He groaned. "I really should go to bed at more civilized hours."

"You probably should, yes," I said, "but that would require not getting home at two in the morning."

He gave me a sheepish grin and put his arms behind his head. "I'd have stayed out all night if someone hadn't scared the living daylights out of me about her lost key." He made a face. "Of course, I might not have slept any more."

"If you're going to brag—"

He just smirked and I chose not to prod. "Look, I have to go out. The furniture I bought from the Martins has been delivered to Mom's house and she insists I come check it out. And then I have to go somewhere at eleven. Do you have a lunch date or something?"

"No. Nick is probably going to spend all morning calling people advertising about giving away pets. He said he'd call me this afternoon. We'll probably go out and buy aquariums for the rats. So he can move his and I can move mine, and I can stop camping on your sofa to keep the animals apart. I mean, I'm sort of assuming you can handle E and Pythagoras."

"I can handle Pythagoras, though, for proper results, he might need a psychiatrist," I said. "And E will be going to his father, probably tomorrow. Which reminds me that I need to buy the materials and start the French polishing."

"Uh . . . good idea that."

"Isn't it? I feel I would be a lot more awake, if you hadn't been babbling on about the corpses of Almeria and Jacinth being buried under those trees."

He looked baffled. "I was? Wow, I must have been more slaphappy than I realized. Wow. I wasn't, like, wanting to look under the tree or something, right?"

"No, you were just being very mystery-reader morbid about it. My parents would have been proud."

"Right," he said. "All right. I'll keep the monkey till after noon, then I'll find out what plans, if anything Nick has."

"You two are . . . I mean . . ." I said.

"Oh, it's early yet," he said. "Ask me again in a year, but I think there is an outside chance he is the one."

"Oh," I said. "Oh, good." For some reason, though, I felt oddly bereft. As though I was about to lose my best friend.

"If you need me," I said. "Call Mom's place or my cell."

CHAPTER 15

Curiouser and Curiouser

I am not sure what I was expecting to find in Mom's garage, other than furniture, but I am sure I was expecting *something*, because I was disappointed when I opened the garage door and saw exactly what I had seen in the carriage house. Only by the brighter light of early morning coming unimpeded through the garage door, I saw that, if anything, the find was better than I thought. I would make a lot of money out of this deal.

There were two rolltop desks. I wondered if Ben would be interested in one of them, since he had made sounds about making his guest room into a home office. There were two vanity tables, kidney shaped, on spindly legs. A couple of what looked like dining room tables, and fry me in oil and call me Lorena if there weren't a breakfront buffet and a tall kitchen cabinet with oak shelves that seemed designed to display compotes, or more likely someone's collection of plates. Added to this, there was a love seat with rosewood frame, and two large, antique, wood-framed mirrors. There was also an assortment of smaller furniture. Occasional tables, tea carts—a profusion of them.

I realized I was looking at it all with an idiotic smile, when my mother said, "Is it everything you expected?"

I nodded. "Everything I hoped for." I went into the garage, and went around the furniture, looking at everything.

That's when I realized I was looking for something like ax marks on the tables and furniture, as unlikely as that was. But there was nothing to be seen, nothing out of the usual. But why should there be? I doubted any of the furniture dated back farther than the fifties, when old Abihu might have been alive, but surely not in charge of the house anymore. This would be stuff that John Martin's father had bought. Except maybe the mirrors. I stared at the mirrors, wondering if they had once reflected Almeria and what Almeria might have looked like.

"When are you going to start working on this?" my mother asked.

I shrugged, without turning. "Probably next week. First I need to finish the piano, so that Cas can fix it on the inside."

"So, you and Castor . . . you're still, you know . . . together?"

I came out of the garage and gave my mother a look. Sometimes there is no possible way of knowing where Mom gets her notions or what she comes up with. Like the idea that Ben wasn't gay, none of it, no matter how many boyfriends he had, or how open he was about it. She either referred to it as his illusion or mine, and would smile sweetly and continue thinking what she wished to.

"I should hope so, otherwise he'd better explain why he came to my house last night to take me out for ice cream."

She sighed, as she closed up the garage. "Well, your going to the tea at the country club made me wonder. You were really very rude to Alex's wife, but I would understand, if you're still in love with him and hope to reconcile."

"Mother, I would rather eat live frogs. With warts."

"Well . . . you know, after you left, she was in tears about the things you said about her dress, and Alex said you gave her a migraine."

Yes, of course. Alex would also say that I was responsible for the swine flu, the Ebola virus, and the common cold. "Mom, you did see her dress?"

My mother looked embarrassed and fidgeted with her engagement and wedding rings, turning them around, because she had nothing else to play with, and she had to play with something when she was embarrassed. "I'm sure it was a very fashionable dress and that it cost her a lot of money. What you must remember, Candy, is that she's your son's other mother, and that if you antagonize her, you're giving her possible reasons to hate your son."

"I don't think she hates E," I said, soberly. Fear, whine about, and hide from, sure. Hate, no. You needed to actually know something properly before you could hate it, and poor Michelle had no clue what made E tick. The fact that I didn't, either, most of the time, made no difference. At least I didn't let it bother me.

My mother gave me a very odd look. "I don't understand you, Candy. You're thirty. I don't know what you expect to do with your life. I have told you before that your father and I will help finance your degree, if you should choose to go back to college." She shook her head.

"Unless, of course, you and Cas are going to get married. Then, you know, you probably should have children right away because it's much harder when you're older, I should know. We always wanted a large family."

I stared at my mother. I was sure that if I looked very carefully in the basement of the bookstore, I'd find a pod person hiding somewhere. First, my parents had married when they were both well past forty, so I couldn't imagine with which body Mom had intended to have that large family. And second, I had it on good authority—my grandmother's—that Mom had never intended to have even the one child, and her pregnancy had caught her so completely by surprise that it accounted for her hysterical behavior over what I was to be named.

And third, I didn't know with whom Mom could have intended to have this large family. My father is a sweet man, one of the nicest men alive. However, he's also not fully rooted in the real world.

If he had been born in the Middle Ages, he'd have been an ascetic monk or anchorite, hidden in his cell, talking to a God only he understood or heard. But he had been born in the twentieth century and come of age in an era when devotion to God was not widespread or expected. So he'd grown up surrounded by books.

When his grandmother had left him a house in her will, hoping it would give him the capital to make something out of himself, he'd filled it with books. And if Mom hadn't come along, hung a bookstore sign over the door, and forced him to move his living quarters to the upper floor and install a cash register by the front door, I suspected that right now Dad would be living like a monk, hidden in the world's largest fire hazard. At least if he hadn't managed to get crushed under a falling pile of books. So far.

Even now, he hated to sell books. Mother made him, but he still hated to do it. Whenever they did a convention or a show and sold a good number of books, he would come home and take a day or two to reassure his remaining books that he still loved them.

I wasn't absolutely sure, in fact, that my father was aware of my existence. Or if he was, that he knew what I was up to at any given time. If I weren't available for him to talk to about mysteries, he just talked about them to whoever else was present.

Sometimes he seemed to be curiously unmoored in time, and think that I was still in high school.

I could imagine that if Mom had succeeded in having the large family she wanted, Dad would wander along in a fog, assuming we were customers come to buy his books and trying to protect them from us.

"We're doing the best we can," I mumbled at my mother, hoping she wouldn't ask who "we" was. In this case it happened to be the royal we, and I was in fact doing the best I could.

"If only you would talk to Ben," she said. "I'm sure that none of this strangeness of his is real. I mean, I think it's some joke he tells you and you believe him."

"Ben has a new boyfriend," I said. "He's Cas's cousin. Oh, and they're adopting rats together. So cute."

Mom's gaze slid across me. It always did that when I said something that she either couldn't accept or didn't know how to respond to. She twirled her rings again, then said, "Want to come and meet Fluffy?"

It was my turn to do a double take. Fluffy had been my parents' cat the whole time I'd been growing up. She was a beautiful white Persian, or at least she started out that way. When she'd gone to the great mouse hunting ground in the sky, she had been a skinny, scrawny little thing with yellow fur, most of her teeth missing, and an undying hatred in her heart for me. Which was perhaps understandable, since I had set fire to her fur, scared her with explosions, and generally driven her insane. Though by the time she died, you really couldn't see the scars, and the only thing she was suffering from was her age, which was pushing twenty-four. Her last act before she died had been to drag herself up the stairs and piss all over my former bed.

Mom said they'd found her dead at the foot of the bed with an expression of profound satisfaction on her grizzled face. That she cried when she told me, was something I didn't want to probe too deeply. But I did want to know why she wanted me to meet a zombie cat. "Mom, Fluffy died. You have her ashes on the mantelpiece." Right under the picture of Ben and me at the prom. We'd gone together because neither of us had a relationship at the time, but of course, it had given Mom ideas. And Mom's ideas took time to die. She probably still imagined Fluffy alive. Or, of course, she wanted to introduce me to the ashes.

Mom shook her head. "No, dear. Fluffy the Second."

"You got another cat?" I said hopefully, since at least this was a better topic than my love life, my professional life, or how Ben would make an ideal partner for me, if I only just took the trouble to understand him.

Mom nodded, and, looking very proud, took me up the stairs to the area that my parents lived in. The house was on a street of redbrick, three-story houses, with attics. Most of them hosted a store on the bottom floor, and Mom and Dad's wasn't an exception. A lot had lofts in the upper stories, but instead, Mom and Dad lived in their upstairs and treated it pretty much like a suburban house.

There was a deep green garden between the garage and driveway and the house proper. We crossed it to reach the foot of a staircase that looked like it had been designed and built by a madman. In a way it had been. Mom had probably—I wasn't sure, since it had happened before I was cognizant—nagged Dad into building it, and Dad had taken the same approach to it as he did to any housework or home improvement she requested of him—he'd done an absolutely piss-poor job, in the serene conviction that if he did things badly enough she would stop asking him to do anything ever again.

Imagine a spiral staircase, built in wood, by someone who had used boards of whatever length and width came to hand, without bothering to cut them down to size. If you add in the fact that the supports for the structure didn't seem to be placed according to any rational system known to man, you'd think the thing should have fallen long ago. Which was true. But over the thirty years of my life, my mother and father had hosted parties and barbecues and the annual get-together for the area mystery writers every last weekend in June, all without the stairs doing more than the usual growling and moaning and swaying. Climbing them gave me the impression of being on a ship on the high seas.

We entered the house through the kitchen, which was the only way to do so since the erstwhile staircase from downstairs, which ended in the living room, had finally been blocked with bookcases, after one too many mystery readers had climbed them and come into our house and tried to buy books off the to-be-read shelf, an offense that even my mother wouldn't tolerate.

Through the kitchen we went past a short hallway, and to the living room. It was, but for the fact that it couldn't be entered directly, a rather formal room, with deeply upholstered sofas of the people-eater variety and a nice, solid coffee table, as well as the ubiquitous bookcases.

Mother's crochet project—at the time her handiwork of choice was fluffy, woolen crochet—lay on one of the sofas. Next to it was . . .

Well, it looked as much like Fluffy as a kitten as it could possibly look without being Fluffy as a kitten. Just in case, I took a look at the urn of ashes, which was still on the mantelpiece.

Mind you, the kitten was considerably smaller than Fluffy had been, even at end of life, and its head was proportionately bigger.

But even though it was asleep when I came in, it woke up and lifted its little leonine head to fix me with a look of pure hatred. Then it rose, tottering on its kitten legs, and extended one paw, hesitantly, with all the claws out, and hissed at me.

It was the most pathetic hiss I'd ever heard out of any cat.

Meanwhile, Mom was saying, "Astounding, it's like Fluffy come again. If I were a believing woman, I'd say it was Fluffy's reincarnation."

I reached out a hand to it and said, "Come on, Fluffs. You don't want to fight with me for two lives. Look, I no longer set fire to things, and I even have a cat." I extended my hand so that it could smell it . . .

Mom was putting iodine on the five, razor-thin claw marks on the palm of my hand when the phone rang.

It was the home phone, not my cell phone. She left me to finish patching myself up, while Fluffy looked up smugly from the sofa. I found I infinitely preferred Pythagoras's neurotic approach to life.

"Well, of course, Ben, dear," Mom said. Followed by, "Are you sure you're feeling well? Right, right, here she is."

She brought the phone toward me, but before she handed it over, she covered the receiver with her hand. "It's Ben but . . . he sounds drunk. Is he taking any medications?"

"No, no," I said. "He was up very late yesterday night, is all. He's probably a little slaphappy." Though he'd sounded perfectly normal when I'd left him.

As I picked up the phone, he sounded definitely far less than normal. In fact, he sounded as if he were more sleep deprived than he'd been the night before. "Dyce," he said. "Thank God it's you. You must not tell your mother anything. I think she's spying for them."

"Them?"

"The killers," he said. "You know, they killed them and put them under the tree, and if you tell her, she'll let them know and they'll come for you, too."

"Ben? Are you all right?"

"Of course I'm all right," he said. "Had a shower. Put some moisturizer on. E still asleep. Must have had lots of ice cream and all yesterday."

"Uh . . . yeah." This sounded more normal, and I wasn't sure that what he had said didn't make perfect sense. After all, my mother had arranged for that tea, and my keys had disappeared during it. I refused to think she had anything to do with the disappearance, but you never knew. And Ben wasn't one to jump to conclusions, so if he thought that my mother was involved, she probably was.

I looked at my wristwatch. It is one of the delights of my existence that the only watch I haven't managed to kill in my thirty years of life is a Mickey Mouse Timex. So good to be taken seriously in social occasions or at the office. It was almost time to go see what Diane Martin wanted with me. "I'll be home in an hour, perhaps less. Do you think you can hold the fort until then?"

"Of course!" he said, sounding offended. "I'm feeding Ratso now. Then I'll feed the others. I think it is time we start trying to give them some dry food, you know. I'll tell Nick to buy some Cheerios."

"Is he on the way there?"

There was a hesitation. "No, he's investigating. You know, with the corpses under the trees and all. They need to be dug up, so I'm sure he's doing that. But I'm sure he'll come here afterward." Pause. "He's a nice man."

"I should hope so," I said and hung up the phone, wondering what had gotten Ben into such an odd state. I wasn't sure I liked all this talk about finding corpses under the trees. Had someone actually found corpses under the trees? Or was it a matter of something Ben had heard? Were the police looking for corpses under the trees? If they'd found corpses and Cas had not called me, he was going to be so dead next time I saw him. I might even plant him under the nearest convenient tree.

"I have to go," I told my mom, as she came back with a Band-Aid to put over the iodine. For a moment I flinched, remembering someone in one of Agatha Christie's books who had been killed by having an infected substance substituted for iodine. But this was my mother. She might be disappointed with my path in life but I was reasonably sure she did not, in fact, wish to kill me.

In point of fact, should Mom ever wish to kill me, she'd probably do it by flinging a book at my head, or if she wanted to kill me slowly, by making me sit while she read me her complete collection of Patricia Wentworth. If she didn't allow breaks for bathroom and food or sleep, that would do me in for sure, since Patricia Wentworth had written more than a hundred books.

"I have an appointment at eleven."

"At the college?" Mother asked. Hope sprang eternal, I guess.

I had to shake my head and dash her expectations. "Uh. No. Just . . . just something that might result in a book."

It might, except that it wouldn't. Not ever.

CHAPTER 16

A Voice from the Past

The Martin house looked exactly the same as it had last time I was there. Well, presumably minus some furniture in the carriage house. Unless it were a magically replenishing carriage house, like a very large and dusty cornucopia.

The housekeeper opened the door and this time didn't look at me as though she thought I should have come to the tradesmen's entrance. Instead, as she closed the door, trapping me in the cool, dark entrance hall, she said, "Oh, dear. I should have told you to wear a skirt and a nice blouse. Miss Martin is rather old-fashioned. I don't know what she'll make of your outfit."

Since my outfit was a T-shirt and a pair of jeans, both clean and not mended, and I was wearing my nicer leather jacket, I didn't answer her. If Miss Martin couldn't handle it, then Miss Martin, clearly, ought to get out more.

The woman didn't say anything else, and I followed her up two flights of stairs. One level up, the house seemed to open up and become much nicer, due to a massive oval skylight centered directly above the staircase, which bathed it in light. The staircase, itself, was probably walnut, well polished, with a red runner down the center held in place by little, polished wooden rods.

Our steps echoed hollowly as we climbed the staircase, all the way to the third floor. The stairs ended on a broad corridor from which a number of doors opened. The doors were double and tall enough to accommodate a twelve-foot-tall visitor—should one drop by. The red rug motif continued, though this time the rug was a Persian runner in predominantly red tones.

I thought that the whole place felt more like a museum than like a house.

The housekeeper turned right, then right again, went to the door, threw it wide and announced, exactly as if she were in some kind of reenactment, "Miss Candyce Dare, madam," and bowed and stepped aside to let me enter.

It would not have surprised me in the least if I had been admitted to a throne room or one of those huge ball-rooms filled with people where everyone turns to stare at the newly announced person. But no. It was just a bed-room. A bedroom that had to be at least three hundred square feet, but a bedroom nonetheless.

The room was filled with flowers and baskets of flow-ers. I had an impression all those flowers had cards with names attached, too, and wondered who'd send them to an elderly invalid woman.

Against one wall was a bed—massive and curtained in white lace. The sort of bed one imagined all those cute little princess suites, in white and silver, that used to be sold for spoiled little girls, were modeled upon. Only this bed was much larger. As was the armoire and the dresser.

Miss Martin was reclining upon a rosewood frame velvet upholstered love seat. She had a lovely shawl over her shoulders and a pretty fluffy blanket across her legs.

The resemblance to the romantic Victorian virgin my mind had been expecting stopped there. In fact, Miss Martin, looked like one of those women who get stronger as they get thinner and dryer. She had white hair cut so short it formed a sort of fuzz on her head. Her nose was aquiline, and her eyes a piercing blue. She reminded me of someone, though I couldn't quite place whom. She waved for me to sit down on an armchair that matched the love seat and was placed directly facing it, so that she could hold court, I suppose.

For the longest time, she looked at me and said nothing, and I contented myself with looking back at her, unblinking.

At long last she sighed. "So you are Elizabeth Dare's little granddaughter." She nodded. "I never thought that son of hers would get married. He was an odd bird."

"He still is," I said, calmly.

She gave me the once-over with those blazing blue eyes, as though saying, "So that's how you want to play it." I smiled back at her, and she looked away, toward the heavily curtained window near the end of the love seat.

"I heard about your project. The book you're intending to write about Mama."

"It's actually not a book about your mother, Miss Martin," I said, softly, remembering what they'd said about her having had a stroke. "It's about unexplained criminal occurrences in Colorado, specifically in Goldport. You know, one of those unsolved-mysteries things. People like reading that sort of thing. I thought I would mention your mother's disappearance, as well as the disappearance of Mr. Jacinth Jones at the same time."

I don't now what reaction I expected. If I had wanted to provoke shock or horror, I'd have been disappointed. She remained absolutely impassive. Of course, the Martins would have told her about what I was looking into, so she would be unsurprised.

"Your nephew told me what you said to him," I said. "About your mama."

She sighed. "Sometimes," she said, "it's very hard to tell the truth to the young. And sometimes, despite one's best intentions, one doesn't."

I looked at her in silence. I didn't know what to do with that, particularly since compared to her, I was definitely very much "young." I made a note that she might feel it necessary to lie to me, but was completely unprepared for what came next.

"That small table against the wall, Miss Dare. You'll find a picture in a silver frame there. The frame has a bas-relief of calla lilies. If you would be so kind as to bring it over here."

I went over, picked up the frame that showed the picture of a blond woman, obviously from the beginning of the century, and brought it back. Miss Martin made no effort to pick it up, and instead motioned for me to sit again. "That is a picture of my mother," she said, in the grand manner of someone announcing that they've just discovered the meaning of the universe and it all boiled down to penguins.

All the same, whether she wounded a few quarts short of a gallon or not, I was interested in the picture. So this was the Almeria who'd written the note I'd found in my piano. I looked closely at it. It was nothing like I expected. Given her son's looks—and even her daughter sitting before me had a trace of what must have been near enough a naturally golden skin—I would have expected Almeria to be an olive-skinned, black-haired beauty.

She was none of the above. She looked exactly like the kind of woman that, after meeting, you say *She's very nice.* Blond hair and a rounded face, large blue eyes, a nice enough nose, and the kind of expression that every child dreams his mother will have while he tells her of his exploits.

Her attire, too, was nothing exceptional. A skirt and jacket, with the jacket cut loose and the skirt covering her to the ankles. She wore a hat that looked like a feminized version of a fedora.

I stared at the picture wondering if, truly, anyone could think that Almeria had ever had a grand romance, much less an adulterous one. She looked kind, nice, sensible. The type of woman who would remind her husband to take his vitamins and always make sure that her children went to school with an appropriate, healthy snack.

Even in modern days I had trouble believing she would be a force to reckon with in, say, the PTA. More likely she would not be able to make meetings because she was sewing a dress for her daughter, baking those cookies her son really liked, and making sure her husband's notes were collated and ready for his big meeting.

As far as her appearance went, she was, in fact, a nonentity, not even different enough to be considered exceptionally good- or bad-looking. I frowned at her and found myself wondering if perhaps she had been stalking Jacinth Jones. What was really behind that letter, with its passionate closing of "Yours, Almeria."

"My mother, Miss Dare," Miss Martin said, in an authoritative voice that made it impossible for me to correct the mistake of my honorific, "was an exceptional woman. She was not a native of Colorado. Grew up in Philadelphia. I daresay when my father met her, he thought he was getting a rather conventional wife. He couldn't have been more wrong."

She looked up at me, and her blue eyes sparkled. "Her exterior might have been placid and accommodating, but she was a woman of ideas. For that time and place, very revolutionary ideas. She thought, for instance, that child labor should be stamped out. She thought that all children should have access to a good education and that, given a good education, most poor children could perform at a level far higher than their place in society. Though she was not foolish or blindly idealistic. She understood the need for proper nutrition and hygiene with the rest."

"I don't know how long it took my father to realize that the woman he had married was nothing like the woman he had thought he was marrying." She looked ahead of her and at the heavily curtained window, again. "She was private. Didn't think it was the place of a lady to speak of her politics, her religion, or any of her beliefs. She had her generation's—" a rueful smile "—and, indeed, my conviction that a woman's intellect is, perforce, always inferior to a man's. Even if she were aware that this was not true in every case, she was too much of a lady to mention it. So in public, she pretended to believe in everything my father said and support all his causes. She stood by him, the unexceptionable political wife, while he ran for office.

"In her private life, she was quite different. Though she couldn't, of course, get involved with organizations in an ostentatious way that would be seen as her endorsing them, particularly organizations that she thought would offend my father. So she started, I think, small, the way people do. She would find a place for a pregnant housemaid to deliver and someone to adopt her child, then receive the housemaid back into the household when it was done. She would give money to servants in distress. She had means of her own, a legacy from a great aunt. Some money, some grants and securities, and whatever they called stocks at the time. So she could do all of it without consulting my father, who didn't need nor take any interest in her money."

"But then she met someone she could use as a cat's paw in her causes. He was a mulatto—to use the old term—man, just arrived from the East. A good-looking man, with charisma—I remember his entering a room, and all eyes turning to him as though it were his natural right. Mr. Jacinth Jones." She sighed. "Not quite of our class, of course, but moving fast. And only Mother . . . and I suppose my brother and I, as we came along and grew old enough to understand . . . realized that he was mulatto. He spoke to her unreservedly in their private moments, to which they, you know, often admitted us."

I wasn't sure that she understood the implications of what she was saying, so I looked at the picture in my hands and made a noncommittal sign of paying attention.

"I'm sure it started quite innocently. He funded charities privately with her money and served as her face out in the world. There was a poor children's nutrition fund, which provided meat and fruit to children of miners and . . . well . . . women of ill repute. Then there were the education initiatives that mostly consisted of paying parents a certain amount to prevent their removing their children from school after elementary school. She subsidized the children's progress—in books and such—through junior and senior high schools, and, in the ten or so years that she and Mr. Jones devoted to the cause, I suspect—though I was too young to understand properly and don't recall exactly—they must have financed more than a few college educations and professional instructions for poor children."

She reached for a stick that leaned against her chair. It was a carved mahogany cane, looking too balanced and beautiful to have grown naturally in such a twisting shape. It was capped with silver at top and bottom, though I guessed at the bottom it was more ringed, with a rubber ending. I thought she was going to rise, but she didn't. Instead, she banged the stick on the floor as though for emphasis. "It would have taken more than human strength to work that way with another young, attractive member of the opposite sex and not to have fallen in love."

The declaration hung, bold in the room, and I fancied that the woman in the frame would have flinched from it, if she could. Or perhaps the bland smile she showed for the photo would have expanded.

"I don't know why Mama married Papa. Surely there must have been reasons, but their society was very different from what it is now, different, even from my own time, so that it's hard for me to bridge the gap between what I knew of her and what she might have been as a young woman.

"It is entirely possible that she loved my father, I think, when she was a young girl. She was very young when she got married, sixteen, and he would have been a thirty-year-old man, established and wealthy. He must have spoken to her of his ranches in Colorado and of the silver mine that had made his family fortune—though by that time he had branched into other forms of investment. He would seem . . . adult." A small smile. "We all know how attractive that is to the very young."

I nodded, not that I knew a heck of a lot about it. After all, most of my life, I'd found myself in the strange position of being the adult around my parents and their friends, and I didn't find it particularly enthralling. The adults I knew growing up were more likely to be lost in their own heads or their own hobbies and have little to no contact with the world. Wonderful people, some of them and creative types many of them, but not the stuff that authority is made of.

"So she married him, and she found herself in a marriage in which she had very little in common with her husband. He pursued his financial goals and his politics, and his only interest in her was that she keep a nice house, be a good hostess and, of course, give him children.

"Meanwhile, there was this young man, somewhat dangerous by virtue of his origins, who was cultured and intelligent—I remember his declaiming poems for my mother—and more, he was interested in the same causes that fascinated her, and always ready to support her, help her, and boost her reasoning. You must see that this would be irresistible." She spoke almost pleadingly.

I set the picture in its frame facedown on the love seat and tried to put a stop to the justifications, "Miss Martin, in this day and age few women would think badly of another woman who strayed during her marriage, when that marriage was almost by default an arranged one."

She looked at me for a moment then nodded and said, slowly, "Yes. Yes. So you understand . . . I mean, it was inevitable that they'd get involved. And just as inevitable that it would lead to problems, eventually, perhaps to tragedy, depending on how it was discovered." She sighed.

"Tragedy is what ended up taking place, because my father, you see, learned that Mama was . . . uh . . . expecting."

She blushed delicately. Unless the news missed something enormous, she'd been single her whole life. "And something about it made him suspicious. Perhaps it was the timing, or perhaps the rumors about Mother's private meetings with Mr. Jones had come to his attention." She shook her head. "I don't know which. But after all that time, he was alive with suspicion.

"He was a successful man. In many ways, I think a very big man, and in his own way as forward-looking as my mother, even if with slightly different . . . priorities. He wanted to advance the city of Goldport and make it a world jewel." She shrugged, as though conceding that he might not have fully succeeded in that. "He was proud. And at any rate, I understand that . . . well . . . I've never been married, but it's not hard to understand how upset a man can get over infidelity. And so I think he went a little out of his mind. He threatened to kill them both with an ax."

"Yes, your nephew told me," I said. "If the new baby didn't look like the other children."

Miss Martin shrugged. "But you know, he would never have actually done it. He was an educated man and too refined to engage in . . . that sort of thing."

I couldn't tell if the sort of thing she spoke of so disapprovingly was axing people or merely the physical exertion involved in the activity. I didn't weigh in either way. Instead I looked at her and she sighed.

"Mama had to do something, of course . . ."

"So she ran away with Mr. Jones."

"She tried to." The blue eyes looked at me a long time, unflinchingly. "To understand this, first I must tell you that I did indeed tell my nephew a different story. I think it is very bad to have a boy think the worst of his father.

And besides, he was very young, and I don't think anything would be served by telling him the truth.

"Secondly, you must understand that I was very much my mother's . . ." She smiled a little. "Favorite child and confidant would be a way to put it, though at this time it makes one feel quite out of countenance to admit one was the favorite anything, as though it were an unearned privilege.

"It was very simple, you know. I was born premature, very small, and it was unknown, for a long time, whether I'd survive. My mother . . . She became attached to me when she thought she might lose me. She took me everywhere with her. She called me Baby, even after I was no longer a baby. I was, in a way I think, her consolation and her support, even though I was only eight when she died."

"Died?" I said.

"Of course. Surely you have realized this. Mama and Mr. Jacinth made plans to get away, but their hand was forced, a day or two earlier. All I remember was Mother dressing me in an extraordinary amount of clothes. Right now we'd call it layering, I believe. Petticoat upon petticoat and skirt upon skirt and blouse upon blouse, all my best. She dressed the same way herself, in addition to packing a small valise.

"I think this was sensible, because, as you must realize, clothes were worth a lot more then, and I suppose she intended to sell some of the more expensive clothing, which would bring less attention than selling jewels, to finance their escape. Meanwhile, Mr. Jones, I now understand, though I didn't at the time listening to their conversation, had been liquidating some of his assets and converting them to money orders payable to bearer.

"I don't know where they meant for us to go. All I know is that I was wakened not too long after going to bed, and that my mother dressed me in an absurd manner, before sneaking out through the deserted kitchens and through the servant's entrance. At the time I was surprised that she didn't wake my brother Edward, also. Edward was ten and we slept in the same room, separated by a screen. But she kept very quiet so he wouldn't accidentally wake.

"She didn't call for the car or have another arrangement. We walked the distance to Mr. Jones's house. And I know you might think a distance of a few blocks was inconsequential, but in fact because the neighborhood he lived in was less than stellar, Mama was in the habit of having the chauffeur drive us there, then wait at the street for us to emerge again." She smiled slightly. "That's probably how Papa found out about these meetings, of course, though it wouldn't occur to Mama to do otherwise."

"Well," she said, "when we came in, I soon realized that it was two days earlier than Mr. Jones had expected Mama to appear, so he wasn't quite prepared. They didn't exactly argue, because he was trying his best to accommodate her, you know. So they sat at the table, and he made coffee, and they drank it, and I grew very sleepy, so Mama laid me down in the love seat in the living room. I woke up sometime later with a very loud thump.

"I ran to the kitchen, and Mama and Mr. Jones seemed to be sleeping across the table. I saw someone run out the back. He looked . . . from the back, like my brother, Edward. I went back to Mama and Mr. Jones, but they wouldn't wake up. I don't know when I realized they were dead, but I did, after a while." Her voice and expression betrayed the confusion and despair the little girl she'd once been must have felt. "I was very little and I didn't know what to do, so I went to Papa. There was a bicycle in the yard and I knew how to ride, so I rode the bicycle back home, and snuck in through the kitchen door, which was unaccountably left open, and into Papa's room.

"It took me a while to make him understand what happened and I must say, to his credit, that he didn't seem to doubt me enough to call Mother or give the alarm in any way. Instead, he went to her room and looked in her wardrobe, then he looked at what I was wearing. And then he told me to go back to my room and take off my clothes. Hang them in the usual way, which he said he trusted a big girl like me to do." She nodded approvingly at her father's manipulation of her feelings. "And to go back to bed, and he would take care of it all. I don't know what he did, but I know that the next day when Mother was found missing, it was understood she had left town and deserted him. After a few years he got a divorce based on abandonment and he never remarried."

She was silent, like a recording that had come to the end.

"Why?" I asked.

"Why did he do that? I expect to avoid a scandal. Oh, you young people don't understand what a scandal meant in those days, but it could have made it impossible for both myself and my brother to ever hold our heads up in society. As it was—" she made a wry mouth "—I suspect I would have been considered a liability in the marriage market, because my mother had run away. As it turned out, I never got an opportunity to enter such a state. But still, Father made the scandal as small as he could. There was never any proof, and very little idea, that Mother had joined Mr. Jones when he disappeared. Rather, it was thought—and Father was quite good about giving enough hints of this to make it the accepted version—that while she was . . . enceinte and the balance of her mind was thus disturbed, as is normal for ladies in that condition, my father's intemperate words on the subject of rumors of her friendship with Mr. Jones had so alarmed her that she had left their abode.

"My father must have paid someone because the investigation, which he had, of course, made, revealed traces of a lady boarding the train alone, and traveling alone all the way to Philadelphia. It was believed she had there joined her family who had helped her hide, perhaps by sending her abroad to England, where her mother came from, or some other place where she would be out of my father's reach."

She was quiet a long time again, as if she had said everything she intended to say. But I took a deep breath and plunged in. "No," I said. "What I meant is why are you telling me this. Your . . . housekeeper told me over the phone that you thought someone should write your mother's story. And surely you know that if I'm undertaking to write about this, I can't promise to keep secret the parts you wouldn't wish revealed. So why tell me, if you didn't tell your own family?"

She shook her head. "Young woman, when you get to be my age, and your brother has been dead a year, and you can tell you don't have much longer in this Earth, you start prizing the truth above all the convenient lies with which you've lived." Her voice rang out loudly. "I had a stroke, about six months ago. And sometimes I have recurrences of certain convulsions, similar to what strikes epileptics. My doctor tells me there is no reason I shouldn't live another ten years, but I think I know when I'm nearing the limits of my allotted time on this Earth." Her face looked suddenly chiseled and terrible, in a way, as though she'd turned to stone. "I realized, as I recovered from the stroke—and of course I was very confused as I came out of it—and past times as present as . . . well, the present, in many ways . . . I realized that I knew a secret and that this secret might die with me.

"All my life, people have pitied me for being abandoned by my mother. And those that know a few hints of the case have considered her an adulteress and worse, a woman of light morals. I think it is high time my mother's reputation was restored, and I'm the only one who can do it. You see, it took me years to realize what had happened, but I am now sure that Edward must have woken up enough, as we left, to follow us, and that he must have realized my mother was about to leave without him.

"Now, I understand why she wouldn't take him. Not only was she more attached to me, because of my frailty at birth and beyond, but he was the boy and heir. My father's heir. My father would never have let her leave with him. If she had, he would have moved heaven and Earth to find them. But if she took only me, he was much less likely to consider pursuing her for fear, of course, that it would come out that she had eloped with another man. But at ten I doubt that Edward could understand that. And he was very passionately fond of our mother.

"He must have felt like he was being betrayed and abandoned. What I think happened—although, you know, it might have been quite different—is that he had got hold of something that was a poison somewhere. Boys at that time were . . . well . . . more vigorous than boys are currently. They played with dangerous things and had fewer of the common feelings of kindness we expect from children now. I know we had arsenic in the house. It was used to poison rats or sometimes squirrels. So I think he had some with him and, in his ire, put it in the coffeepot from which they were drinking.

"The pot was on the stove behind them, as they sat side by side, discussing things. Edward used to play games of being an Indian—Native American you would now say, but in those days—at any rate, he used to play at being an Indian sneaking around. There were all these stories about how Indians could walk through the forest without cracking a twig, and he used to practice it all the time." She frowned. "I thought it was very silly." She shook her head. "But I think that's what he did, and poisoned the coffee in the pot . . ."

"How can you say that?" I said, and I think I surprised her as much as I surprised myself with the vehemence of my words. "How can you say that about your brother?"

She smiled a little, looking at me. It was the indulgent smile of an adult to a small child. "You must forgive me, but I wasn't aware that I was saying anything especially bad about him, except that he was a child and loved his mother dearly and reacted in an inappropriate way when he thought that she didn't love him. He never again—to my knowledge—killed anyone else."

"No," I said. "I mean you're making this accusation against him when he can't defend himself, and you're going on old, old memories. For all you know you dreamed it all." I registered the faintly scandalized look in her eyes and pushed on. "There have been studies—I've read about them because I have a child of my own—and children do that sort of thing. They confabulate dreams and realities, what they heard told and what they witnessed, all of it in a big jumble. They do it, and they don't think about it, and years later they'll swear that what they remember is true. Maybe you dreamed it all when you heard your mother had disappeared. It would be a way to cope with your feelings of abandonment. You really have no proof that what you are saying is true."

A smile slid across her lips. "Only this," she said. "What happened best explains how my father and my brother treated me from then on. Though I'd always been a slight young girl, I was perfectly healthy and at the time of Mama's death I'd started to go out in society a little. Oh, not on my own, of course, that was just not done. But Mama had arranged for me to take dance lessons and painting lessons, and I was mingling with girls my age.

"After Mama's death that all changed. Not for my brother, so there was no fear of a scandal being kept alive by us being seen in society. No. The fear was more that I would form a friendship, that I would marry, that I would tell what I knew.

"The excuse given was that I was very frail and couldn't go out, and I myself believed it until I was well into my thirties, at which time a habit of reclusiveness had formed. I had my books, and my interests, and didn't see any reason to mingle in the common way. But if I tried or became close to someone, my brother always found a way to discourage it. The only way I could see to escape was to do what Mama had planned and to leave, taking very little with me. But I wasn't prepared to sacrifice my comforts." She shrugged. "It took me years to realize that both Edward and Father simply wished to ensure I didn't tell anyone what I knew."

"And so you are telling me for revenge?" I said.

She shook her head. "Revenge upon whom? My brother is dead, and even if it becomes known, it was a murder he committed at ten under circumstances that these days would condemn him to nothing more than some intensive counseling and perhaps psychiatric care. My nephew and his wife are very private people. In fact, because they are afraid that their staff is insufficient to prevent the seizures I suffer from, and because they are so often absent at the ranch, they are closing this house and putting me in a quite nice assisted-living facility. Sunset Acres, I think it is, on the edge of town. They have activities and a very good library." She smiled. "Maybe I will have a social life for the first time since I was eight. At any rate, I don't think my nephew would care. He is . . . has always been a man of few social graces. I don't say this to disparage. It is simply his character. He was a silent and sullen boy, and he's grown up to be a silent and sullen man. He will not care what anyone thinks of his father, as long as his horses continue receiving proper care." She spoke with amusement, as if she were talking about a little boy's hobby. "And as long as they continue winning prizes." She nodded, emphatically.

"And Mama's reputation will be saved."

There didn't seem anything I could say to that. Of course, I had no intention of writing a book at all, something that would probably disappoint her. I had a sudden, sharp suspicion that she was counting on this book to make her the belle of the assisted-living ball.

But then again, could I blame her, considering the blight of her life? She had never been the belle of the ball, and if she finally had a chance in her nineties—well, better than never, I supposed.

I stood up, feeling like I should be pulling my gloves on, and noticed that she was looking at me curiously. "You have a lovely complexion, Ms. Dare," she said.

I stopped. Couldn't help it. No one had ever told me that before. Oh, my skin was good enough. Except for a brief and disgusting outbreak of pimples at nineteen, I had weathered adolescence unblemished. And because I lived in the age of effective remedies, the brief acne had left no mark.

Whatever Ben had to say, at thirty I was not old enough to have to worry about wrinkles, so I had none, and my skin looked unexceptionable—not at all something to remark on. It was sort of like being told, "Ms. Dare, I see you have a head and four limbs."

"Thank—Thank you," I stammered, not knowing what else to say. Mom got told she had a lovely complexion all the time because she did. She was all white and peach and looked like she couldn't be real and someone must have painted her in porcelain.

Miss Martin's hand went out to the stick, and it made a little *thump thump* on the floor, as though she meant to make me pay attention, or perhaps she meant to wake herself up. I had a notion that she had got in the habit of using her walking stick as a punctuation mark. "Do you use any of those miracle treatments that they offer now? Botox or what have you?"

I didn't know how old she thought I was. Besides, if she really wanted a rousing discussion about beauty products, she should get hold of Ben. He could probably tell her what every moisturizing cream did, and about each clarifying lotion she might purchase. So I just said, "I use moisturizing cream, when I remember to."

She raised her eyebrows. "I see. Yes, I see. Well, you know what I tell my nephew's wife, it is never to early to start making sure one doesn't age badly." She smiled at me. "If I hadn't taken to applying several clarifying lotions and such as early on as my twenties, I'd probably look like parchment now."

And since she didn't—her face looked like a version of

my mother's, peaches and cream, only a little older and a little dustier—I had to bow to her knowledge.

"I've found though," she said. "That the best beauty product of all is to wash my face with rosewater in the morning. I don't know if it's the lovely smell, but I feel refreshed and buoyed all day."

I admitted it might be the smell, thinking she was after all years ahead of all the aromatherapy people, and I'd left her to her thoughts.

First I had, of course, to say good-byes, and receive her compliments to my mother and my grandmother, whom she seemed to have forgotten had died. I didn't enlighten her. She told me she was too weak and unbalanced, since her stroke, to go more than a few steps, and even that only with the walking stick. I didn't see any reason to destroy her illusions of the outside world and the longevity of her friends, when she was not likely to ever leave this room and confront them.

Instead, I smiled and nodded a lot, returned the frame and picture to its table and finally, after being led by the house-keeper along echoing corridors, walked out of the house and into bright sunlight. It felt like I had left age and oppression behind and come out into a beautiful day. I felt like saying, as Elizabeth I is said to have when they brought her news of her sister's death, "This is the day the Lord has made, and it is marvelous in our sight."

I didn't even think of her story again until I was in the car and headed home.

CHAPTER 17

Breaking the Shell

I didn't have very long to think about it, either. Only the short drive between the Martin house and my apartment. But even in that brief time, I thought that there was something wrong about the story. But it was not something I could have put my finger on. Instead, I decided I'd go home and write it all down, then highlight the parts that were giving me issues.

The minute I opened the door to my apartment, though, I completely forgot the old murders and homicidal ten-year-olds.

Usually when I left E with Ben—or anyone else—I'd come home and find the adult slumped on the sofa, staring blankly into space, while E ran circles around the table. Up until six months ago, when he'd refused to talk in front of strangers—or at least to talk in front of anyone but me, an uncommon but not rare form of selective mu-

tism that I was told struck only very intelligent children—
he'd run around the table making senseless noise. Now he
was more likely to be repeating something he'd heard that
struck his fancy or that was guaranteed to get a reaction.
When Ben had been so incautious as to say, "Oh, holy
fuck," in front of E, it had become E's favorite exclamation
for months and months, dropped willy-nilly into all sorts of
situations.

This time, E was sitting huddled, on the sofa, clutching
Pythagoras to his chest—and Ben was walking in circles,
round and round the coffee table, babbling. For a moment,
I thought it was a joke and that they'd staged it to see my
reaction.

Then I realized what Ben *was* babbling. "Buried under
the tree," he said. "I'm sure of it. That's why the trees grew
together like that. What do you say?" he asked, even though
neither E nor I had said anything. "Yes, exactly, reaching
out. Trying to give a sign. Poor things. Murdered with ax.
Buried under tree. Almost a hundred years of silence." He
looked over at me, and madness shone out of his eyes, a sly
madness that I wasn't sure was trying to play me—or
someone else. "Mustn't tell them. No, no, no, mustn't tell
them. You know what they'd do. They'd lie. And they'd
grind the bones to make soup." He rubbed the middle of his
forehead, which was a gesture that Ben had made as long
as I'd known him, and that meant he was worried and had a
headache coming on. "I'm confusing things, aren't I. It's
not the giant. There are no giants here. All very small men,"
he said with patrician disdain. "And they buried them under
the tree." He looked at me, and his look seemed completely
open and innocent. But the madness was still there, perhaps
worse than ever. "You don't understand, Dyce. They're

suffocating. I must save them. Imagine dirt in your mouth. All that time."

I was in shock. I should explain that of all forms of mental illness, any type of dementia, has always terrified me. There is a feeling that there is something there that is both more and less than human.

Worse yet, it was Ben who seemed to have slipped a cog. Ben who was always so precise, so exact, so full of understanding and planning of the world around him. It made me want to turn and run, fast, get in the car, and never stop until I was very well away.

But I couldn't do that. Something happens to you when you become a mother. Unlike what several popular comedians maintain, it doesn't give you superpowers or make you special in the sense of giving you something extra. It just divides your consciousness into two.

Oh, you don't hear through your child's ears or see through their eyes, though often if feels like if you just concentrated a little bit you ought to be able to. But you do feel as if your mind is in the two bodies at once and your imperative to live is then part of two bodies. Worse, the body that your senses are actually connected to is not the most important.

I used to admire, and still do, women who give their lives for their children. But I don't know how much a choice they have. I know that at that moment, as much as my mouth went dry and I wanted to drive far away and call a doctor and Ben's mom from a distance, most of all I wanted to grab my child and get him out of there, or at least make sure he was safe.

He was sitting there, huddled, his eyes enormous, holding on to Pythagoras who, in turn, stared at me with an expression that seemed to say, "This is another fine mess you got us into."

I started edging around Ben who had resumed pacing. "Yeah, see, it's why I have to go there and free them. Because they called to me. And I have to go. You can't ignore your duty to the dead." He looked up and repeated emphatically. "To the dead."

I didn't care. I'd reached E. I grabbed him and Pythagoras together in a bundle in my arms and started running hell bent for leather to my bedroom. I needed to call someone to come help, and I thought that it was more than likely Ben, in his seeming paranoia, would not let me.

I locked my bedroom door, and set E down. I registered a moment of satisfaction that Ben wasn't trying to break it down. Given those massive shoulders of his, I doubted the Victorian hinges and lock would keep him out for long. But he wasn't trying to do that, nor did I even hear him come close and knock.

I fished in my purse for my phone.

"Mommy, what's wrong with Ben?" E asked. He continued clutching Pythagoras and looked forlorn and confused, as if it might have been something he'd done. He also still had raspberry stains all over himself, so Ben hadn't bathed him.

Afterward, when he calmed down, I was going to try to pry the sequence of the morning's events out of E. In retrospect I cursed myself not to have seen the beginnings of this in Ben's phone call to me at my mom's. But he had sounded really tired, but still almost rational then.

I wondered what could be causing it, as I dialed the first number that came to mind. If Ben were on some sort of medication, I would have assumed he had taken too much. But as far as I knew, he wasn't. So what could have caused him to flip out so completely?

Ben was human, as much as he wished to deny it, but he had never been an unbalanced sort of human. In fact, when people talked of the man who kept his head when all around him were losing theirs, it was Ben they were talking about.

"Hello," Cas's voice jolted me out of my thoughts.

"Oh, thank God," I said, realizing after the fact that it was his number I had dialed, and that I'd called his cell phone and not his work number.

"Yes? Dyce? What's wrong?"

"Ben has gone crazy."

"What?"

"I don't know, Cas. He's walking around the table in the living room and ranting about people buried under the trees and how terrible it is to have your mouth full of dirt."

"What?" Cas sounded as if he thought that I had gone over the edge.

"I know it doesn't make any sense. But that's what he's saying, and he seems to be hearing voices, and his eyes are all weird, you know, like there is something sly inside his mind, and . . ."

"Uh . . . Don't do anything. I'm coming right over. Uh. I'd better bring Nick."

"No," I said, desperately. If this were something caused by a mini-stroke or something, I could just imagine what Ben would do to me once he came to his senses. He'd say I had let his prospective or perhaps actual boyfriend see him at the worst of possible times. "No, please, I'm sure Ben wouldn't want—"

"Too late, honey. Nick is right here. I think I'd need a full squad of armed guards to keep him here."

I heard something in the background that indicated Nick's agreement.

"Whatever," I said, giving up. "Just get here quickly, because he's going crazy and I don't know what to do and he doesn't take drugs, so it has to have been a stroke or something. Oh, please, come," I said.

And at that point, I heard the front door slam with a bang. Turning off the phone, I unlocked my door. The living room was deserted, and out in the driveway, I heard an engine start up.

"Oh, holy fuck," I said, and before I knew what I was doing, I had picked up E, who was still holding Pythagoras, and taken off toward my own car.

CHAPTER 18

It's a Mad, Mad, Mad, Car Chase

I honestly don't remember getting in the car, or get-ting E into it, with his seat belt buckled. All I remember is peeling out of my driveway like a bat out of hell.

Some part of my consciousness, way at the back, was aware that I might be giving E material for several years of therapy. Right at that moment, I couldn't care less. I grabbed my phone from my purse and put it on the seat next to me, even as I did a one-handed left turn out of my street onto Fairfax, about the time I realized that I was in more trouble than I thought.

I've heard Fairfax is the longest, straightest street in North America. I wasn't too sure about that, since I had heard the same claims for other streets in other parts of the country and suspected that other countries too were full of it—claims and streets both.

But I did know that Fairfax *was* the most heavily traveled, non-highway street in the city. It had been constructed, I'd once been told, by having oxen drag a broad log more or less in a straight line. The idea had been to create a street wide enough that two carriages could pass one another with ease.

Now it accommodated four car lanes, two in each direction, as well as having sidewalks in front of the mostly small, independent shops that lined each side. What this meant, at the best of times, is that I had to be careful when driving on it. More than once I'd gone so close to a car in the next lane, that my mirror had been flipped flat.

And that was at low traffic times. Now it was the lunch rush hour. There was little room to maneuver and the best way to change lanes is to have been born in the other one.

This wasn't slowing Ben down at all. He forged merrily ahead, speeding up, changing lanes and, for a brief and glorious moment, driving the wrong way in the opposing lane. Which only convinced me more that he had gone completely mad. Normally Ben would have preferred opening his own veins as a sacrifice to a pagan god than risking a tiny dent or a hair-thin scratch on the impeccable panels of his cream-colored BMW.

The funny thing, I thought as I drove after him, taking risks I normally wouldn't take and bullying my way into lane changes to a cacophonic sound of horns, was that he wasn't hitting any other cars. My grandmother had a proverb that said something about the good Lord keeping the falling sparrow, the innocent child, and the madman in the hollow of his hand, and I guessed she was right. There were collisions in his wake—the sickening grind of metal on metal and a very decisive crunch, though I didn't slow down enough to see who had crashed and where—but none of them affected Ben. He put his arm briefly out of his window and waved. Not at me. As far as I could tell he was waving at helicopters.

"Mommy, Mommy?" E whined from the seat next to me. He was strapped in, still holding Pythagoras, the cat's frightened little face peeking out just above the belt.

"E," I said, in my best voice of authority, "pick up Mommy's phone and press redial."

"What's *redal*?"

"No, no, no. Redial. It says right there on the button."

I made a dangerous lane change to catch up with Ben who had suddenly decided that he must be in the left lane.

"Mommy! E can't read."

"Why the hell not?" I asked. "You are three!" And then, as he started crying, I said, "Sorry, sorry, sorry. But you're a big boy and you do know your letters. Look for a button with a word that starts with *R* and has no number."

He sniffled. "Oh."

From the corner of my eye, I could see him pressing a button, then holding the phone to his ear.

"Mommy? Cas says what?"

Ahead of me, Ben took a right turn from the left lane—across a line of traffic that honked the hell at him—onto Sparrowhawk Lane.

"Oh, shit, hell, and damnation."

"Mommy says . . ." E spoke into the phone. "Mommy says . . . Mommy says *bad* words." In increasing desperation, I tried to find a way to turn onto Sparrowhawk, but couldn't because, of course, the line of cars had closed in my way and I wasn't a madwoman—though I was getting pretty damn close.

"I can't do," E wailed. "Mommy driving. Mad."

At this point I'd lost Ben. Even if I made it into Sparrowhawk, which led to a pretty neighborhood street, likely he would have taken a random turn into one of the other small streets, and I would be completely out of luck.

On the other hand, I could turn ahead—there was a light and I could turn left at the left arrow—and pull onto a side street and think. And talk to Cas. "I'm sorry, Bunny," I said, as calmly as I could, while I executed this maneuver. "Tell Cas that I'll talk to him in just a second."

I pulled onto Narrow Way, a street full of tall, two-floor brick houses, set in spacious gardens. It wasn't as high rent as Waterfall. I knew that because they didn't have lawns. But they had nice trees, and the houses themselves looked well kept.

I parked, then reached for the phone, which E gladly gave me. He started frantically petting Pythagoras, who looked like a cartoon cat. All four of his legs protruded from under the belt, and his face looked goofy. He didn't seem like he was in distress, though. His face had that "I hope I'm not bothering you expression" it normally wore.

"Cas," I said.

"We're on our way to your house," Cas said. "I take it that Ben's no longer there? Because you're driving somewhere? Judging by the honks?"

"Just got off Fairfax."

"Are you the disturbance the traffic helicopters—"

"No," I said. I felt suddenly very tired. "That was Ben." I gave him a quick account of my friend's adventures. "I don't know where he's going or why, but he's not in his right mind, and I don't know why." I realized I was crying and felt fairly upset at myself for it, but there was no way of stopping. "I mean, he's always been a nut, in a way, but not this kind of nut, if you know what I mean."

"I know exactly what you mean. Nick and I were talking and it sounds from what you told us like Ben is on an hallucinogen of some kind. Would he ever—"

"Never," I said. "He doesn't even like pain meds, because he tends to have weird reactions to . . . Oh."

"Exactly. Do you know if he's taking anything? Headaches? Arthritis?"

"Not that I know." I wiped my tears to the back of my hand.

"Uh. . . . If he gets picked up he might get booked on drug charges. It would be good if we could find him before that happens."

"Yeah," I said, bawling my eyes out. "I don't want to call his mom. I don't want her to get all worried for, you know, something I don't understand."

"Yeah," Cas said. "Tell you what. Where do you think he'd have gone?"

"No idea," I said. "He was raving on about those trees in front of Jacinth Jones's house, but he can't possibly have been headed there. I mean, if he was doing that, taking Colfax was insane."

"Dyce, from what you've been saying, I doubt Ben is thinking logically at all."

"Um," I said. "We don't have anything to lose, do we?"

"No," Cas said. "I say we go to the house where Jones used to live, and see if he's there. If not, then we start driving in a rational manner through the neighborhood, okay? Make a grid or something. But for now, the best bet is that house."

"All right," I said.

I looked over at my son. He was looking back at me, his eyes huge and full of tears. "Bah—Ben gonna be awright?" he asked, his pronunciation of Ben's name momentarily returning to his very early age.

"I think so, sweetie. Should you have Pythagoras inside the seat belt? It looks like it would hurt to be strapped in that way." It suddenly occurred to me that E should be in his car seat in the back. I hoped no policeman would stop me. At least no policeman I wasn't currently dating.

"Peegrass likes it," E said. And because he was sniffling and because the cat didn't look any more bothered than usual, and also because I wasn't sure what the cat would do if he were set loose in the car, I nodded. "Okay. We're going somewhere now to see if Ben is there. If he isn't, then we'll have to figure out another way of finding him."

"An' if he ax murdered?"

"What?" I said, as I drove across Colfax and headed for Jacinth Jones's house, which was about ten blocks away and a few turns, through side streets.

"Ben say someone killed. E afraid."

Pythagoras chose this moment to corroborate E's fear by making a ridiculous little meow.

"Don't be, honey. It all happened a long time ago." But I wondered if that long-past death could be reaching toward us. I didn't understand how long-dead people could affect Ben's behavior, but clearly they were. Maybe I had to start believing in ghosts . . .

CHAPTER 19

Horticulture Is Your Friend

As soon as I turned on the street where the Jones house stood, I knew we had made the right call. Ben was standing by the twin trees. I couldn't see what he was doing—for all I knew some sort of ghost dance around them.

"Stay in the car, Bunny," I told E.

"Why Ben . . ." He struggled for the word, then gave up. "Funny?"

So many answers to that. But I didn't think that telling him it was probably genetics, given neither of his parents were exactly average, would have satisfied E. I thought carefully and spoke slowly as I parked. "We think he ate something that gave him a bad reaction. Allergies, you know, like when Mommy sneezes and cries near feathers?" He nodded. "Well, sometimes it makes people crazy."

I dialed the phone, as I got out of the car, and I told Cas, "Bingo."

"Right, be there in a few seconds."

I saw Cas's small white SUV turn onto the street, as I hung up. He parked it at a jaunty—and illegal—angle by the curb.

"I'm afraid to go nearer," I told him as I stood at the edge of the lawn, on the sidewalk. "Whatever Ben's problem is seems to include acute paranoia. Earlier he was afraid of my mother and there's a lot of talk of an unspecified *Them*. I'm afraid he'll take off."

Cas nodded. From where we stood, we could see what Ben was doing. Even Cas realized, without my needing to tell him, that something very serious was wrong. Because Ben had a shovel—large, with a shiny red handle—and was digging madly into the half-frozen ground around the trees.

Where Ben got the shovel was a complete puzzle. That he was using it was alarming to say the least. His ancestors might have been Vikings or Irish peasants. He had the shoulders and the build of those people. But he did not have the disposition. Oh, he worked hard. Mad hard, from what I understood, but his work consisted of planning investments for people, and the fact that he prospered even in these times meant he was good at it. His muscles came from exercise in a climate-controlled gym, not from anything that might be considered manual labor. Plus, he was digging into the brown clay soil while wearing his best pants, a dress shirt, and an impeccable tie.

The only explanation was insanity.

I stared in horror as Ben threw another shovelful of dirt over his shoulder and continued digging.

He was muttering to himself while he did so, something about finding them, how he must find them. I had no doubt that he was talking about dead people—Jacinth and Almeria no doubt.

Nick was acting like Fluffy the First when Mother put down her dinner, but I was in the way. She used to do this odd two-step, where she walked toward the dish, then remembered I was there, and stepped back, managing to forget while doing it that I was in the way. Then she would step forward again.

Nick would take two steps forward toward Ben, put his hand to his forehead, and do the two-step back, then start forward again, then back again.

Cas, on the other hand, was talking on the phone. "Code fifty-nine. No, I don't think violent, but at serious risk for attempting to escape."

Nick gave him a look, squared his shoulders, and walked over to Ben's car. He opened the door, reached in, and came out with the keys, which Ben had left in the ignition. He walked back toward us. "That will stop him trying to drive away," he said. "You have your keys, right?"

"Yeah, the kid and the cat are in the car, but I have keys."

"The cat?" Cas said, hanging up.

"They were holding each other when I took off," I said. "What the hell do you think he's doing? And why?"

"Digging for bodies," Cas said.

"Yeah, but why?"

"You said he had some weird reactions to meds in the past," Cas said. "Ask Nick what happened to his father once when he took cough syrup with codeine in it."

Nick spoke without taking his eyes off Ben. "It was like giving him speed. He walked around and around, babbling in Greek, though neither Mom nor I spoke it. But he was no way as bad as this. If this is the reaction to some medicine, Ben sure needs to be careful. Hell, he'll need a statement from a doctor before taking aspirin. I'll make sure of that."

I passed on the "I'll make sure of that" because in context with the worried eyes and the look like Nick didn't know whether to rush forward and forcibly restrain Ben or bawl his eyes out, it was more an expression of concern than of ownership.

At that moment an ambulance and a fire truck turned into the street, sirens blaring. I heard Cas shout above the din, "I told them to not use the sirens!" But it didn't have any effect on Ben. He didn't even turn to look.

Two paramedics got out of the ambulance at a trot and advanced toward Ben.

"I told EMS it might be a reaction to medication," Cas said. "So they won't tranquilize him."

Which probably explained why they'd sent two of the burliest paramedics I'd ever seen.

Even though, as they flanked Ben and managed to take the shovel away, they couldn't move him. He was shouting something I couldn't make out, both because his voice sounded oddly hoarse and because he was looking away from me.

I think Nick and I started forward at the same time. We did say, "It's all right, Ben," at the same time, but so much for the claims of his oldest friend—it was Nick that Ben turned toward, dragging the paramedic hanging from his right arm about a quarter turn.

"Nick," he said. "Nick!" He was red-faced, sweating, and wild-eyed, and I couldn't tell if he was calling to Nick out of affection or anger. But then he said, "Nick, tell them I'm not crazy."

Nick stopped. I thought he was going to do the two-step again, only he didn't. "You're not insane, Ben," he said. "But you're not well, you must know that. We need to take you to the hospital. You're having a reaction to something."

Ben shook his head. "Head hurts. Eyes blurred. But I'm not crazy. Look."

He pointed. Nick and I both looked in the hole that Ben had managed to dig—a surprisingly deep hole. Hell, a miraculously deep hole, considering that it had been dug by just one man in the frozen ground of a Colorado winter. At the bottom of it there was something yellowish, paler than the soil. No, several somethings.

Nick jumped backward. "It's a hand."

"Yeah," Ben said. "I'm not crazy. It's a hand. They're there. They were buried there."

Cas was on the phone again. "Human remains," he said. "We have reason to believe they maybe have been victims of foul play."

Ben took a deep breath. It was as if he'd been animated by his obsession and now had run out of purpose. He still looked crazy, but he looked docile-crazy. As the paramedics started dragging him toward the ambulance, he looked back over his shoulder. "Nick," he said, "don't let them arrest me."

Nick looked at Cas. I didn't know what passed in that look, but Nick ran after the paramedics. "I'm coming with him," he said. "I want to write down anything he might say that . . . that might give us a clue."

As they got in the ambulance and left with the fire engine, which according to Colorado law had to follow any ambulance sent out, I turned to Cas. "Did you have to say that you had reason to suspect foul play?"

He nodded. "Oh, yes. From here on out, things will

have to be done a particular way, you know, the excavation and examination of the remains, if there's the slightest chance there might be a murder charge involved."

"A murder . . . charge?" I said. "But if Ben found Jacinth and Almeria and they were murdered, it was almost a hundred years ago."

He shrugged. "There is no statute of limitations on murder. I know that there's little chance the murderer is alive, but still . . ."

I shook my head. "If what Miss Martin told me today is true, he isn't," I said. I told him what she had said, even as a police car drove up and started disgorging more people than any clown car had ever managed. I should have made a remark about policemen violating the law on maximum occupancy for cars, but I didn't. Instead, I told Cas the whole story.

Cas frowned at me. "It could certainly be the truth. But you don't seem to believe it?"

"No," I said. "There's something about it that's bothering me, though I can't put my finger on it. She might be telling the truth, of course. It might be that what's putting me off on it is this idea that she is trying to get her revenge on her father and her brother now that they can't defend themselves."

"Well . . . would you blame her?" Cas asked.

"No, but . . . it's possible that's all it is. I find it—distasteful."

"On the other hand," Cas said, "it would explain why someone put the word out to my captain to stop you. I don't care how little of a social butterfly John Martin is, no man alive wants his father branded as a murderer."

"Yeah. It would explain that, but—"

"But?"

"Something about it still bothers me, I just can't tell you what it is."

A tall man that I'd only seen in passing at the station before approached us. He wore a khaki-colored shirt and khaki pants and looked almost terminally relaxed, even though he was carrying more shoulder bags than I'd ever seen a human being carry. I knew who he was—Rafiel Trall, the other senior investigator in the Serious Crimes Unit of Goldport Police Department. He was hot in yet a completely different way from Cas and Nick, and worried though I was about Ben's state and whatever was bothering me about Diane Martin's story, I couldn't afford sparing a thought to the awesome taste of the woman—probably a woman though it could be a gay man—who did the hiring for Goldport Police Department. Clearly, whoever it was had a requirement that went, "Must be this hot to wear the badge."

"What are the chances if it was foul play that the murderer is still alive?" Rafiel asked. "Or that this will ever get to court?"

Cas looked over at me. I don't know what he read in my expression, but whatever it was made him turn to Officer Hotstuff Number Three and say, "Treat this as though the bastard is still out on Main Street handing out poisonous candy, Rafiel."

Rafiel smiled. "Right you are. So, isn't it your case, too?" He gave me a curious look and then, clearly recognizing me as Cas's girlfriend, a purposely naughty wink.

Cas took a deep breath. "Right," he said. "Right. Let's do this." He squeezed my upper arm and then let go, the objection to public displays of affection in full force before what must be at least half of his department.

"I'll go," I said. "I can't leave E and Pythagoras in the

car much longer." A look in their direction showed me both little faces pressed against the glass window. "And besides," I said, "I have no idea what Ben did in the house before I got home."

CHAPTER 20

Of Rats and Men

In the car on the way home, I questioned E. I asked him what Ben had done before I'd gotten home.

E shook his head. He had added a full hug to Pythagoras's restraints, and I was now wondering if the belt against the cat's chest was restricting oxygen to his brain. Because any cat worthy of the name would, right about now, be clawing at my son and doing his best to take his eyes out. Instead, Pythagoras remained still, with that ridiculously apologetic expression on his furry face, emitting a meow now and then that probably meant, "I'm sorry, could we hurry this up, I have a meeting of the bedwetters club later."

"I was 'sleep," he said. He had stopped crying but still looked scared. I guess it was very strange for a little boy to find himself in this position. "I was 'sleep an' I woke up an'"

Ben was talking to you onna phone. He was feedin' Ratso,
He put him down an' feed Ratfink."

I nodded. That E knew the rats on sight didn't surprise
me at all. "He was gonna feed me, too. He put Ratfink in
the glass box to play, an' Ratley was runnin' round in circles. With his tail sticking out. An' I thought it was funny
an' Ben did, too. An' he gave me a muffin and milk, an' . . ."

"Yes?"

"He left the kitchen. He said he had some work to do.
An' . . . an' when I went after, he was walkin' round the
table."

"Yes?"

"He yelled at me. He said I was a bad boy 'cause I was
spying for them." E started bawling again. "He yelled at
Peegrass, too, an' Peegrass jumped on my lap an'"—he
paused to breathe—"an' then, and then you got home."

It was the longest and most correct speech I'd ever
heard E make.

"Ben is going to be all right. They're going to take
good care of him." I patted his knee with my free hand, as
I drove. "And we're going home, and I'm going to give
you a bath, put you in clean clothes, and find you some
lunch."

At the mention of lunch, Pythagoras, proving that there
was still enough oxygen left in his brain for him to understand essential words, said, "Meeeeeewwwww?"

"Yes, of course, Pythagoras. We'll get you lunch, too."

But at the back of my mind, I was thinking of Ratley,
running in circles with his tail sticking out.

As soon as we got home, I opened a can of food for
Pythagoras, but I asked E to wait a minute while I looked
in the aquarium.

Ratley was still running around, steadily, in circles

around the aquarium, always in the same direction. His tail was sticking straight up, rigid. I picked him up—and his legs continued moving. I looked into his eyes and met with the same mania that had shone in Ben's. Right. I smelled Ratley. Why did I do that? Because I caught a faint whiff of something quite unrodentlike about him. Closer up, he smelled pleasant like . . . some sort of beauty product? I dropped him back in the aquarium, and grabbed the phone. "Cas, Cas, I think I know why Ben was acting the way he did. I think there was something in one of the skin products he used this morning."

"What?"

"Ratley is acting just as weird, his tail is stiff and sticking straight up in the air, his little hair is standing on end and he smells . . . perfumy. I think Ben fed him first, right after he did his morning moisturizing routine, and . . ."

"Dyce, I'll come right over, but before I do, call this number. It's Nick's cell phone. Tell him Ratley's symptoms. He needs to know about this."

Right. I called Nick, who sounded somewhat startled at hearing my voice over the phone, then said, "Oh . . . Okay, look, I'm going to get a pharmacologist on the phone, tell him again Ratley's symptoms."

I did, explaining in detail how he was—still—running in circles with his tail right up in the air. He had to have been doing that for three hours at least. I wondered how long his poor little ratty heart could hold out. I asked the man. He said, "um," then, "um," again and then. "This sounds very familiar. Let me consult my online database."

Moments later, he said, "I think he was given topiramate," And to my silence added, "It's an anticonvulsant. Acute intoxication presents as psychosis. Seeing things, hearing voices. Paranoia. Anxiety. Mania. And it will have that effect on rats, too, I know because I worked in a lab where we tested it."

"What is it used for?" I asked, wondering where Ben could have got hold of such a substance, much less how he'd confused it with his moisturizer.

"To stop convulsions in epileptics," the man said. "Or seizures in someone who had had a stroke. Probably topically applied, in case the person is not able to swallow. The presentation of an overdose is similar to schizophrenia." He said, "He ought to be started on a course of clozapine, which is indicated anyway since it's an anti-psychotic and bicuculline, which blocks GABA receptors. The research seems to indicate that topiramate toxicity is due to its GABA-like properties. If the treatment is started now, we can see how he reacts by morning. If it's acute topiramate intoxication, he should be normal in twenty-four hours or less."

I wanted to cry with relief. "What about Ratley?"

"The rat?" the man sounded surprised.

Nick on the phone again. "I'll call a friend who's a vet and send him over to look after Ratley. Okay, Dyce?"

"If you can."

"Of course I can. And then I'm going to call Cas and have some of the squad come over. I might come myself, if Ben seems to be settling down. We're going to do a thorough work-up on your house, and anything Ben might have touched."

"Uh . . . why?"

"Because if it is topiramate intoxication," he said, gravely. "It sounds an awful lot like he was poisoned. Remember your missing key, and the fact that the aquarium was broken and Pythagoras let out of the bathroom?"

"Oh." I said. Something was bothering me, something

deeper than the fact that my son was covered in now almost day-old raspberry stains, which at a guess I wouldn't get a chance to wash off any time soon. I asked Nick, and there was almost a smile in his voice as he answered, "No, it would be better if you don't use the sinks or bathtubs or anything Ben might have used."

"Uh, then you'd better hurry up, because sooner or later the kid or I are going to need to pee."

The smile in his voice became broader as he said, "I'll get someone there as soon as humanly possible."

CHAPTER 21

Rats, Raspberry, and Polish

The vet appeared before anyone from the police, though. He was a slim young man who seemed nonplussed, but nonetheless firm about what needed to be done.

He squeezed my hand in a handshake and said, "Hi, I'm Doctor Zed. Or at least that's what they call me. My name is Zebadiah Smith, but all my patients—or rather their owners—call me Zed." He looked a little nervous, delivering himself of this speech, and even more nervous as I took him to the aquarium and he looked at Ratley. He picked him up while Ratley's little legs continued pumping away.

"I have to say this is a very unusual case, but I've learned to trust Nick's hunches. I have specific instructions on how to treat the rat. I'd like to wash him immediately, but Nick wants me to take a scraping first and then to wipe him with tissue that we save. Is that all right with you?"

"Of course," I said. "Just so long as you can take care of Ratley before he has a stroke or something."

"Oh, he's at no risk of a stroke," the vet said. "He's much more likely to have a heart attack."

But Ratley didn't have, either. Instead, he continued frantically pumping his legs while the vet took as good a scraping off his fur and skin as he could, then wiped him with a paper towel—because our tissues had lotion—and finally with baby wipes, leftover from E's potty-training days. Finally he gave Ratley two shots, talking all the while.

"Working on very small animals is difficult because of the dosage," he said. "But fortunately the doctor in charge of your friend's case knew how this substance affected rats. So he knew what the dosage of the antidote should be—or he did after he consulted some of his old course notes."

"Right," I said.

"So when I stopped by the hospital they had the syringes all ready. They have your friend on an IV drip."

I nodded while I watched Ratley slowly stop moving his legs and relax, then eventually fall asleep in the vet's hand, I hoped that things were going equally well for Ben.

"I'll come by tomorrow," the vet said, putting Ratley back in the aquarium. "Just to see how he's doing. This is my card. Call me if you think that anything looks wrong, all right?"

"You do house calls?" I asked.

He grinned. "Not exactly, but I owe Nick a few. No, don't bother paying. He told me he's going to be adopting the little fellows."

He put fingers in the aquarium and petted the rats one at a time. "I must say you've done a fine job with them. Orphan rats are notoriously difficult to bring up but these little fellows look great. Tomorrow I'll bring you some chow to start weaning them to, all right?"

I nodded again and he left. Only to be replaced seconds later by the crime-scene investigation team from the good old Goldport Police Department, led by Nick.

"Ben seems to be doing much better," he told me as he took pictures of various things, from the place where Ben had slept, to the area in the bathroom where he kept his toiletries, to the kitchen and the dishes on the sink, to the apparatus for feeding the rats, which had been left strewn about the counter. Which was only one more sign that Ben hadn't been—Ben. "After less than an hour on IV. Of course, he could be responding to the antipsychotic, but the doctor doesn't think so. He really seems to have been poisoned. Now, tell me which of these he uses," he said, throwing back the lid of Ben's beauty products case with gloved hands, while his technicians fanned out over the house, dusting for fingerprints and doing heaven only knew what.

"All of them, I assume," I said. "Otherwise he wouldn't cart them around. Though it's perfectly ridiculous. He has Irish skin. It will be years before he starts looking his age."

Nick grinned. "Yes, but which ones does he use every day?"

"Uh . . . I don't know. The moisturizer for sure. I've seen him when he's really hurried, and he always puts at least the moisturizer on. He calls it slapping on some grease."

Nick pulled the plastic from the case he was carrying around into which he'd shoved the paper towel used to wipe down Ratley. He smelled the towel, then smelled

Ben's moisturizer. "I think that's it," he said, closing the baggie again and collecting the moisturizer. He put it into a separate baggie. Then for good measure, he went over the whole case and the mirror and the sink taking finger-prints. I am probably the only woman ever who, while watching a criminal investigation, was embarrassed by the number of prints the fingerprint powder revealed all over the bathroom mirror.

The police left, and I'd just managed to get E into a warm bath and wash the raspberry stains off him at last, when the phone rang. I picked it up expecting it to be Cas or, on the outside, Ben.

It was Mrs. All-ex, sounding brisk and businesslike. "Candyce, I was wondering if we could have Enoch back today, and then we'll keep him for three weeks if you wish, or just till Tuesday in the normal schedule if you prefer, and save the extra days for when you need them?"

I normally hated giving E up, though I had been plan-ning to let them keep him for three weeks during which time I could get the piano done. But that had been before Ben had gone psychotic and scared my son half to death. Besides, there was Peegrass. I really couldn't swear the cat wouldn't go—more—neurotic without the presence of his favorite boy.

The fact that he was walking back and forth across the bathtub ledge while E played with his rubber ducky in the soapy water didn't reassure me. What Pythagoras was say-ing was, "meow, meow, meow," but what it managed to convey was, "Was that bathtub properly disinfected? Good God, woman, do you know how many carcinogens might be in that rubber ducky *and* does the soap have any danger-ous chemical components."

I figured if I let E spend too much time at All-ex's, Pythagoras would worry himself to death over what kind of treatment E might be getting. A brief, fleeting fantasy of sending Pythagoras to All-ex and Mrs. All-ex was discarded. They would probably take him to the Humane Society and I'd gotten somewhat attached to the neurotic fool. He could keep me company while E was gone.

"No, that's fine, you may pick him up and keep him till Tuesday," I said.

E looked up stricken. "Mom! Peegrass. And rats."

"Oh, don't worry," I said. "I'll take good care of them while you're gone. And you get to take Ben's gift with you. You know what a big backyard Daddy has."

If there was some hesitation in Mrs. All-ex's voice as she said she would be here in two hours, I gave her time to neither back off nor ask me what Ben's gift to E had been. Instead, I hung up the phone on E's jubilant shout, dressed and combed my son, and gave him a very late lunch of hot dogs. E's secret recipe for hotdogs means that the weight of the mustard must exceed that of the hot dog and the bun combined. Fortunately I had learned from past experiences, so he was swaddled in an old towel before I sat him down to eat, and when he was done the damage was limited to his hands and face. Which I'd just washed when Mrs. All-ex arrived to pick him up.

The look of shock on her face when she saw Ben's gift—both the electric motorcycle and the miniature leather jacket—will warm the cockles of my heart when I'm old or even possibly in hell.

However, she couldn't complain without feeding into E's mulish insistence it was either the motorcycle or Peegrass and the rats. She thought she was getting the least evil of the options, the poor fool.

As for me, I saw E stowed away—apparently the big

reason for his needing to go to his father right then was that his father was hosting a dinner for his boss, who liked families and liked to know that his employees had, as the man put it, an interest in the future through their children.

Mrs. All-ex confessed this without blushing, and I waved good-bye to them with a song in my heart, thinking of All-ex's manicured backyard lawn and the plastic, ridged wheels of E's electric motorcycle. Sometimes things happen to the best possible people.

Now that I was alone I had time, and I decided to do my thinking where my brain seemed to work best—in my work shed.

CHAPTER 22

Pianissimo

The piano stood there, peeled and patient, waiting for me. I felt as if things were working themselves out at the back of my mind, but I was not sure what I could do to hurry the process. It felt—as it had felt before, when I was working through some problem that was so big and complex I couldn't see my way out of it with simple logic—as though my subconscious were working furiously and not letting me out on it.

To while away the time, I set my printouts on French polishing on top of the piano. Long ago, I'd admired the mirrorlike finish on Ben's mother's piano and been told that it was French polish. Because I was then young enough to think that French polish must be done in France, I'd remembered the term forever, since I'd spent quite a bit of time considering how one might ship a whole piano to France, then back again.

Now reading the instructions, I learned that French polish was both the finish with the best acoustic qualities, and therefore the best to put on musical instruments, and that it was susceptible to a list of ills—alcohol, heat, cold—all manner of things could damage it. I found myself wondering if I could just give it a thin coat of that plastic substance they used to put on bar tops, sometimes with coins underneath. While epoxy was by no means—at least I thought—the best acoustic anything, it was practically indestructible. I'd once finished a living room table in epoxy, back when I still shared a home with All-ex. The result was a piece of furniture capable of surviving everything including but not limited to parking your car on it. Not that I'd ever tried that, of course, but it had survived two years of All-ex's putting his feet on it while watching sports on television, without showing the slightest mark.

The instructions themselves were bewildering and at least two sites seemed to imply that you could set your house on fire in the process. Given my propensity to set my parents' house on fire—I had done it at least half a dozen times as a child—I decided to shy away from those methods that said anything about heating or melting. At any rate, some of the other material led me to believe that the dangerous stuff was a form of shellac—the base material of French polish—that was only available in the United Kingdom.

It was all completely bewildering, so I set it aside. Instead, I started making a shopping list, consisting of shellac flakes and rotten stone and pure, virgin olive oil. The last one surprised me as an ingredient but the arguments in its favor made sense. And some of the problems mentioned could probably be avoided by its use.

The flakes were going to be the biggest problem to

find. I looked at my watch and realized that the hardware store would still be open. I couldn't lock my door, because I didn't have a key to get back in, and now that I was aware someone had broken into the house in my absence, I didn't feel right leaving Pythagoras and the rats behind, at the mercy of whoever might come in.

After all, I had promised E that I would look after the animals. So I did the only rational thing. I took the aquarium with the rats and put it in the backseat of the car and strapped it in. Then I shooed Pythagoras into his carrier, took that out to the car, and strapped it in beside the aquarium. I tried to ignore the fact that this reminded me of a *The Far Side* cartoon where trucks of rodents and flightless birds have an accident in front of a house where a cat is waiting. On the other hand, at least I'd managed the same in more compact space. On yet another hand, judging by how Pythagoras had cowered from the rats the one time the poor things had had the run of the house, perhaps I should be more worried about him than them.

With my strange passengers, I headed out to the hardware store. This hardware store was as old as the town or perhaps older. It was run by a man named Julius whom I had always assumed had served in the Revolutionary War. He looked exactly like the wounded soldier in the *Spirit of Seventy-six* poster, only I had to assume he'd found a way to grow back his leg. This didn't seem unlikely, as he'd been as old as he looked now—probably mid-fifties—since I was a little girl and had come in with Grandma to pick up some wax polish for her antique furniture. But he had to be more like in his seventies or even eighties.

He also cut keys and carried a line of old drawer pulls that rivaled anything I could find online in the manner of reproductions. Apparently collecting them and finishing them was his hobby, though getting him to sell them was as hard as convincing Dad to part with a book.

However, with one thing and another, I spent a lot of time in his store. Sometimes I thought I was the only customer under seventy, the others being little old ladies who came in for everything from cleaners to lightbulbs, instead of going to the grocery store, or even to the bigger chain hardware store across town.

Part of this was the service. I greeted Julius—I'd sometimes wondered if he was the original and if his last initial was *C*—and asked him where the shellac flakes were. He didn't even turn a hair at the idea that I wanted to buy something so quaint, but led me right to them. He also found the best rotten stone for me. "They say to use pumice sometimes," he told me. "But rotten stone is ground finer."

Then he had insisted on selling me several pads of cloth, and instructed me on how to use them. "You want several pads, because by the time you're done applying all the polish, your arm will be right sore and these pads will be in tatters."

He seemed to relish the idea of my arm being sore far too much for my taste, so I tried to divert him. "Funny weather we've been having, huh?" I said, falling back on the standby of every tribe of man since the beginning of time. It was particularly effective in Colorado. Most people—probably because of *South Park*—think Colorado is all ice and snow almost year around. At higher elevations, it might be so. In fact, I had often read about Colorado towns that were snowed completely under from the beginning of September to the end of May every year. The articles I read tended to talk about the absolute necessity of beer to keep the population of those towns what passed for sane during the months of isolation.

But Goldport, and for that matter Denver and Colorado Springs—though in varying amounts for each town—had a lot of snow fall, but also had an almost instant melt. It was rare for the snow to linger on the ground for more than a day or two. If it did so at all, it was in January.

And it was neither unusual nor remarkable for the day to start at seventy degrees and be minus two by nightfall, or vice versa.

Julius perked up, as I knew he would. "Oh, yeah. Boy, the weather. Now it's cold, then it's hot, then it's cold again. I was telling Miss Martin just yesterday as it played havoc with my leg." He made a gesture, pointing at his leg that made me wonder if he was really the man in the *Spirit* painting. Nah. Impossible.

"John Martin's wife buys her own hardware?" I said, somewhat surprised, to say the least.

"No, no, Miss Diane Martin. She comes in now and then. Fussy. All these old women are, of course, and she wants her furniture polished just so."

I wondered if he'd taken leave of his senses. The invalid I'd seen, the woman who was getting ready to go into assisted living couldn't possibly be walking around polishing her furniture.

"Course, last time she just came in for me to cut a key," he said. "Said she had lost hers." He shrugged. "Old women lose everything, too."

I shook my head. He had to mean Mrs. Martin. I hardly call her an old woman—but Julius was definitely an old man and it made me a little sad to think he might finally be failing. But I had no intention of arguing with him, so I left the store carrying my purchases and drove home by way of the grocery store, where I bought the virgin olive oil.

When I got home, Cas's car was in the driveway, a sight that always makes my day better. He came over, opened my car door and stood looking at the backseat with a smile. Pythagoras said, "Mew," in the tone of a cat who wishes to complain of a great injustice done to him and I told Cas, "He's lying, you know. I never did leave them in the car with the windows up. I opened them a crack, because even in winter, in the sun, cars can get very warm."

He just shook his head as he picked up the aquarium and left me to collect the cat carrier. "Mrs. Dare and her mobile animal zoo."

I made a face at him. "Well," I said. "I do what I have to do. Besides, after dealing with you, Ben, and E, the zoo is the least of my worries."

We settled the animals in the kitchen—Pythagoras in front of a plate of flaked tuna—and Cas said, "By the way, you left the door unlocked. Which I'd think you wouldn't do, after someone came in and tampered with Ben's beauty products. And yes, we're already looking at the possibility that his ex is back in town. He was last heard from playing the French horn in the symphony in Belize, but this seems to smack of him."

"Yeah. It would drive him nuts to come back to town and find Ben is dating again, wouldn't it?" I said, as I made tea for both of us.

"Probably. So, right now he's our number one suspect. But you really shouldn't leave your door open, meanwhile."

"Well, I don't have a key," I said. "That's why I took the rats and Pythagoras. I mean, it's not like there's anything else to steal in the house."

"No, but someone could mess with your tea, or the milk . . ."

"If it is Ben's ex, he'd know he doesn't make tea from bags."

"All the same," he said. "You shouldn't leave the door unlocked. Do you want to have to chase Ben across town again?"

"Well, presumably," I said. "If whoever did whatever they did to Ben's moisturizer already has my key, my locking up or not wouldn't make any difference."

"If.they have your key," Cas said. "Which is a big *if*."

"They got in somehow."

"Doesn't prove they had your key," he said. "It's entirely possible that they'd simply found the door unlocked. I mean, weren't you the last one out when we went for ice cream? And carrying E, yet. You don't have a key, so you couldn't possibly have locked the door. My fault, of course, but I forgot."

It was possible. "Well, I still haven't found the key."

This was the wrong thing to say to my law-and-order love. It started a search of all my pockets, while the tea cooled in the teapot, despite the very pretty chicken-shaped tea cozy that Ben had given me in what I liked to believe was a fit of humor.

Cas finished with my purse, and after spilling all the contents on the kitchen table, he reached down and triumphantly held the key aloft. "Ah-ha!" he said. "See, you do have your key."

I frowned at him. "I'm sure I looked in the purse."

"It was under the lining. You're always losing things there. You need to either mend the hole or get a new purse. Remember when your phone was ringing and you were convinced it wasn't in your purse, so your purse had to be echoing the ring of the phone at home?"

I gave him a glare. "I was very tired."

He smiled a little. "We've both been working too hard. And I have bad news for you."

"Oh, no."

"Oh, yes. Even though E isn't in the house, I can't spend the night. You see, the tests we've already done on the bones Ben found seem to show the presence of arsenic. There were two skeletons, one a woman's and one of a man. The man's bones were wearing the remnants of an overcoat, which had a label still visible. It was tailored for Mr. . . ."

"Jacinth Jones."

"Bingo. It's quite possible the old lady told you the truth, however questionable her motives might have been, you know."

"Yeah," I said. It was starting to seem like it.

"So, between that and the fact that someone broke in and tampered with Ben's moisturizer, we have our hands full tonight. I doubt I'll even get to sleep. But I'm taking a couple hours off to take you to dinner, because I convinced Rafiel I really needed it." He smiled. "Besides, I've covered for him more than once or twice. The man must have the busiest love life west of the Pecos." He rolled his eyes. "I don't think I would want that. Not for me, the kind of romance you have to manage with a Rolodex and a file cabinet."

So we went to dinner, and talked about E and the rats, and gossiped about Nick and Ben, hoping they would end up together, the way you do about family and best friends. "Nick went to the hospital to spend some time with Ben, while I came here. He'll be on duty pretty much all night, too."

It wasn't till Cas was dropping me off at my house that he said, "Oh, by the way, the techs say that the dead woman was pregnant. Pretty far along."

This left me feeling sad as I went into the house and cuddled up with Pythagoras.

I had been a little upset at Ben spending so much time hanging around my house and alphabetizing my spices while he was single, but I had a feeling I was going to miss him. I was certainly going to miss him while dealing with cats and rats.

"Oh, my," I told Pythagoras, who gave me a "meow, meow" that indicated he was afraid the lions and tigers and bears would show up later.

All in all, it was a very quiet evening. I fed the rats, noting that Ratley was a little lethargic but seemed otherwise unharmed. I'd have been lethargic, too, if I'd spent three hours running. No, given my decidedly unathletic body, I'd be dead if I'd spent three hours running.

I fed Pythagoras, again, because he seemed to think it was one of the great injustices in the world that he shouldn't get fed as much as baby rats. "You're going to be a butterball," I told him. "We'll end up confusing you with the turkey and cooking you for Thanksgiving." Seeing his stricken expression, big eyes staring up at me in terror, I said, "Joking. But you are going to destroy your cattish figure, my dear."

He didn't seem fully reassured and was scrambling sideways and skittish the rest of the night.

I put my pajamas on and climbed into bed to reread Agatha Christie's *Sleeping Murder*, which was my idea of a rousing good time when alone at home on a winter's night. When you're practically raised by mystery books you acquire these kinds of quirks.

Pythagoras clearly decided that no one who was such a fuddy-duddy as to read Agatha Christie when she couldn't have a good time with her hard-working policeman boyfriend, could possibly harbor such vigorous and innovative notions as cooking neurotic cats.

He put his paws on the bed and asked permission to jump on and, when I granted it, climbed up and nestled under my arm. It wasn't really comfortable but it was very comforting.

So comforting in fact that I fell asleep like that. And woke up, two hours later, wide awake and convinced that I was in danger.

CHAPTER 23

Something Wicked This Way Comes

I sat up in bed so violently that I startled Pythagoras who complained of my rudeness. Not sure what had alarmed me, and half-convinced I must have dreamed it, I petted Pythagoras while looking around the room. Everything was exactly as it had been when I'd fallen asleep, and I didn't have a sense that there was anyone in the house. Well, anyone other than me, seven rats, and a truly confused cat.

Then why was my heart drumming up near my throat and why was I suddenly convinced that I was in great danger and needed to get out of the house?

I thought backward through the various things that had been in my sleeping mind when I woke up. The most important of those was a key. My key.

Cas had found my key in my purse, but I'd swear it wasn't there the day before. Which meant . . . what? I thought back to the hardware store and to Julius saying that Mrs. Martin had been in to copy a key. Well, he had said Miss Martin, but of course that was impossible. Old people made that kind of mistake all the time. Given that he had to be at least two hundred, it was a minor slip. So . . . I petted Pythagoras and thought on. Mrs. Martin had come in to copy a key. Which had allowed her to have the housekeeper return said key to my purse when she had let me in to talk to Miss Martin. Probably the younger Martins had manipulated the older woman into asking me to come visit. They would never have expected her to tell me the truth.

And that brought me to two realizations. Mr. Martin had to know about his father's guilt, of course. He'd been doing whatever he could to minimize chances his father would ever be exposed.

So I'd gotten my key back. Which meant that someone had already used it. To poison Ben's moisturizer cream, thinking it was mine. Maybe the old lady had overheard something and that was why she questioned me about my skin care! It almost made sense.

I had insisted on investigating and poking my nose into an almost hundred-year-old murder. But if all of a sudden, I became a raving lunatic, no one would listen to anything I said about anything I might have found. At least, I hoped that the intent had been to make me sound crazy, so no one would pay attention to me, rather than kill me. It had been a masterful plan except for the fact that the moisturizer in the house was not mine but my male houseguest's.

By now, though, whoever it was would know that they missed their target and even possibly that the skeletons in their closet had been found. This would not have made them happy. And they still had a key to the house . . .

My subconscious had finally come through and all of my scattered thoughts and suspicions were clear. I was out of the bed and packing. Pythagoras must have caught on that I was scared and trying to leave, because he climbed into the suitcase, forcing me to go find his carrier, shoo him into it, then finish filling a suitcase with enough clothing for a couple of days, just in case Cas had to work late tomorrow night, too.

The clock on my bedside table said it was midnight, and that meant that my parents would still be up, reading or discussing the latest mystery. In fact, I suspected discussing mysteries was what my parents did instead of sleeping, if they didn't discuss them while asleep.

Of course, my taking refuge with my parents was the rough equivalent of Christians taking refuge in a lion's den, or perhaps a virgin taking refuge in a bordello. Mom could drive me insane in no time flat, and I could only imagine how the two of them would take to Pythagoras and the rats. But the fear gnawing inside of me told me it was better to go home to Mom and Dad and let Fluffy the Second—now improved and with more fluffiness—pee on my bed than to stay here and end up maybe dead.

So I set out, in the middle of the night, with the aquarium and the cat carrier once again strapped side by side in the backseat, and Pythagoras muttering softly under his breath that it was truly an injustice and undignified too for him to be transported under these conditions and that if the car was going to be a rodent express he would want no part of it.

CHAPTER 24

The Prodigal and Her Animals

I was received as if I'd announced I'd come to my senses and was finally moving back home and—probably—after suitable nagging by my mother, going back to college.

My mother is very good at believing the things she wants to believe and ignoring signs of any reality that is different. For instance, she often says that she and my father had wanted a large family. Knowing my father, I strongly doubted this. In my more uncharitable moments, I thought I had been conceived after Mom had glued books all over herself, and while Father was reading them something had gone wrong. Or right depending on your opinion.

Since one of her fondest wishes—right after the golden dream that I would marry her favorite child, Benedict Colm—was that I would move back home and go back to college and take a degree in English or library science or something else that could use in the store, she received me exactly as if I had finally chosen to do this. And while she didn't kill the fatted calf, she received the ratty guests with something approaching euphoria.

After I'd climbed—*creak, creak, shake, shake*—the rickety, father-built stairs all the way to the top carrying the aquarium and the cat carrier (and made a second trip with my suitcase containing clothes for two days and the equipment to feed the rats), Mom had opened the door with a bright and fixed smile, and said, "Oh, hi, dear. I'm so glad you finally got in."

Note that she didn't say come back or even come home, but "got in," as though I already lived there and had merely gone away for some hours. All those crazy people who claim you should act as though things were true and, presto, chango, they would become so, were amateurs compared to my mother.

She proclaimed Pythagoras the most beautiful cat in the world and quite the companion for her own precious little Fluffy, even as the king of neurosis—newly released from his carrier—was walking experimentally around the kitchen muttering apologies. "So sorry to be here without being invited. No manners, that girl. Of course she should have called in advance. Oh, look, a cat dish—" fearful look around "—from its dainty size and pink color I deduce it must belong to a ferocious man-eating tiger—" mad scared look in my direction "—you wouldn't let me be eaten, would you?"

As for the rats, Mom was not crazy enough to touch them—not even, in fact, to go near their aquarium or get so near to them as to help me carry the aquarium to my attic bedroom. She had instead taken my suitcase while I carried the rats—with all of them crowding the glass and wondering where they were—up two more flights of stairs. Despite this distance and her rather obvious aversion to them, she proclaimed them darlings and the cutest things.

And once they were set on my desk and I—who didn't trust Fluffy nearly as much as I trusted Pythagoras—had closed the door and sat on the bed to feed the rats, Mom had stayed behind to talk to me.

"Are you . . . are you intending to keep them?" she asked me, in a tone that implied she wished I wouldn't, but was afraid to say it.

"No. Half of them are going to Ben and half to his new boyfriend."

"Boyfriend?"

"A very nice police officer. Cas's cousin. Greek. I think I mentioned him?"

It had taken my mother about ten seconds to process this information. You could tell she had arrived at one of her conclusions when her eyes lit up and she lifted her eyebrows and said, "Ah, Greek." As if that explained everything.

"Born and raised in the States," I said. "But his parents are of Greek origin."

"Well," Mom said. "We know everything about the Greeks. Alexander the Great . . . Huge influence on Greek culture. Anna Apostolou made that very clear."

I refused to speculate on what Anna Apostolou had made very clear. In fact, I already had a pretty good idea, because I'd read a book by the author, sometime ago, called *Murder in Macedonia* and it contained enough sodomy to make Ben blush. I let that matter drop, because if we went into it, we'd end up discussing modern life as viewed through mysteries, which was always one of my mother's problems, anyway.

So instead, I'd said, "So they'll be taking the rats, and I can keep Pythagoras, though I think, really, he's more E's cat. He's always sleeping with E or sitting on him."

"Um . . ." Mom said. "We can change the guest room so that it's E's room. Unless you want to move there and have E sleep here."

Given a choice, of course, if I ever *have* to move back to my parents' house, I fully intend to stay in the attic and keep E with me. Neither of us needed to listen to my parents never-ending discussions of mysteries at all hours of the night. It had scarred me, would continue to scar me, and might very well scar E.

"Not needed, Mom. E is staying with All . . . with his father until Tuesday and I don't expect to stay here more than one night at the most. I'm just here because uh . . ." I tried desperately to think of an excuse that wouldn't get me questioned about the murder and everything that had happened, and wouldn't get my parents all excited about having me in the middle of a real mystery. "The heating is out at my place. Nothing bad, the rental company should have it fixed it by the day after tomorrow, but I needed a place to stay for a couple of nights." After which I would have had my locks changed, something I planned on doing by the dawn's early light. And also by the dawn's early light, I was going to call my boyfriend. First, to tell him the locks had been changed, just in case he found it necessary to go to my house. And second to tell him that either John Martin or possibly his wife was behind the poisoning, probably to hide the fact his father was a murderer.

It was just like an Agatha Christie novel with all the pronouncements on how bad blood could be passed on. Though, of course, in almost every Agatha Christie novel that theory was disproven and the child of the murderer or suspected long-ago murderer turned out to be completely innocent. But maybe Agatha was wrong and Rex Stout, American and supposedly a lot more progressive, whose villains often were the children of the damned was right.

(I told you that listening to all those late night discussions had scarred me. . . .)

I realized my mother was launched well away in one of her tirades. "It's just not right, my dear. I mean, we all lived in college neighborhoods when we were college students, but it's like living off noodles, you can't go on doing it the rest of your life. You should move back here and go back to college. Better for you and for your son."

I marveled at the idea that living in a college student area was considered juvenile, but going back to live with my parents was not. But again, it didn't bear discussing.

She finally left me, after she had expressed—at length— her opinions about my completely unacceptable lifestyle. All the rats were fed. Pythagoras was waiting patiently at the door. A fresh batch of scratches across his nose told me that the resident kitten was less than ecstatic with the idea of a new playmate, and also that she found it less than pleasing to be apologized to constantly.

After I'd let him in, I cleaned the blood off his nose with a tissue. "You shouldn't have gone near the little demon," I told him. "I think she's the incarnation of the most cantankerous cat ever to walk the Earth. She probably only scratched you because she knew you were my cat."

He said, "Mew," which in this case meant, "It's all

right, kind lady. I shouldn't have tried to become friends with the little lion. She's a bit territorial, but then I probably deserved it."

And on that imperfect but perfectly amicable understanding, we'd gone to sleep. I'd dreamed confused dreams about moisturizer dripping from a hand, each of the droplets becoming poison.

When I woke up, I'd dialed Ben's number before I realized he probably wouldn't have his cell phone with him in the hospital. But judging from the very gruff, "Yes," he did. And he also sounded less than pleased with being awakened at—I checked—seven in the morning. "You're alive," I said,

"Of course."

"And in your right mind?"

This brought about a semi-cackle. "More or less. As much as I can be when people keep waking me every hour to take my temperature and blood pressure and stick me with a needle. But I guess everything is clear, because they say I should be discharged around noon. That means I can go home and sleep and be fine to go to work tomorrow." There was a brief silence, and I was thinking of hanging up, when he said, "Dyce . . . the . . . uh . . . There really were skeletons, right? Nick told me, I think, but I still wasn't very lucid when he was here last night."

"There really were skeletons," I said. "Apparently a man and a woman, the woman very pregnant, Cas says." I shuddered. "That probably means that they found baby bones, too."

"Poor bastards," he said softly.

"Yeah." And because I couldn't bear the solemnity in his voice, nor the stupid feeling that I should somehow have been able to save these poor people who'd died before I was even a twinkle in my grandmother's eye, I said. "And I hope in the future you understand the dangers of beauty products, young man."

This brought another cackle, and a protest, "I don't think there are teams of people roaming around poisoning cosmetics."

"Oh, you never know," I said. "I'm glad you're sounding like yourself."

"So am I," he said. "I have blisters on my palms. Nick says they're from a shovel. A shovel, me! A bit more of that stuff and I might have become a raging heterosexual, and then what would that do to my self-image?"

"Don't worry, honey," I said, tartly. "You're likely to die first."

He laughed again and said, "I'll come by later after they discharge me. We can go to lunch at Cy's." Cy's makes organic burgers and it's sort of our local corner of paradise. Ben lived in hope it would cross with Dairy Queen and merge the name, but he loved the burgers anyway.

"Yeah, that would be nice."

I got up, showered, and dressed and went into the kitchen in search of something that would pass for breakfast, before I went out to look for an early rising locksmith. And I had to call Cas.

Father was in the kitchen, eating buttered toast and drinking coffee. He looked up, startled, at my approach and once more proved my suspicion that he wasn't so much absentminded as unmoored in time. Any time he met me around his house, he was as likely as not to ask me how my history test had gone, and mention my ninth grade teacher and her concerns on my work.

He looked up and for just a moment his unfocused gaze told me had no idea who I was, or perhaps even what

I was. This was probably why he preferred books to people, because books have covers and titles on those covers, which makes them much easier to identify.

Father looks like me, or at least that's what people tell me. This resemblance had stopped me, in my most snarky moments, from making even worse surmises about my parents' sex life and my birth.

However, *looks like* is a vague thing. For me to look like my father, I would need to lose most of my hair, leave the rest short, and comb it so that it stood on end. My face would need to look like Ben says it's going to look in no time at all if I don't start using moisturizer, and I'd need to start wearing large, square, black-rimmed glasses. Right now, from behind his glasses, his eyes blinked distractedly at me. He raised a finger, as if he were experimentally, feeling the wind. "Sherlock . . . No, that's not your name, is it?"

"Candyce, Daddy," I said, helping myself to coffee. One of the things my parents do well is get coffee from the Beanery, which has its own blend—the smoothest, least acid coffee on the planet.

"Oh, yes, that whole silly thing with that ridiculous candy shop." He sighed. "I suppose it's a good thing that your mother agreed to come back, though."

He seemed to be asking me for confirmation. "I think so," I told him. "I might not have had the most standard upbringing in the world, but without it I'd be someone else, and I like myself."

"Good, good," he said.

Then, when I sat down with coffee and my toast, I guess he felt it his paternal duty to ask another question. "So . . . so . . . have you got any boyfriends?"

"One, Daddy. Castor Wolfe. He's a detective with the Goldport Police Department. Serious Crimes Unit."

"Ah, good. A policeman is always good. We really should give him that new police procedural your mother read and passed to me. I think it's a good book, but I wonder about some of the details. Do you think he'd be willing to discuss them?"

In the blissful certainty that my father would almost immediately forget that Cas existed, I said, "Probably, Daddy. I'll ask him."

And with that, Father finished the rest of his coffee and went downstairs to man the bookstore. Or more likely to walk aimlessly amid the crowded bookshelves, picking out a book now and then and—if he got half a chance—discouraging prospective buyers from purchasing any of his darlings. I'd seen him do it and it was a masterpiece of the anti-salesman art. First he'd find out what the customer liked to read and then no matter what the customer selected assure him or her that the book was just not going to be to his or her taste.

It didn't work for the regulars, but it worked for practically everyone else, because, after all, who believed that a bookseller did *not* want to sell his books?

Fortified with coffee, I took my phone out of my pocket, and called Cas.

CHAPTER 25

Wild, Wild Hypothesis

"No, Dyce, I don't think so," he said, after he heard my full theory of why John Martin was the culprit, with the help of his wife, who had the key made.

"Just like that?" I said. "You listen to my whole idea and you say, "'No, Dyce, I don't think so.' Why not, I'd like to know?"

He sighed. He got very cranky when he'd spent the night without sleep. "Mostly because Mrs. Martin had a heart attack yesterday morning, when she was starting her work at the library. She was rushed to hospital, where she's in intensive care with her husband by her side. I don't think she left the hospital with her oxygen mask and tank, to get a key cut. Even old Julius would have remembered that."

"Oh," I said, as my lovely theory deflated. "I wonder then who Julius thought was Miss Martin . . ."

"I have no idea," Cas said. "However, I do agree with

you that the key having disappeared and the tampering with the moisturizer may be related . . . it doesn't make me happy. Your place is just not secure enough. If you want to continue renting it, you could make it a business deduction and store furniture in the front while you do your work in the back. But I think, frankly, it makes more sense for us to look around and see if there is the same sort of space somewhere else at around the same price, that can be turned into a storefront. I'm not saying to stop putting your pieces for sale up in Denver, but you might as well have a little place here to sell them, too."

"And where would I live?" I asked, baffled.

"With me, of course. Haven't we talked about this?"

Suddenly, there were a heavy weight on my stomach. Oh, not that again. I felt stupid telling Cas I wouldn't move in with him without a wedding ring. It made me feel like someone of Miss Martin's generation. And yet, I *wouldn't* move in with him without a wedding ring. . . . "I haven't decided yet."

"Uh . . . I see," he said. "Well, we'll talk about it to-night. You can go back home, I should be able to spend the night. And I'm taking some comp time tomorrow, so we can have the locksmith come by then."

Like that, he destroyed my plans for the day. Which was just as well, because a second later, my mother came up the stairs and into the kitchen. "Dyce, my dear, your father and I really need to go over to Mail Depot, Etc., and see if the new shipment of *Too Cold To Die* has arrived. It's selling faster than we can keep it on the shelves, and your father, you know, doesn't like to be down to the last book. It would be so much easier if the company shipped with one of the other carriers, but it's all UPS, and of course, instead of delivering yesterday they left us one of those yellow little tickets saying that the package is at Mail Depot, Etc. And it's in your father's name, so he'll need to go. There's no use saying he doesn't, because I've tried to get those books out of hock on my own and they always say it has to be the person to whom it's addressed. And it's no use, either, your telling me I should just let your dad drive alone, because the last time I did that he ended up driving to the book mall, all the way in Denver, and coming home with a thousand dollars of books that weren't even for resale."

I avoided laughing at my father's typical behavior and instead tried to figure out what Mom meant by that long ramble. "Uh . . . and you're telling me this, because?"

I had the terrifying feeling that she wanted me to drive my father to Mail Depot, Etc., or, worse, keep him on track while he drove there. If it was awkward to spend time in a kitchen over breakfast with a man who has known you since you were born and has no idea who you are, it is twice as disconcerting to do it in a moving car. Particularly when that man, probably on purpose, suddenly accuses you of having carjacked him and threatens to put his head out the window and scream he's been kidnapped unless you take him exactly where he says.

Mom must have read my fear in my eyes. She smiled. "I'd never ask you to drive your father," she reassured me. "I know how difficult he can be. But we just opened the store, and I would hate to close it again, even for an hour. We have to do it, of course, when we're here alone, but since you're here today, I don't suppose you'd stay in the store while we go?"

Alarm shed off me in waves, replaced by relief. "Oh, that," I said. "Of course."

I made sure that the rats and Pythagoras were safe, then went downstairs to man the counter.

Bookstore work at nine in the morning on a Sunday is probably the most boring thing in the world. My mother and father were the only ones on the street who opened their store that early on Sundays. But Mom said there was a link between preachers and turning people to thinking of murder. Probably when the sermons were too long. She said they got a steady crowd starting with those leaving the early Catholic and Episcopal services, through the noontime when the Baptists left theirs, and then again in the early evening when the more exotic denominations were done.

I suspected it was because mystery fanatics are such that their idea of a satisfying day off always revolves around a good book. So, faced with the expanse of Sunday afternoon, they came in search of that good book to read.

Mom was right. The store started getting people in waves. Not singly, but in groups of fifteen or so, between which the bell behind the door would be completely silent.

I don't mean that they came in a group. They would arrive, by ones or twos, and make their purchases, one by one or two by two. Then the shop would be silent for a while. Fluffy had been the bookstore cat and kept my parents company during the lulls, but the new and improved Fluffy the Second hadn't yet been trained in her duties of sleeping in the chairs arranged in front of the fireplace to the left of the entrance or winding in and out of people's steps as they walked around looking at books. So I was completely alone.

It was a little nerve-racking, too, because when you are out back, trying to help someone find the book they were looking for, the register is completely unprotected. Anyone could get into it or take out money and what could you do about it?

I was thinking of that as I finished ringing up the sale for the man I thought was the last customer of the previous batch, when I saw someone move at the back of the store.

This shouldn't have been alarming, but it was. After all, customers wandering around the back of the store is normal, part of the wonders of capitalism. Only the person back there now—it looked like a tall man in blue jacket and pants—seemed to be trying not to be seen. In fact, he seemed to be trying to hide in the area where mother had put a little curtain to conceal the shelves containing the plastic dishware and such that she sets out when the bookstore hosts a signing.

I really wished I was not alone, but then I reminded myself most people doing secretive things in the bookstore were trying to shoplift, or maybe deface one of the books. Very few people came into a bookstore to murder the owner, much less the clerk.

The worst thing that people can say about mysteries is that they don't read them because they're too violent. Unlike fantasies, those who write or sell them have never been accused of being witches who must die.

So I took a look to make sure the new batch of customers weren't coming up the walk to the store, and then I went to the back, hesitantly. Closer up, it was clear the man was wearing some sort of uniform, like that of a repairman, and that he had a cap of the same color as his pants and jacket jammed down on his white hair. "Sir," I said. "Sir, is there any way I can help you?"

The man turned around, and said, in a surprisingly high, well-bred voice, "Yes. You can die."

I was so shocked by the words that it must have taken me several seconds to recognize the well-bred features of Miss Diane Martin.

By that time she had a gun out and was pulling the trigger.

CHAPTER 26

Hide and Book

You don't know the abilities you have till you need them. If anyone had told me I could see a finger start to squeeze the trigger of a gun and throw myself sideways fast enough to avoid the bullet, I'd have told them they were insane. But that's exactly what I did and, while she took more shots at me, making books fly all around, I managed to stay out of their way, mostly by crawling on the floor and rolling.

But this strategy had its limits. I had my cell phone in my pocket, but I couldn't get to it while I was crawling and listening for her steps. Her steps. She was walking around. Which meant that Old Julius had been right and that it had been her who had come to his store to copy a key. My key.

I had a sickening feeling that she had gone to the house earlier, that she hadn't found me there, and that she had come to the store, maybe intending to ask Mom and Dad if they knew where I was. And she had found me.

There was a lull in the firing. I wondered if she was reloading. I knew virtually nothing about guns. Not that I thought they were repulsive, or had any objections to them—at least when I wasn't unarmed and at the mercy of a crazy woman holding a gun—but because like forensics and my parents' other favorite subjects, I'd heard so much about them from the moment I could listen to anything, that I had found myself unable to take the subject seriously.

Damn, I thought as I crawled behind a further set of bookshelves. *Now I will die because I don't know if she's reloading. If she's reloading, I could charge her.*

I looked around and realized I'd cornered myself in a cul-de-sac formed by bookshelves and the innermost corner of the store. Trapped, like a rat. One of the slower rats, like Rat Face. I could hear her approaching. She wasn't firing, probably because she had figured out where I was.

Except . . . Except that behind me was the door to the powder room. Now, if you're thinking that by going into the powder room, I'd simply manage to trap myself even more, behind a very small door that bullets could pierce, in a tiny room, where bullets would ricochet, you'd be absolutely right . . . except for one thing.

My parents were unable to comprehend the concept of any corner of the bookstore being devoid of books. Hell, they were unable to think of any corner of the house—any house—being free of books. So the powder room—which was, in fact, a full bathroom, had a large, sturdy utility shelf in the space where the tub had been piled high with the sort of books that my parents also had up front in the free bin. That way if a light-fingered customer came out of the bathroom with a book shoved down his pants or up his shirt, they wouldn't have lost anything. On the other hand, if a customer came out of the bathroom complaining of the lack of good reads, they would direct him toward the books that were for sale.

I'm not sure how often it worked, but I was sure about the utility shelf, which was rated to take three hundred and some pounds.

I stood up, and quickly slipped into the powder room, locking the door behind me. Once inside, I clambered up the shelf like a cat, trying to make no noise and refusing to apologize, as Pythagoras would have.

The top of the shelf was almost at the ceiling, and I wedged myself behind the row of books Dad had piled on it, hoping that any bullets ricocheting wouldn't hit me.

I took the phone out of my pants and dialed Cas. No answer.

A bullet came through the door, and shattered a mirror—seven years of bad luck. Another shot, and there went the lightbulb. Another one I could hear hitting the floor.

My captor wasn't talking. I wanted her to. I called Nick. No answer. I called Ben.

"Dyce," he said. Sounding almost bubbly happy. "I'm just waiting for the doctor to come and discharge me so I can go home."

"I'm in my parents' bookstore," I said. "And Diane Martin is shooting at me."

I spoke as low as I could, to avoid helping the old lady get a fix on me, but of course, she heard my voice and knew I was still alive, so she took another shot.

"Holy fuck!" Ben said. "Someone is shooting."

"Yes, Diane Martin. I need help and I can't get Cas or Nick on the phone."

"The old lady? Impossible. Don't move. I'll—I'll do something. Your parents' bookstore?"

"Yes. And it is her." But he had already hung up. It occurred to me that he'd arrive too late and I'd be dead and then no one would believe Diane Martin had killed me. It would be the perfect crime simply because being old and frail would protect her from suspicion.

So I burrowed farther behind the books, and I said, "Please stop. Why are you shooting at me?"

"Why not," she said. "You wouldn't listen. You wouldn't stop. I gave you a perfectly good story, but you wouldn't believe it." A shot bounced off the cement block walls. "Why wouldn't you believe that my brother killed Mama and that man?"

"Because you told me you slept in the love seat," I said. "You couldn't have. There were pictures of it in the file. Jacinth had been sorting papers there. There was no room for a person to sleep." Hah! Once again my subconscious came through! That's what had been bothering me about her story. I could hardly wait to tell Cas. If I wasn't dead, that is.

My reward was a scream of rage and another shot that—judging from the explosion of ceramics, and the sudden gurgle of water had hit the toilet tank. "They sat there," she said. "And they talked about how they would go back East, or perhaps to Australia. Taking me with them, as if they were doing me a favor. My brother could stay in Goldport and live the life he'd been accustomed to, but me, they were going to take with them, to be the daughter of a couple with no antecedents and no connections, to be nobody like the miner's daughters that my mother was so fond of feeding. They said that they would take the bare minimum of money to buy boat passages for all of us. They talked of raising sheep!" She shot again.

I remembered the girl at the end of Agatha Christie's *Easy To Kill*, who had found the best way to prolong her own life was to make the murderer talk, and that the best way to make the woman talk was to flatter her. I'd read about a million mysteries, but Agatha Christie stayed with me, maybe because they were the books my father had read to me when I was a toddler, or maybe because she understood murderers. Like her hero, Miss Marple, she understood evil. She once said that all murderers were horribly lonely. They had killed. They had broken the ultimate human taboo. And if they got away with it, they couldn't talk to anyone about it.

Imagine killing when you were just a little girl, then living with that knowledge all your very long life. If I was going to die, I had to leave behind some proof of what Diane Martin had done, so long ago.

I dialed my home number, waited till the machine picked up, then said in a trembling voice, "You must have been very clever," I said. "To have been able to kill them, when you were only eight years old. And get away with it."

Bitter laughter answered me, but no shot. She wanted to talk, I realized. "Few children could have done it," I said.

"Oh, yes, but I was always gifted. Far smarter than my brother. Or Mother. I was like my papa. I loved him and she was going to leave him for that—nobody. I remembered that a few weeks before when the workman had been preparing a room for the new baby, that our nursemaid told us to be careful about the green wallpaper that was being stripped away. She said that the glue could be dangerous—that is was poison.

"Jacinth Jones had wallpaper in his living room, too. I said I was tired and wanted to lie down. Then I tore some strips from the wallpaper, and brought it back to the kitchen, hidden in my pockets. They were still talking, trying to figure out exactly where they would get the money for everything. I told them I couldn't sleep, and asked if they wanted me to make coffee. I'd done that for them, during their meetings, before, when they were talking about their charities.

"I put the strips in the pot and I boiled them with the coffee and then I ran home and told Papa, just like I told you. Only I didn't say anything about Edward, because my father knew Edward, and Edward was a scaredy-cat. He would never have followed Mother out of the house. Papa realized what had happened. He covered things up, but afterward he stopped me from marrying, stepped in and claimed I was an invalid and suffered from a nervous disorder."

"So you got away with it," I said. "But why would you sacrifice it all now, just to . . . to get me? They've found the bones. You know that, right?"

"Oh, yes. John called from the hospital to tell me. He thought poor Papa had done it, he was afraid I'd have a shock. I—a shock." She laughed again.

"But you know there is going to be an investigation. By coming after me this way, you're only giving them reason to believe you did it. And it will destroy what life you have left."

"Life! Hah! My stupid nephew is selling my house from under me, and putting me in some place filled with imbecilic old people. What is life to me?"

And she started shooting. Again, and again and again, until—like a miracle, like deliverance, like all the best things in the world rolled together—I heard sirens. Ambulances, fire engines. Police cars. My relief was so great I almost fainted.

No more shots rang out, but I wasn't sure I was in the clear till there was a tap on the door, and two male voices clamored, "Dyce!" at once. "Dyce, are you okay?"

It was Ben and Cas, and I opened the door and fell into Cas's arms as Ben leaned against the nearest bookcase.

I was too relieved to be able to make much sense of the paramedics strapping a still form into a carrier, but I said, "She . . . she killed herself?"

"No. She collapsed when we came in," Cas said. "She fell, had a seizure, and was gone."

The paramedics hadn't covered her face and as the stretcher went by, her piercing blue eyes seemed to look at me with disdain. I shuddered, while Ben squeezed my shoulder, the way he does when he's too overcome to speak.

At that moment my parents came back. I heard a box of books drop on the counter and then my mother's voice, "Oh, for heaven's sake. Why is there water pouring out the front door?"

"You know Sherlockia!" Father said. "You're lucky she didn't set fire to the store."

CHAPTER 27

Start

A month later, Cas and I had finished the piano, which had been moved into his house. He'd invited me, and E, and Ben and Nick over for dinner to celebrate what he called the advent of the Steinway.

We'd had an excellent dinner, which Cas had cooked, and then he and Ben had played the piano, commenting on the sound in specialized terms I didn't even begin to understand.

Then we'd just sat around, drinking coffee and talking. Except for E who was sitting in the middle of the floor playing with wood blocks that Cas had unearthed from somewhere and brought out for the occasion. E built towers while we talked.

"It was really stupid of me not to have thought that people recover from strokes. She might have been unable to walk at first, but later she could. I doubt even her nephew and niece knew."

"I'm sure they didn't," Cas said. "What baffled me was the whole business with the key. I looked into it, even though the case is closed. But there was an off chance that the whole family was in on poisoning Ben. After all, it did come out that it was John who tried to put pressure on my boss to stop you. He was concerned about his grandfather's reputation."

Ben shuddered. "I had blisters. On my palms."

Nick put his hand on Ben's nearest knee. "A traumatic experience," he said, and was, I think, only half teasing. "You'll probably have flashbacks," he added, that time fully teasing. "Good thing I'll be around to console you."

"So what did you find out?" I asked Cas, because when those two started they weren't likely to stop, and they got very silly.

"Well, at her age, and with her very short hair, she could pass for a man. I showed her picture around to some of the people who had served at the tea and they all remembered seeing this old-geezer server and wondering how he'd got hired." He shrugged. "Apparently as well as being a murderer, she was a good pick-pocket. She probably returned the key to your purse, when she sent you to get her mother's picture."

"I guess we'll never know if she made those threatening phone calls, too," I said.

Nick chimed in. "Probably not. Cas checked the phone records. I still think they had something to do with the animal poisonings." He sounded frustrated. He still hadn't gotten his man—unless you counted Ben.

"Poor Almeria and Jacinth," I said. "To die just when they thought they were going to be happy."

"She completely misjudged her precious little daughter," Cas said. "But let's leave sad subjects behind. E, have you thought of the offer I made you?"

"Uh?" I said.

E looked up from his towers. "E keep Peegrass . . . in your house?"

"Wouldn't dream of it any other way," Cas said.

E nodded. He considered things. "You be E's dad?"

"Nah. You have a dad. You can call me Cas."

"Castor Pollux Wolfe, what in heaven's name are you asking my son? You can't adopt him!"

"No. I asked him if I could marry his mother!"

"What?"

"Well, I tried to ask you in various ways, and I thought you were refusing me, but Ben said you were just being obtuse, so I'm asking E for your hand, in the presence of witnesses." He gestured toward Ben and Nick. "So, E, may I have the honor of marrying your mother?"

E looked from one of us to the other. "E needs electric car," he said.

"No!" Cas and I said at the same time.

"'Nothah cat?" E tried.

"Hmmm," Cas said. "Pythagoras might not like that."

"A rat?" E stilled missed the rats. They were happily residing elsewhere, some with Ben and some with Nick.

"Maybe. I hear that Rat Fink may be having babies."

E sighed in that way that meant he had to give it a sporting try. Then he cocked his head sideways and said, "You want to marry Mommy?"

"More than anything in the world."

E waved a little hand grandly. "Awright."

"My son," I said, speaking between my teeth, "is not my guardian. You can't ask him for my hand. You—"

He dropped to one knee in front of the sofa and took hold of my hand. "Candyce Chocolat Dare, will you do me the very great honor of marrying me?"

I said yes.

How to French a Piano
and Other Things You Probably
Shouldn't Be Doing

Before I get to the how-tos, I should preface it with this being based on my experience, which was mostly bad, and on research since then that has taught me to do it properly. French polishing is, however, more of an art than a science and your mileage may vary.

To begin with, I married a pianist. Married him with my eyes open, too, since, even though he was a mathematician by day, he composed a piece for me when we were courting. But then we found ourselves in the normal vicissitudes of a young couple starting out. We could weather most of the relative privation, except for one thing—the lack of a piano. This drove my husband insane and even the fancy keyboard he bought couldn't make up for the lack of the Steinway he had played at his mother's house.

In despair I set aside some money—let's just say it was the type of sum that won't buy you a key at most piano stores—and started looking high and low, through used stores, thrift shops, and want ads. I stopped just short of Dumpster diving, but not by much. Most of the pianos had a cracked soundboard, which I understand is normal in that this portion of the piano is very susceptible to temperature changes not to mention movers dropping it, but more on that later.

We finally found an upright with a whole soundboard in a price range we could afford. It was unbelievably dirty and covered in its sixth or seventh coat of very bad paint. Also when we opened it at home, there was a rat's nest inside. Fortunately with no rats in it anymore. Also, though I regret to report it, there was no hundred-year-old letter.

My husband thought he could rebuild the inside of the piano, which amounted to buying anything that could have decayed, shrunk, or warped in the last hundred years. I thought I could French polish it. Turned out he wasn't wrong.

My attempts at French polishing on the other hand, were less than successful. The oil "pasted" on the wood. The pumice stone refused to come clean and I couldn't find shellac flakes in our small town to save my life. The piano ate up most of my life for six months. I did finally get it done, but my method being "mess up, clean it up, do it again," is probably not replicable.

Since then I've found out how I should have done it and also some of the mistakes I made.

The piano looked great, by the way, and played wonderfully, but it got dropped by movers three houses ago and, wouldn't you know it, the soundboard cracked. Fortunately by then we could afford a better—or, my husband says, just showier—instrument, in this case an early twentieth-century player piano.

As for French polishing . . . I might try it again if my husband finds that baby grand he's been dreaming of, since the only way we'll be able to afford it is covered in six layers of paint or currently on fire.

So, after my cautionary tale . . .

Why French Polish?

French polish started as a finish applied to guitars and other fine acoustic instruments. The reason for it was because, the wood being part of the resounding portion of the instrument, it was important not to change its properties with the finish. Finishes that went on top, creating a shell upon the instrument would change the resonance.

The shellac part of the French polish, though, gets pushed into the interstitial bits of the wood, so that it becomes part of it and doesn't change it.

Now, I'm not sure how important this is for a piano, as opposed to the smaller instruments, but smarter minds and more acute hearing senses than mine say it's essential.

Step One: Catch a piano

If you're not yourself well versed in the innards of pianos and what they should look like, find a friend who is and take him or her along. Ignore all the snide remarks about looking for pianos in all the wrong places, and about how it would be much easier to make an ox cart look like a piano than to make the wreck you're contemplating presentable.

Make him or her concentrate on the essentials—soundboards, ivories, and what the replacement cost would be for these parts. Make notes. Do not convince yourself that everything can be fixed with five cents and elbow grease.

Step Two: Remove the crud

There will be crud on your piano. How much crud and which type of crud is open to discussion. If the original finish remains, you might simply be dealing with a lot of dirt and a finish in bad shape. If that's the case thank your lucky stars.

French polish is very easy to damage. It is also, fortunately easy to repair. Wet a soft pad in denatured alcohol. Ring it. Rub it gently on the finish—after you've cleaned— in the direction of the grain. Do not rub so much you remove the finish. Just one or two gentle passes. If you're lucky, that will fix the original finish and you can take credit for all the hard work.

Step Three: When all else fails

So, you were unlucky. Whatever was on the piano was more dirt than finish, or perhaps it was covered in sick pink paint made from melting Saturday-morning cartoon horses.

I'm afraid, my friend, it is time to refinish. First you must remove as much of the paint off the piano as you can and as little of the wood—so as not to change the resonance.

Get your piano-connoisseur friend again and make him/her take out every portion of the piano that can be taken out and put in a safe place. Make them draw a diagram so they remember where it goes. Tell them it's good practice for when they open their piano repair shop. Ignore protests that he/she is a surgeon by trade and a piano shop is not likely in his/her future. You're only looking out for your friend's best interests, after all.

Now this is one of the cases in which I'd recommend a commercial paint remover. Look for something with "no drip" in the name. If you absolutely can't find anything, then mix equal parts mineral spirits and denatured alcohol, thicken with plenty of starch so it's about the consistency of runny batter. Brush onto piano taking care that you don't do more than an area you can scrape before it dries. Scrape. Repeat. If needed wash with mineral spirits/denatured alcohol afterward, using a very fine grade of steel wool. If needed sand lightly using your finest grade of sand paper.

You are now ready to French polish, may heaven have mercy on your soul.

Step Four: What you're going to need

When I tried to do it I was using a British book, which told me to buy some form of shellac on block that had to be melted over the fire. I couldn't find it anywhere, so— being me—ordered it from England. Don't do it. My kitchen cabinets were never the same again, even if I got out most of the scorch marks.

What I finally realized I needed was as follows: shellac flakes. These are usually available in fine woodworking shops, as well as online. Denatured alcohol. Several pads of very soft wool cloth. Olive oil. (I used mineral oil at first and it gummed things up something awful.) Pumice or rotten stone. (I'm not absolutely sure there is a difference, technically, but in our store the package labeled rotten stone is ground much finer than the pumice, so I tend to prefer it.) Elbow grease and plenty of it. If you have an enthusiastic male teenager, get them to do the actual work while you supervise for which you'll need a sufficient quantity of your favorite alcoholic beverage.

Step Five: Do it

The process for French polishing is very simple, just like the process for teaching your cat to waltz is very simple. It is the execution that might take trial and error and, in the case of your cat, Kevlar armor.

Depending on whether you want your shellac heavier or finer—and I believe for pianos the heavier is preferred— mix either two pounds of shellac flakes per gallon of alcohol, or one pound of flakes per gallon of alcohol. Mix only what you're going to use immediately. Some people prefer to let the mix sit for twenty-four hours.

Dissolve shellac in a heat-proof glass jar—a canning jar will do—tighten the lid and place it in hot tap water— that is the water that comes out of your tap on the hot setting.

DO NOT—I can't emphasize this enough—use boiling water and/or put your mixing jar on the stove. Not unless you really want an explosion in your kitchen. And if you do, find another way to do it.

Once dissolved, transfer your shellac to a cheap plastic bottle of the squeeze type.

Now, apply a layer of that shellac to the piano, using a cloth pad. Do it only one surface of the piano at a time, such as a leg, or the keyboard cover. This "wash" will protect the piano during the more lengthy process.

Let it dry. After half an hour, repeat the process. Then again. Perhaps another time for good measure.

Wait a few hours or overnight.

Now, take your cloth pad. Make sure it is 100 percent wool, since synthetics might act oddly.

Now, wet your pad with alcohol. Sprinkle on the rotten stone—onto the pad, not the piano—and rub it with your finger, so it's well spread and forms a transparent layer. Now press the pad onto the piano and rub in clockwise circles.

And rub. And rub some more. This might be where you want to find the teenager and that drink.

If you get too much pumice in any area, add more alcohol and work it to another area that might need more pumice.

Now, either get a new pad, or apply a new cover to your pad. Used T-shirts would do. I would prefer a new pad with a cover of used T-shirts, but your mileage may vary.

Take your heavier mix of shellac, now, and load your pad, then put a few drops of alcohol on your pad. Then a drop of olive oil. Just wet your finger with olive oil and rub on pad. Now, smack the pad against your GLOVED hand to distribute the shellac. You need the pad loaded, but not too loaded. Kind of like the state you should achieve while watching the teen do this.

Glide the pad onto the surface of the piano, working on a little area at a time to prevent its sticking. Do not stop. Or at least, do not stop with the pad on the piano.

After you're done with a portion of the piano, remove the excess oil by running a pad with just a little bit of shellac and a few drops of alcohol all over the section.

Let the whole thing rest for a couple of hours. No, you don't get to rest. You start on another section.

Repeat until the result is pleasing to the eye; the teen,

if you're employing one, falls down of tiredness; and/or you're too sloshed, if you've been loading yourself as well as the pad, to see whether the surface looks right.

At this point it is a good time to get hold of your piano-knowing friend and get him to do the totally inconsequential work of getting the piano to play. Failing that, you can also pay a professional to do it, though it will probably be pricier than a new piano.

French polish can also be used for other pieces of furniture such as sideboards and tables, though I have no idea why you'd do it unless you're in the habit of playing your dining room table.

If so, by all means, carry on.